' Before I agree to help you, I need to be sure there won't be trouble."

" ...u can't be sure." She strained against him, s ...ing off heat waves where their bodies to ched. Whatever was happening, Brandon c ld not bring himself to step away and let h r go.

" ou can't be sure of...anything." Her voice v s breathy, her words tangled skeins of l gic. "You can't just bend life to your will, andon. Things happen, and sometimes you ve to let them. You bet and you lose, you ve and you get hurt, or you hurt others."

ince when did you become so wise, hoolmarm?" His lips brushed the soft hair at temple as he spoke. "You don't strike me a lady who's done a lot of living."

r *a lot of loving*, he thought. Lord, the ssons he would teach this woman if things ere different between them!

Elizabeth Lane has lived and travelled in many parts of the world, including Europe, Latin America and the Far East, but her heart remains in the American West, where she was born and raised. Her idea of heaven is hiking a mountain trail on a clear autumn day. She also enjoys music, animals and dancing. You can learn more about Elizabeth by visiting her website at www.elizabethlaneauthor.com

A recent story by the same author:

ANGELS IN THE SNOW
  (in *Stay for Christmas* anthology)

HER
DEAREST ENEMY

Elizabeth Lane

⊚™ MILLS & BOON®
Pure reading pleasure™

All the characters in this book have no existence outside the imagination of the author, and have no relation whatsoever to anyone bearing the same name or names. They are not even distantly inspired by any individual known or unknown to the author, and all the incidents are pure invention.

First published in Great Britain 2008
Harlequin Mills & Boon Limited,
Eton House, 18-24 Paradise Road, Richmond, Surrey TW9 1SR

© Elizabeth Lane 2005

ISBN: 978 0 263 86280 5

Set in Times Roman 10½ on 13¼ pt.
04-0908-69751

Printed and bound in Spain
by Litografia Rosés S.A., Barcelona

HER
DEAREST ENEMY

Chapter One

◇◇◇◇◇

Dutchman's Creek, Colorado, 1884

It was late afternoon on an October day when sun-light pooled like melted butter in the hollows of the land. The children of Dutchman's Creek savored its warmth as they trooped down the path that led from the one-room schoolhouse to the wagon road. They laughed and chattered, their feet swishing happily through the thick carpet of dry leaves.

In the west, rising from foothills brushed with pine and aspen, the jagged peaks of the Rockies jut-ted against the indigo sky. The mountains were al-ready white with snow; but here in this high valley the beauty of the day was like a last, lingering kiss, bittersweet, as only Indian summer can be.

A vagrant breeze swept through a clump of big-toothed maples, swirling leaves into the air like flocks of pink-and-crimson butterflies. The school-house door, which the last departing child had left ajar, blew inward, causing Miss Harriet Smith to glance up from the half-graded stack of arithmetic papers on her desk. What she saw through the open doorway made her heart plummet like a mallard shot down in flight.

There was no mistaking the identity of the angry figure striding up the path toward the schoolhouse. Brandon Calhoun, who owned the bank, the hotel and, so it was whispered, the saloon, was the tallest man in town, with shoulders like a blacksmith's and rough-hewn features that captured the eye of every woman he met.

Under different circumstances Harriet might have been flattered that the most powerful man in Dutch-man's Creek had come to pay her a call. But she knew exactly what was on Brandon Calhoun's mind. She had been dreading their confrontation all day. Now that it was at hand, she had only one regret—that she hadn't taken the offensive and bearded the lion in his den. After all, she had her own concerns, her own pride. And, truth be told, she was as worried about her brother Will as he was about his precious daughter Jenny.

Harriet's nervous fingers tucked a stray lock of dark brown hair behind one ear as she watched his approach. Dressed in the slate-gray suit he often wore at the bank, he walked leaning slightly forward, like a ship battling its way in a storm—no, she thought, more like the storm itself, raging up the path, his elegant black boots plowing through the fallen leaves, creating chaos in their wake. His brow was a thundercloud, his mouth a grim slash in his chiseled, granite face. All he lacked was a fistful of lightning bolts to hurl at her with the fury of Jove.

As if this debacle were *her* fault!

Harriet's heart drummed against her ribs as she settled her reading spectacles on her nose, dipped her pen in the inkwell and pretended to write. Her pulse broke into a gallop as he mounted the stoop and crossed the threshold. Fixing her gaze on the scribbling pen nib, she forced herself to ignore him until he spoke.

"I want a word with you, Miss Smith."

"Oh?" She glanced up to see him looming above her, his face a study in controlled fury. Slowly and deliberately, Harriet removed her spectacles and rose to her feet. She was nearly five feet eight inches tall, but she had to look up to meet his withering blue eyes.

"You know why I've come, don't you?" he said coldly.

"I do. And I've spoken with Will. There'll be no more sneaking out at night to meet your daughter."

"You've *spoken* to him!" Brandon Calhoun's voice was contemptuous. "I caught your brother in a tree, last night, talking to Jenny through her open window! If I hadn't come along, he'd likely have climbed right into her bedroom! If you ask me, the young whelp ought to be horsewhipped!"

Harriet felt the rush of heat to her face. "My brother is eighteen years old," she said, measuring each word. "I can hardly turn him over my knee and spank him, Mr. Calhoun. But I do agree that he shouldn't see Jenny alone. We had a long talk last night after he—"

"A long talk!" He muttered a curse under his breath. "You might as well have a long talk with a tomcat! I was his age once and I know what it's like! There are girls down at Rosy's who'll put him out of his misery for a few dollars and others in town who'd likely do it for nothing. But, by heaven, I won't have him touching my Jenny! Not him or any other boy in this town!"

His frankness deepened the hot color in Harriet's face. In the eight years since the death of their parents in a diphtheria epidemic, she had devoted all her resources to raising her younger brother. She had done her best to teach Will right from wrong. But there were some things an unmarried sister couldn't say to a growing boy—things that required the counsel of an experienced man. And there had been no man available.

With a growl of exasperation, Brandon Calhoun wheeled away from her and stalked to the window, where he stood glaring out at the autumn afternoon. Sunlight, slanting through the glass, played on the waves of his thick chestnut hair, brushing the faint streaks of gray at his temples with platinum. How old was he? Old enough to have a seventeen-year-old daughter, but surely no more than forty. There were deepening creases at the corners of his eyes, but his belly was flat and taut, his movements graced with a young man's vigor.

Harriet had come to teach school in Dutchman's Creek less than a year ago. Except for the schoolchildren, she was not well acquainted with many of the town's citizens. But a woman at church had told her that the banker's wife had died six years ago and, despite the fact that any number of ladies had set their caps for him, he had raised his daughter alone, just as she had raised Will. Maybe that was part of what had drawn the two young people together. Will and Jenny had met last summer and had been close ever since. That they were becoming too close was as much a concern to Harriet as it was to Jenny's father.

Silence lay cold and heavy in the little classroom as Harriet pushed herself away from the desk and took a step toward him. Her legs quivered beneath her, threatening to give way. She willed herself to stand erect, to thrust out her chin and meet his blistering gaze with her own.

"Believe it or not, I'm no happier about this situation than you are," she declared. "For years, I've been planning for Will to attend college. He's finishing up his preparatory work by correspondence now, so that he can enter Indiana University in the spring to study engineering. If you think I'd have him jeopardize his future by getting mixed with some girl who doesn't have the sense to—"

"Jenny isn't *some girl!*" he snapped, cutting her off angrily. "And as for sense, she's every bit as bright as she is pretty! I want nothing but the best for her, and that doesn't include your calf-eyed, tree-climbing brother! By heaven, she deserves better!"

Harriet felt her anger rising as his words hung in the air between them. So the truth had come out at last. Brandon Calhoun was nothing but a strutting, bombastic snob who placed himself above common folk like Will and herself and judged his daughter worthy of a Vanderbilt heir. Merciful heaven, what grandiose delusions! He was nothing but a big fish in a very small pond! If she weren't so furious, she could almost feel sorry for him!

"You've made your position quite clear, Mr. Calhoun," she said in a voice that crackled like thin ice. "At least we seem to agree on one thing. I'm as anxious to protect Will's future as you are to promote your daughter's."

Her subtle shift of verbs was not lost on him. His cobalt eyes darkened and she braced herself for another blast of hostility. For a long moment the only sound in the room was the droning buzz of a horsefly trapped against the windowpane. Seconds crawled past. Then, as Harriet held her breath, his rigid shoulders sagged. He exhaled raggedly, thrusting his fists into the pockets of his fine gabardine jacket.

"Jenny's all I have," he said. "She's the only thing in my life that I give a damn about. If you had children of your own, you'd understand how I feel."

If you had children of your own. Harriet winced as if he had caused her physical pain. She had put aside the hope of having her own family when she'd taken on the task of raising Will. Now, at twenty-nine, she knew that time had passed her by. She had become that most disparaged of creatures—an old maid.

Pressing her lips together, she gazed past him into the blur of sunlight that fell through the uncurtained window. She had always despised self-pity and refused to indulge in it. But the wretched man had known exactly where to jab and he had jabbed with a vengeance. Harriet had no doubt that he'd meant to wound her.

He cleared his throat, breaking the leaden silence between them. "This so-called talk you had with your brother. What did he have to say about his intentions?"

"That he loves your daughter. That he wants to marry her."

He sucked in his breath as if he'd been gut-punched. "And how did you answer him?"

"How do you expect I would answer?" she retorted. "I told him it was foolish to even think of love at his age, let alone marriage! Getting involved with a girl at this point could ruin his plans for the future—indeed, it could ruin his whole life!"

"And did you resolve anything with him?" Brandon Calhoun's voice was flat and cold.

"Only that there'll be no more sneaking out at night to see Jenny. Will tends to be headstrong. As his sister, I've learned that if I draw the reins too tightly he's quite capable of breaking them and going his own way."

"So the reality is, he's eighteen years old and the only control you have over the boy is what little he allows you." He shot her a withering scowl. "I thought as much."

Harriet fought the urge to fly at him and rip the smug expression off his face with her bare hands. "Whatever you're implying, Mr. Calhoun, my brother is a decent, responsible young man!" she snapped. "Ask anyone who knows him!"

"I already have. Hezekiah Moon at the feed store says your brother's the best worker he's ever hired. He's always on time, he has every account figured to the penny, and he can load a wagon in the time it takes the customer to have a smoke. But that doesn't mean I want the young whelp sniffing around my Jenny!"

"So what *is* it you want?" Harriet demanded, suddenly out of patience with him. "If you've only come to grouse and complain, please consider your mission accomplished and let me get back to work!"

He retreated a step as if startled by her sudden vehemence. Then he swiftly recovered and seized the offensive. "I wouldn't have wasted my time in coming here if I didn't have something in mind," he said, shifting his weight uneasily, like a boxer. "Since you don't keep your money in my bank, I can only judge your financial situation from what I see. You live in a rented, two-bedroom shack next to the cemetery. You don't own a buggy or even a horse, and as for your clothes—"

"My clothes are clean and modest and in good repair." Harriet's fists clenched against the skirt of her faded gingham dress. "If I don't look like a page from a fashion magazine, that's none of your concern, nor is the way I live! Aside from the matter of Will and Jenny, you and I have nothing to say to each other, Mr. Calhoun! Now kindly get out of my classroom and leave me in peace!"

He loomed over her, making everything in the room seem small. Blue lightning crackled in his eyes. "For what it's worth, Miss Smith, I own this building and the land it sits on," he said. "That would make it *my* classroom. And I don't intend to leave you in any kind of peace until you've heard me out."

Harriet willed herself to ignore her liquid knees and slamming pulse. She faced him squarely, her chin up, her features composed, her eyes meeting his in a steady gaze. But when she spoke, her shaking voice betrayed her. "Go on, then. I can hardly throw you out with my bare hands."

One dark smudge of an eyebrow slid upward in unspoken challenge, as if to imply he'd like to see her try manhandling him; but when he spoke, his manner was cold and formal. "Very well. I'm prepared to make you and your brother an offer. I think you'll agree that it's more than generous."

"I'm listening." Harriet felt as if the ground had dissolved under her feet, leaving her with no solid place to stand. He was so imposing, so damnably sure of his power to turn her to quivering jelly. She found herself wishing he would give her an excuse to slap his insolent face. Of all the girls in town, why had Will chosen to fall in love with the pampered only child of a man like Brandon Calhoun?

He took a deep breath, the air rushing into his powerful chest. "Here's my offer," he said, pulling a folded paper out of his vest. "Leave town within the week, the two of you, and I'll pay your way to wherever you want to go. If your brother agrees never to contact Jenny again, I'm prepared to pay for his college education. Every penny of it."

Harriet stared up at him, shocked into silence by his audacity. The offer was more than generous; it was unimaginable.

She struggled to keep her wits about her, but her head had already begun to spin—as he had doubtless known it would. Over the years she had saved her own money for Will's education, living like a pauper so that she could send every spare cent to the Denver bank where she kept her savings. By now, she calculated, she had enough to pay for three years of college. Somehow, with Will working summers, they would manage the fourth year.

But if Brandon Calhoun were to pay for Will's education, the money she had saved would be hers. Dear heaven, she would be able to travel—to England, to Italy, to all the places she'd dreamed of seeing. Or she might even be able to buy her own small house, with space for a garden and no landlord to trouble her for the rent. It would be like a dream come true.

All she needed to do was to strike a bargain with the devil.

He was watching her, his steel-blue eyes wary but confident. Harriet could almost read his thoughts. This sorry spinster, so drab in her worn gingham frock, could not possibly be foolish enough to turn him down. Just like anyone else, the woman had her price. For a few thousand dollars he would be rid of her and her troublesome brother once and for all, with no stain on his own conscience or reputation.

Brandon Calhoun thought he could buy them off, as if they were common trash; as if they were so poor and so devoid of pride that they would take his charity—or bribery, to call it by its real name. She was as anxious to keep Will and Jenny apart as he was, but not at such a price. What a smug, self-righteous prig he was!

The wave of outraged pride that welled up in Harriet almost swept her off her feet. "How dare you?" She flung the words at him. "I am not for sale, Mr. Calhoun, and neither is my brother! I have enough money saved to pay for Will's education myself. And as for our leaving, I have a two-year contract and twenty-three children who will be without a teacher if I desert them. If you're so anxious to keep your daughter from associating with common folk like us, you might want to consider leaving town yourself!"

He glowered at her, his face burning as if she had slapped him. Harriet fought the impulse to shrink away from him. Even with her heart pounding and her legs buckling beneath her petticoat, she could not let this man intimidate her.

"Very well," he said in a flat, cold voice. "I made you a fair and generous offer and you rejected it. All I have left to say is, keep your brother in line for his own good, Miss Smith. If he so much as speaks to my daughter, I'll have the law on him!"

With those words, Brandon Calhoun turned on his heel and stalked out of the schoolroom.

Harriet stood rooted to the floor, gazing after him as he disappeared down the path in a swirl of fallen leaves. Her hands were shaking and the inside of her mouth felt as if she'd swallowed a fistful of dry sawdust.

Stumbling backward, she collapsed onto the

cramped seat of a first-grade desk. Outside, the sun was sinking below the peaks. Its fading light cast dingy shadows on the schoolroom walls. The breeze that blew in through the open doorway had turned bitter. Harriet wrapped her arms around her trembling body, too stunned to even get up and close the door.

Had she done the right thing? Heaven help her, should she have swallowed her pride and accepted Brandon Calhoun's offer?

Her spirit sank deeper as a gust of wind rattled the trees, ripping leaves off the branches and scattering the math papers on her desk. Maybe she should have put the banker off, told him she'd think on the matter and let him know. At least she should have spoken with her brother before making such a rash decision—but no, that would have changed nothing. Will was head over heels in love with the banker's pretty, shy daughter. Young as he was, he had his own share of family pride. His answer would have been the same as hers.

Now what? How could she keep her brother from pursuing Jenny Calhoun—especially when Jenny seemed as eager as he was?

Harriet's head throbbed at the thought of what lay ahead. Brandon had spoken truly about one thing. Will was eighteen years old, practically a man, and the only control she had over him was what little he allowed her. Her only hope was that her headstrong brother could be made to listen to reason.

Keep your brother in line for his own good, Miss Smith. If he so much as speaks to my daughter, I'll have the law on him!

The words rang in Harriet's ears as she staggered to her feet, shoved the door closed and bent to gather her wind-scattered papers. Could Brandon Calhoun really put her brother in jail? There was no law, surely, against two young people falling in love, but as the most influential man in town, the arrogant banker had the means to accomplish anything he wanted.

Would he carry out his threat, or worse? Either way it was a chance Harriet could ill afford to take. She had no means of knowing what lay in the darkness of Brandon's heart. The only certainty was that she had made a very dangerous enemy.

Chapter Two

All the way home Harriet struggled with the question of what to tell her brother. Given the power, she would have chosen to wipe out the shattering encounter with Brandon Calhoun, the way she might erase a child's botched arithmetic problem from the blackboard. That way, Will would never know what she had thrown away out of pride; nor would she need to make it clear that she was still dead set against his courtship of Jenny.

But that kind of denial was useless. One way or another, Will was bound to ferret out the truth. It was best that he hear it from her.

The wind plucked at her thin skirts, raising gooseflesh on her legs as she passed along the weathered picket fence that ringed the cemetery. Blowing leaves danced among the tombstones like ghostly spirits in the twilight.

Harriet pulled her thin wool shawl tighter around her shoulders. She'd been told that winters were long and harsh in this high mountain valley, but she had comforted herself with the thought that Will would be with her through the cold months to shovel the paths, chop wood for the stove and provide companionship on dark, snowbound evenings. Now she found herself wondering if it might not be best to send him to Indiana before the storms set in. He wouldn't be able to start college until spring term, but maybe he could find work and a place to board until then. It would be a dear price to pay, for she truly wanted his presence over the winter. But at least he would be far away from Jenny Calhoun and her fire-breathing dragon of a father!

Harriet's resolve began to crumble as she opened the door of the unpainted clapboard house and stepped over the threshold into its dusky interior. The place would be so lonely without Will. Worse, he was only eighteen, little more than a boy! And they had no relatives anywhere who might take him in. Sending him away to school was one thing, but simply putting him on the train was quite another. If he left now, he would be entirely on his own, easy prey for any opportunist who happened along! Merciful heaven, how could she just turn him out into the world, so innocent and untried?

Harriet was still struggling with the dilemma twenty minutes later as she sliced the bread and set the table for supper. The fire in the stove flickered on the rough-cut walls, lending a touch of warmth to the bleak kitchen with its small alcove that served as a parlor. Brandon had been right about the house. It was a shack in every sense of the word. Even the homey touches Harriet had added—the calico curtains, the crocheted afghan draped over the rocker and the framed family photographs on the wall—could not relieve the drabness or stanch the cold draughts that whistled between the boards.

She had rented the cheapest place she could find so that she could save the remainder that was needed for her brother's education. True, she may have carried frugality too far this time. But there was nothing to be done about it now, except to thank the good Lord that she and Will had a roof over their heads, food on the table and the bright promise of days to come.

She was stirring last night's leftover beans when she heard the scrape of Will's boots on the stoop. Harriet could tell from the weary cadence of the sound that he'd put in a long, hard day at the feed store. At an age when many boys were sowing their wild oats, Will did the labor of a man. But he would not always have to earn his bread by the sweat of his brow. She would see to that. She owed that much to their parents, who had cherished such hopes for him.

Will stumbled inside as if the wind had blown him through the open doorway. His hair and clothes were coated with dust from loading sacks of feed. His body sagged with weariness, as if he had spent the past nine hours carrying the weight of the world on his young back.

"Supper will be on by the time you're washed," Harriet said, wishing she had a better meal to offer him than bread and beans, and more cheering conversation than what she needed to tell him. But the present trouble was Will's own doing, she reminded herself. Much as she loved her brother, she could not condone what he had done or shield him from the consequences.

As she was ladling up the beans, Will emerged from the back of the house, his face scrubbed, his dark hair finger-combed and glistening with water. His lanky frame folded like a carpenter's rule as he sank onto the rickety wooden chair. He was still awkward, like a yearling hound, with big feet and big hands and a body that was all bone and sinew. His face might one day be handsome, but for now there was an unformed quality about his features. His nose seemed too big, his jaw too long and gaunt and his chin was punctuated by an angry red pimple. Only his eyes, like two quiet black pools, showed the true character of the man who waited within the boy.

He was too thin, Harriet thought. He worked too hard and laughed too seldom. And now he was hopelessly, determinedly, in love. Heaven help them all.

She murmured a few words of grace over the food, then waited until he had buttered his bread and taken a few bites of food before plunging into her account of Brandon Calhoun's offer and her own defiant refusal.

She had expected him to be upset, but he ate as he listened, chewing his beans and bread in silence as the story spilled out of her.

By the time she'd reached the end of it, Harriet felt as if she had lived through the encounter a second time. Her pulse was ragged, her breathing shallow, as if an iron band had been clamped around her ribs. Gazing into Brandon's angry blue eyes had been like facing a charging buffalo or leaning into the face of a hurricane. Even the memory left her nerves in tatters.

"The man was simply monstrous," she said. "He threatened—actually *threatened*—to see you in jail if you came near his daughter again, and I've no doubt that he has the power to do just that. Be careful, Will. Brandon Calhoun owns a good piece of this town. He has influential friends and people who are in his debt. A word from him and your whole future could be ruined."

Harriet's gaze dropped to her untouched plate as she struggled to collect her emotions. All her life she had protected her young brother. Now he was nearly a man, but it was clear that he still needed her protection and good judgment.

She raised her eyes to find him sopping up the last of the beans with the crust of his bread. His face wore such a faraway expression that Harriet found herself wondering whether he had heard a word she'd said. Will had seemed unusually preoccupied of late. She had chalked it up to the vagaries of puppy love.

But maybe there were other things troubling him. Maybe she should have been talking less and listening more.

"Are you all right, Will?" she asked, feeling the weight of sudden apprehension. "Is there something you need to tell me?"

He raked his lank, dark hair back from his brow. For the space of a breath he hesitated, chewing his lower lip. Then he shook his head. "No, there's nothing," he muttered. "Nothing you can help, at least."

"Maybe it would be best to send you to Indiana now, before the snow sets in," Harriet said, grasping at the possibility. "You could find a place to live, get a better-paying job than the one you have at the feed store—"

"I'm not going to Indiana, sis," he said quietly.

"Well, of course you don't have to go right away." She was babbling now, unwilling to face the reality that lurked behind his words. "As long as you're there in time to get settled in before the beginning of the term—"

"I'm not going to Indiana." There was a grim finality to his words, as if he were telling her that someone had died.

"But—" she sputtered in disbelief. "What about your schooling, Will? What about your future?"

His eyes were like a wall behind their dark pupils. "I'm not going to college. I'm staying right here in Dutchman's Creek, with Jenny. We're going to be married."

* * *

Brandon strode through the fading twilight, his boots crushing the aspen leaves that littered the path like spilled gold coins. Damn Harriet Smith, he thought, muttering under his breath. Damn her to hell, and double damn that randy, calf-eyed brother of hers!

He'd done his best to reason with her, but the woman had more pride than common sense! Now Brandon found himself at an impasse, with only one way out.

His offer would have made things better for everyone concerned. He had made it in the spirit of fairness and generosity. But Miss Harriet Smith had reacted as if he'd just proposed to buy her spinsterly body for a night of unbridled lust. Her eyes had drilled into him, their expression making him feel as crass as a tin spittoon.

Who did she think she was, anyway? For all her shabby clothes and skinned-back hair, there was an aura of fierce pride that clung to the tall schoolmarm; something regal in those large, intelligent eyes that were the color of moss agate flecked with copper and set in a pale, cool ivory cameo of a face. And there was something almost queenly in her graceful, erect carriage. Given the right clothes and a decent hairstyle, she might be a handsome woman, he mused. But never mind that fantasy. The high-minded Miss Smith might be made to look like the Queen of Sheba, but she had the disposition of a hornet. He wanted nothing more to do with her.

He walked on as the glow of sunset faded into gloomy autumn twilight. From up the roadway, at the top of the hill he could see the glimmer of lamplight in the windows of his stately redbrick home—not a grand place by Denver standards, but by far the finest house in Dutchman's Creek.

Most nights it gave him a sense of satisfaction, seeing what his hard work and shrewd business sense had built. He had come to Dutchman's Creek and started the bank during the silver boom; and he had invested its profits wisely enough to thrive even after the mines played out and the economy shifted to farming and ranching. He owned a handsome assortment of properties in the valley and was wealthy enough to live anywhere he chose. But he was a man who liked to put down roots, and his roots were here.

Most nights he would sit down with Jenny to share the hot meal that Helga Gruenwald, their aging housekeeper, had prepared. While they ate, Jenny would chatter about the day's events, her girlish voice like music in his ears.

Most nights he looked forward to coming home. But tonight would be different. Brandon's footsteps dragged as he realized those sweet evenings with his daughter were about to end, perhaps forever.

All the way home, he had wrestled with the wrenching decision. If he could not get rid of Will Smith, then he would have no choice except to send Jenny away before things got any further out of hand.

His sister in Maryland had offered to take Jenny in so that she could attend a nearby girls' preparatory school. Jenny had shown no interest in going, so Brandon, reluctant to part with her, had not pushed the plan. But now…

He paused in the shadow of a gnarled pine tree. His clenched fists thrust deep into his pockets as he gazed up at the cold, silver disk of the moon.

She was so innocent, his Jenny. A reckless, uncaring boy could easily take advantage of her. Someone needed to tell her the facts of life for her own protection. But who? Brandon sighed wearily. It would hardly be proper for him to instruct her. And he could not imagine the grim, taciturn Helga broaching such an intimate subject.

He should have remarried after Ada's death, he thought as he forced his steps toward the house. Not for love—he had long since given up on that sentimental nonsense—but he should have taken a wife for Jenny's sake. He was just beginning to realize how much the girl had missed having a mother in the past six years. In remaining single, he had shielded his own heart but he had failed to meet his daughter's needs. No wonder she was so vulnerable, so hungry for the affection he'd had too little time to give her.

With a leaden spirit, he mounted the three steps to the wide, covered porch. Even the aroma of Helga's succulent pot roast, which enveloped him like a warm blanket as he opened the door, did nothing to raise his spirits.

The house seemed strangely quiet. To Brandon, it was as if the silence floated ahead of him, casting its phantom shadow down the tiled hallway with its oak-paneled walls and tall grandfather clock, through the parlor with its hefty leather armchairs and into the dining room where the long table seemed to dwarf the slight figure in pink who sat in a high-backed chair on its far side.

Only as he saw her did Brandon realize how much he'd feared that his daughter might not be here to welcome him.

"Hello, Papa." Her voice was thin, her smile as tenuous as a cobweb. The two of them had not spoken since last night when he'd caught her opening her window to young Will Smith. In a rage, Brandon had ordered Will off the property and sent his daughter back to bed. Even later, when the house had quieted down, he had been too upset to go talk with her.

"Hello, angel." Brandon tried to sound natural, but his voice was hoarse with strain. No words could change what had happened last night. The trusting relationship they'd shared for so many years would never be the same again.

They sat on opposite sides of the table, the painful silence a wall between them as they picked at their food, pretending to eat. Helga, who took her own supper early, shuffled in and out with the dishes, her wrinkled face as impassive as a slab of burled oak.

Brandon studied his daughter furtively over the rim of his coffee cup. She looked like one of her own precious dolls in her starched pink pinafore, her pale gold curls caught up and bound by a matching ribbon. But her face was blotchy and her cornflower eyes were laced with red, as if she had spent much of the day crying. He ached, knowing that nothing he had to say would ease those tears.

Only when Helga had retired to her cozy room at the rear of the house did Brandon venture to bring up the matter that was tearing at his heart.

"I've been thinking..." He paused to clear the tightness from his throat. "I've been thinking it's time you went to stay with your aunt Ellen for a while."

Jenny's blue eyes widened. Her lips parted in protest, but Brandon cut her off before she could speak.

"It's high time you continued your education," he said. "Your aunt Ellen has a fine, big house, and I know she'll be happy to have you. You can make new friends at school, and there'll be dances, parties and picnics—plenty of chances for you to meet suitable young men."

"I don't care a fig for dances and parties." There was a thread of steel in Jenny's voice. "Will is a suitable young man, and I happen to love him."

"You're too young to know anything about love," Brandon snapped. "Will Smith is a small-town yokel with no more manners than a mule. Once you've met some proper gentlemen, with the means to give you the life you deserve, you'll come to realize that and you'll thank me for saving you from your own foolishness!"

He saw her face blanch, saw the whitening of the skin around her lips, but he plunged ahead before she could raise an argument. "Pack your things, Jenny. You won't need much in the way of clothes—your aunt can help you buy new things in Baltimore. We'll be leaving for Johnson City tomorrow, in time to put you on the afternoon train. Helga can go along to make sure you arrive safely. I daresay she'll enjoy the trip."

"No."

Brandon stared at her as if she'd just slapped his face. Jenny had always been the most respectful of daughters. He could not recall even one time when she had openly defied him—until now.

"Excuse me?" His words emerged as a hoarse whisper.

"You heard me." He saw the tears then, welling up in her eyes and spilling through the golden fringe of her lashes. "Sending me away won't make any difference. It's too late for that."

"Too late?" The pounding of Brandon's heart seemed to fill the room. "What do you mean, too late?"

Her voice caught in a ragged little sob. "I'm going to have a baby, Papa. Will's baby. And we're getting married whether you like it or not."

Chapter Three

Late that night the season's first winter storm spilled like a feathery avalanche over the granite crags of the Rockies. Ahead of the snow, a howling wind swept down the canyons, stripping the leaves from the aspens and maples, scouring away the last remnants of Indian summer.

Harriet lay awake in the darkness, listening to the sound of the wind clawing at the shingles on the roof. Not that she would have slept in any case. Things had gone from bad to worse with Will that evening. Now, as she relived the memory for perhaps the hundredth time, her stomach clenched in anguish.

Will's announcement that he was not going to college had unraveled the whole fabric of Harriet's life. Her first reaction had been shocked disbelief. She had tried to reason with the boy, but to no avail. His stubborn young mind was set and, as that reality struck her, she had broken down and railed at him.

"You're throwing it all away, Will!" She had flung the words like daggers, wanting to wound him as he had wounded her. "Our parents' dreams for you, my hard work and sacrifice to make them come true— all of it for a golden-haired bit of fluff with no more sense than a chicken!"

Will had taken her tirade calmly until she had attacked Jenny. "You're talking about my future wife!" he'd snapped, the color rising in his pale face.

"Have you lost your reason?" Harriet had retorted. "Brandon Calhoun will have you drawn and quartered if you go near the girl!"

Both of them had risen to their feet. His dark eyes had glared down at her as if she were a simple-minded fool. "Jenny's a woman, not a girl. She's reached the age of consent, and if we want to get married, there's not a damned thing Brandon Calhoun or anyone else can do about it!"

"Not within the law, maybe. But I got a taste of his methods this afternoon. The man is absolutely ruthless! Cross him and he'll do anything, legal or not, to destroy you!" Harriet had seized his arm, gripping it as she'd done when he was five years old and she'd saved his life by pulling him out of the millrace. "I can't let you do this, Will! I haven't worked and sacrificed all these years to let you spend your life in a backwater town, married to a spoiled little chit who'll bring you nothing but trouble!"

She had said too much. She'd known it even before she'd felt him stiffen beneath her touch and seen the flash of cold anger in his eyes. But it had been too late to take back the words spoken in a fever of desperation.

"I can't live my life for you," he'd said in a strained voice. "And you've already lived too much of yours for me. It's time to let go, sis. It's time for you to back off and let me be a man."

"But you're *not* a man—not yet!" She'd gripped him stubbornly, refusing to give up. "You're eighteen years old, and you've no way to support a wife, let alone one who's grown up rich and pampered! *Think* about it, Will! Use the brain God gave you, instead of—"

"That's enough." He had twisted away to stand facing her, his face shadowed by an odd sadness. "I'm tired. I'm going to bed. We can talk in the morning."

"But what about your lessons?" she'd protested, ignoring what he'd just told her. "You have three weeks to finish your algebra course before…"

Her words had trailed off as he'd cast her a look of utter desperation, then stalked into his room and slammed the door behind him.

Now, sick with regret, Harriet lay staring up into the darkness. Why hadn't she been more understanding? Why hadn't she listened to her brother instead of raging at him like a harridan? He had looked so weary, as if the weight of the whole world had dropped onto his young shoulders. Her emotional outburst had only added to that burden.

The worst of it was, she had treated him like a child when, in truth, he was already doing a man's work, and doing it well. As for his character, Will had been responsible, honest and trustworthy his whole life. Harriet remembered the summer he was eleven years old and he'd rescued a lost purebred spaniel puppy. He'd fallen in love with the little dog and would have given anything to keep it, but because he'd known it wasn't a stray, he'd forced himself to trudge up and down the dusty streets, knocking on doors until he found the rightful owner. Afterward, Will had been so heartbroken that he'd refused the reward the family had offered for the return of their valuable pet.

It was much the same now, Harriet told herself. Will was infatuated with pretty Jenny Calhoun, but in the end he would see the light and do the right thing, no matter how much it hurt. Meanwhile, trying to force him to a decision would only make him dig in his stubborn young heels. It was time to take a quieter, wiser course of action.

Tomorrow was Saturday. While Will was at work, she would have time to prepare a pot roast with new potatoes, carrots and onions, and to bake his favorite molasses cake. When he came home from work, she would encourage him to talk, and this time she would listen instead of lecture. Somehow she would find a way to break this spell of youthful madness and set his feet back on the path to happiness and prosperity.

As for Brandon Calhoun, he could take his precious daughter and go to the devil! If the man harmed so much as a hair on her brother's head, she would see that he paid for the rest of his life!

A shattering heat, like flame blazing through ice, surged through Harriet's body as Brandon's image took shape in her mind. She had struggled for hours to erase that image—the looming stature that made her feel small and defenseless; the piercing cerulean eyes that rendered her as transparent as apple jelly; the chiseled-granite jaw and the grim yet, somehow, disturbingly sensual mouth.

Harriet had never felt at ease around men, especially men like Brandon Calhoun. Arrogant, overbearing and reeking of self-made success, with the kind of looks that caused matrons to reach for their smelling salts, he was everything that made her want to snatch up her skirts and bolt like a rabbit.

But running away from Brandon was the worst thing she could do. If she so much as flinched under the scrutiny of those storm-blue eyes, he would see it as a victory. She would never again be able to stand up to him in a convincing manner. Despite any show of bravado on her part, he would look down at her and know that her mouth was dry, her pulse was racing and her knees were quivering beneath her petticoats. He would bully her into a corner and keep her there while he did his worst to destroy her brother's life.

Whatever the cost to her own pride, she could not allow that to happen.

Outside, the voice of the wind had risen from a moan to a shriek. Its force caught the edge of a warped shutter, splintering the weakened wood and tearing it loose from its upper hinge. Held by a single corner, the shutter flapped and twisted in the wind, banging against the front window, threatening to shatter the fragile glass panes.

Harriet sat up in bed, shivering in her high-necked flannel nightgown. She was not tall enough to reach the top of the shutter and hammer the hinge back into place, nor was she strong enough to pull the shutter down for later repair. For this, she would have to rouse her angry, exhausted young brother.

Without taking time to find her slippers, she sprinted across the icy floor. A wooden splinter jabbed into the ball of her bare foot. Ignoring the pain, she rapped sharply on the thin planks. She hated the thought of waking Will when he was so tired, but the shutter had to be fixed or it would break the window, letting in the cold wind and the snow that was sure to follow.

"Will!" When he did not respond, she rapped harder on the door. "Wake up! I need your help!"

She paused, ears straining in the darkness, but no

sound came from her brother's room. She could hear nothing except the slamming of the shutter, the scrape of a dry branch against the roof and the howling cry of the wind.

"Will!" She pounded so hard that pain shot through her knuckles, but when she stopped to listen again, there was still no answer. Harriet sighed. Will always slept like a hibernating bear, with the covers pulled up over his ears. She would have no choice except to go in and wake him, as she'd done so often when he was a schoolboy.

The doorknob, which had no lock attached, was cold in her hand. She gave it a sharp twist to release the catch. The warped wood groaned as the door swung open on its cheap tin hinges.

The room was eerily silent, its stillness unbroken by so much as a breath. A flicker of moonlight through the window revealed a lumpy, motionless form in the bed. Harriet's throat tightened as she crept toward it.

"Will?" She tugged at the quilts. There was no stirring at her touch, no familiar, awakening moan. Heart suddenly racing, she seized the covers and swept them aside. An anguished groan stirred in her throat as she stared down at her brother's pillows, his bunched-up dressing gown and his Sunday hat, arranged to mimic his sleeping outline beneath the covers.

Will was gone.

* * *

The frantic pounding on Brandon's front door jerked him from the edge of a fitful sleep. He sat up, still groggy, swearing under his breath as he swung his legs off the bed, jammed his feet into fleece-lined slippers and reached for his merino dressing gown. What could bring someone to his house at this ungodly hour? Had something gone wrong at the bank? A robbery? A fire?

Still cursing, he lit a lantern and made his way down the long flight of stairs. Only Helga slept on the ground floor of the house, and she snored too loudly to hear anything short of an earthquake. As for Jenny…

His chest clenched at the memory of their confrontation over dinner. Lord, what he wouldn't give to wake up and discover that he'd dreamed the whole miserable scene—and that his precious, innocent girl wasn't really with child by a moon-eyed yokel who worked at the feed store and lived in a shack with his prissy schoolmarm sister.

First thing tomorrow he would be driving her to Johnson City and putting her on a train for Baltimore, where his sister, God willing, would shelter her from scandal and see that her baby was adopted by a good family.

As for himself, he would wait until the train had pulled out of the station. Then, by all heaven, he would go after the young fool who had ruined his daughter and make him pay for every despicable thing he had done!

The pounding continued as Brandon lumbered across the entry hall. "Hold your horses," he muttered, fumbling with the bolt. "You don't need to break down the damned door!"

Released by the latch, the door blew inward. A bedraggled figure stumbled into the hallway to collapse like a storm-washed bird against the wall. Brandon stared, his gaze taking in the wind-raked tangle of dark hair above copper-flecked eyes that were wide and frightened, set in a face that seemed too narrow and pale to contain them. The creature wore a threadbare cloak, clutched around her thin body with fingers that looked to be half-frozen. Her lips were blue with cold.

Time shuddered to a halt as Brandon recognized Harriet Smith.

Summoning her strength, she pushed herself away from the wall and stood erect to face him in the flickering lamplight. Sparks of defiance glittered in her eyes, but her teeth were chattering so violently that she could not speak. The shack by the cemetery was almost two miles from Brandon's house. Judging from the looks of her, she had walked the whole distance in the storm.

What was the woman doing here at this hour? Had she changed her mind about his offer? Not a chance of that, Brandon thought, remembering her fiery pride. More likely, her damn-fool brother had just given her the same news Jenny had given him and she'd come for her pound of flesh.

A dizzying tide of rage swept through him. For one blinding moment, it was all he could do not to seize her in his two hands, jerk her off her feet and fling her back into the storm. After all, didn't she share the blame for what had happened? Hadn't she reared the young hooligan who'd impregnated his daughter? Hadn't her coming to Dutchman's Creek set the whole ugly chain of events in motion?

With near-superhuman effort, Brandon willed his impulses under control. When he spoke, his voice emerged as a hoarse croak. "What is it? Are you all right?"

She shook her head, her mouth working in a futile effort to speak. Specks of ice clung to her thick black eyelashes. They glowed in the lamplight like miniature jewels. Below them, her eyes watched him guardedly, emotions he could not read swimming in their coppery depths.

Only one thing seemed clear—if he wanted the woman to talk, he would have to get her warm first. Shaking off the paralysis of surprise, Brandon set the lantern on a table and forced himself to move toward her.

His hands pried her stiffened fingers loose from the edges of her cloak. The soggy garment fell to the floor, revealing beneath it a faded gingham dress, so hastily donned that the buttons down the front were misaligned with their buttonholes. The resulting gaps allowed glimpses of the creamy skin beneath—

far more of it than any lady would want a gentleman to see.

Brandon averted his eyes, but not swiftly enough. She glanced down, to where his gaze had rested an instant before. With a horrified gasp, she jerked her arms across her breasts. Color flamed in her blood-less cheeks.

Without a word, Brandon whipped off his woolen robe and wrapped it around her trembling body. She huddled into its warmth, her eyes downcast, her teeth still chattering.

Suddenly her gaze jerked upward. Her color deep-ened. Brandon bit back a curse as he realized what had caught her eye. The hem of his gray flannel nightshirt hung just past his knees, revealing the lower part of his bare legs and ankles—more naked flesh than any proper lady would be fit to see.

Well, to hell with her, he thought. If the sight of his hairy calves offended Harriet Smith's sense of propriety, that was her problem. It wasn't as if he'd sent her an engraved invitation to come calling to-night. She could damned well take him as he was or come back when he was dressed for company.

It was chilly in the front hall. Gripping her upper arm through the robe, he steered her into the parlor, where a few dying embers still flickered in the fire-place. Two comfortable leather armchairs faced the hearth. Thrusting her firmly into one of them, he gathered some kindling sticks from the wood box and began feeding them into the embers. Little by little, small orange tongues of flame began to lick at the splintered pitch pine. The crackling sound was warm and welcome.

"Will's gone." Harriet's low voice, rising from the shadows of the chair, startled him. "I think he's run away."

Brandon bit back a sigh of relief. It would hurt Jenny's pride to know that Will had deserted her, but in the long run it would make everything easier. Now, surely, she would stop fighting his plan to send her to Baltimore.

He glanced up at Harriet, his expression deliberately cynical. "So the young rooster's flown the coop, has he? Somehow I can't say I'm surprised. I would have wagered he wasn't man enough to own up to his responsibility."

She surged forward, her eyes suddenly angry. "I don't know what responsibility you're talking about, Mr. C-Calhoun," she said, her teeth still chattering with cold. "But I didn't fight my way through the storm to sit here and listen to you disparage my brother! I only came to ask you if you'd seen Will, or if you had any idea where he might be. If you can't tell me, I'll be on my way...."

Her voice trailed off, catching at the end as if she were stifling a sob. Brandon stared at her in amazement. Lord, didn't she know? Hadn't the young fool told her what he'd done to Jenny?

Turning away from the fire, he seized her icy hands—not out of affection or sympathy but in an effort to hold her captive while he pummeled her with the truth. Her thin, cold fingers were all but lost in his big fists. Instinctively they sought the warmth of his flesh, pressing into the hollows of his palms, even as her eyes blazed resistance.

Heat and emotion had brought the color back to her face. With the wind-tossed mane of her hair framing her aquiline features, she reminded Brandon of some wild, mythical bird goddess, held to earth only by his determined grip. Let her go and she would fly away, back into the storm that had brought her here.

Lowering his eyes, he forced his mind back to reality. When he looked at her again it was dowdy, stubborn Harriet Smith he saw. Harriet Smith, his enemy, dressed in his own robe and a pauper's gown that gapped between the buttons.

He pressed her hands so hard that she winced. "Didn't your brother talk to you?" he rasped. "Didn't he tell you about the ungodly thing he'd done to my Jenny?"

"What?" She stared at him, caught off guard. "Will told me he'd changed his mind about going to college. We quarreled…" Her voice trailed off. Her eyes widened in horror as the realization struck her.

"Yes!" Brandon crushed her hands in his, wanting her to feel the kind of pain he was feeling. "Your no-account brother has gotten Jenny with child. She gave him the news yesterday, and now he's skipped out on her, slunk off like the filthy coward he is!"

He watched her crumble then, like a mud figure in a deluge—first her face, then her head and shoulders. Even her fingers seemed to dissolve in his hands.

"No," she murmured dazedly. "Will's always been such a good boy, so upright and honorable. He wouldn't do such a thing, especially to someone he cared about!"

"He would and he did," Brandon snapped, releasing her hands. "I'm only thankful that he's finally out of Jenny's life for good. The young scapegrace has caused her enough grief."

"No!" Harriet was sitting straight now, leaning forward, her eyes like twin flames in the darkness. "Tonight at supper, Will said he wouldn't leave her— that he would *never* leave her. He must have been trying to tell me about the baby, but I refused to listen. I just—"

She halted in midsentence, the color draining from her face. When she spoke again, her voice was taut and strained. "Where is your daughter?"

"In her room where she belongs," Brandon growled impatiently. "I checked on her before I went to bed. She was sleeping like an angel."

It was only a half truth. Jenny had cried herself into silence behind the closed door of her room. Later, when Brandon had passed her door on his way to bed, she had not answered his discreet knock. He had left her in peace, resolving to settle things in the morning.

Only now, as he gazed into Harriet's stricken face, did the truth leap like chain lightning from her mind to his.

Not that! Dear God, anything but that!

Knocking over a footstool in his haste, Brandon dashed for the entry and seized the lantern from the table. Harriet sprang to her feet and plunged after him, clutching her skirts as they pounded up the stairs.

Brandon was not a religious man, but he found himself silently praying as they reached the door of Jenny's room. *Please let her be here. Let her be safe....*

But it was too late for prayers. Even as he fumbled with the knob and flung the door open, he knew what he would find.

Chapter Four

As the door to Jenny's room swung open, light from the upraised lantern cast Brandon's features into craggy relief. Harriet watched from the shadows as waves of raw emotion swept across his face—first disbelief, then despair, then a tide of helpless fury, as if he were biting back a howl. She had never seen a man look so angry, or so wretched.

Harriet braced herself for a tirade against her brother, but it did not come. He only stood in rigid silence, one white-knuckled hand gripping the lantern, one taut muscle twitching in his cheek.

No words were needed. His expression made it clear that when Brandon caught up with Will, there would be hell to pay.

Tearing her eyes away, Harriet stared past him into the silent room. The pretty little bedchamber was in perfect order, as if young Jenny had given it a farewell tidying before she'd vanished into the stormy night. The pink satin coverlet had been carefully smoothed over the canopied bed, with ruffled pillows arranged against a headboard of inlaid mahogany. A lacy afghan, crocheted in shades of rose and mauve, was draped over the back of a carved wooden rocker. Its colors matched those of the oval rug, hooked in an intricate pattern of cabbage roses, that lay on the polished wooden floor.

It was the kind of room Harriet had dreamed of as a child, and never possessed. The kind of room a father would want to provide for a little girl he loved.

Two exquisite French dolls, with mohair curls and bisque porcelain faces, decorated the top of a bookshelf. A third doll, with golden ringlets like Jenny's, sat in a miniature copy of the rocking chair, dressed in a gauzy pink princess gown and holding a tiny doll of her own. Harriet had never seen such elegant dolls. The cost of any one of them would probably be enough to keep a poor family in beans and bacon for an entire winter. Now they sat like abandoned children, their glass eyes wide and vacant, silent witnesses to everything that had taken place in this child-woman's bedroom.

From the far side of the room, a flutter of movement caught Harriet's eye. Her taut nerves jumped— but it was only a lace curtain, blown by a sliver of wind that whistled through a crack beneath the sash.

Jenny, it appeared, had not quite managed to close the window when she'd climbed out into the darkness.

Crossing the floor, Brandon shoved the window down with a snap that rang like a gunshot in the room. Harriet saw him turn, then hesitate abruptly as his gaze fell on a sheet of notepaper that lay on the dresser, anchored in place by the weight of a silver-framed looking glass.

Still gripping the lantern, he snatched up the paper with his free hand. A lock of sleep-tousled hair tumbled over his brow, casting his face in shadow as he scanned the page.

"What does it say?" Harriet's question broke the tense silence.

He flashed her a contemptuous glance, then deliberately crumpled the paper in his fist and flung it to the floor. "Read it yourself if you're so damned curious!"

Harriet bent forward, then checked herself. Brandon Calhoun's insufferable pride demanded that she grovel at his feet. But even now, while her whole being screamed with the urgent need to know what Jenny had written, she could not afford to give him that satisfaction.

Straightening, she took his measure with emboldened eyes. Any other man would have looked ridiculous facing her down in his nightshirt and slippers. But Brandon Calhoun was as fierce as a mythological giant roused from sleep. The sight of his bloodshot eyes, tousled hair and whisker-shadowed jaw triggered a leaden sensation somewhere below Harriet's stomach. She willed herself to ignore it.

"Stop behaving like a peevish child," she ordered in her sternest schoolteacher voice. "I'm just as upset about this situation as you are. What makes you think I want my promising eighteen-year-old brother saddled with a wife and baby?"

He glowered down at her, his lips pressed into a thin, hard line.

"Blaming me is only going to make matters worse!" she declared, thrusting out her chin. "Right now, nothing matters except those two foolish youngsters, their safety and their happiness. Either you accept that and we work together, or, heaven help me, I'll walk out of here and leave you to unravel this mess by yourself!"

Brandon's countenance was icy. Harriet searched his face for any sign that his resolve was crumbling. But she could detect no change in him. Like a wounded animal, he was masking his pain with tightly reined fury. The pain was real; but so, Harriet sensed, was the danger.

The ticking of the tiny porcelain clock on Jenny's nightstand echoed in the stillness of the room. From outside, Harriet could hear the rubbing of a bare sycamore branch against the window—a nerve-grating sound, like the scrape of fingernails against a blackboard. Her damp clothes felt clammy beneath

Brandon's robe—the heavy, satin-lined robe that had enfolded his naked body countless times and carried his essence in every fiber. Its richly masculine aroma surrounded her, swimming in her senses, filling her mind with forbidden images and unnamable yearnings. Suddenly the little room seemed too warm, his looming, male presence much too close.

Harriet tried to swallow, but her throat was as dry as chalk dust. Her lips parted but the power of speech had fled. At the very time when she should be defending her brother, she stood like a tongue-tied schoolgirl, riveted by the raw power in those cobalt eyes.

She willed herself not to avert her gaze or to back away. Brandon Calhoun was the enemy. If need be, for Will's sake, she would fight him like a tigress.

"The…note." She forced the words out with the effort of a six-year-old writing them on a slate.

His eyes darkened in the lamplight. Then, with a weary exhalation, he bent, scooped up the crumpled note and shoved it toward her. "Here. Go ahead and read the damned thing. It won't tell you anything you don't already know."

Still numb with cold, Harriet's fingers fumbled with the crinkled folds. Tilting the paper to the light, she scanned Jenny Calhoun's round, girlish script. As she read, her hands trembled, blurring the letters on the page.

Dearest Papa,

By the time you read this, I will be Mrs. William Smith. Please forgive me. I tried to make you understand, but you wouldn't listen. Will and I love each other. We want to be a family and raise our baby together. This is the only way. I know you'll be angry, but Will is a good man. In time, you will come to like and respect him. Please know how much I love you.

Your Jenny

The paper slipped from Harriet's fingers and fluttered to the rose-patterned rug. When she looked up at Brandon, his narrowed eyes were the color of gathering storm clouds, grim and dark and angry.

"The county line's about fifteen miles north of here." His voice was drained of emotion now. "Johnson City's just the other side of it. On the way into town, there's a justice of the peace who'd marry a coyote to a mule if they had the money to pay him. That's where your brother will likely take Jenny—unless I can put a stop to this foolishness once and for all."

"What are you thinking?" Harriet stared at him, alarmed by his cold resolve.

Brandon picked up the note and crumpled it in his fist. "Jenny didn't expect me to come in here and find this until morning. If I leave now and travel fast, I might be able to catch up with them."

"And then what?" Harriet clutched at his sleeve

as he turned to leave the room. "What do you intend to do?"

"Whatever I have to." He shot her a threatening glance, then jerked away from her and strode out into the hall. Harriet plunged after him, the danger screaming in every nerve. If he caught Will alone on the road with his daughter, Brandon, in his present condition, was capable of killing him.

"I'm going with you!" Catching up with him outside his bedroom door, she seized his arm. "This is as much my problem as yours! I need to be there when you find them!"

"Don't be a fool! You'll only slow me down!" He tried to pull out of her grip but only succeeded in dragging her along the hallway, over the threshold and into his dimly shadowed bedroom.

Harriet struggled to ignore the massive, rumpled four-poster bed, its covers flung back to reveal a slight depression where his body had been lying when her knock had roused him from sleep. "I won't slow you down," she argued. "I can ride as well as any man, and I'm as anxious to find them as you are!"

He twisted away, strode to the hulking wardrobe and flung open the doors. "You're already half-frozen. You can wait here, if you like, but I don't want a whining, shivering woman on my hands, and I won't be responsible for your catching your death of cold."

"I'll be fine. Lend me a warm coat, or even a blanket, and you won't hear a word of complaint from me."

He glanced back at her, his dark brows knit into a scowl. "And if I say no?"

Harriet drew herself tall, clutching his robe around her still-shivering body. "Then, so help me, I'll trail you on foot, in the clothes that brought me here! Either way, you're not leaving me behind, Brandon Calhoun!"

Brandon swore under his breath as he set the lantern on the nightstand and jerked a pair of heavy woolen trousers out of the wardrobe. "If the sight of a man getting dressed shocks your modesty, you're welcome to wait in the hall," he said, scuffing off his slippers to reveal long, pale, elegant feet.

Harriet felt the hot color rise in her face. She took a step backward, then hesitated. Brandon would welcome any chance to get away without her. She could not afford to leave him alone to slip out the back window as his daughter had done.

She shook her head, praying the darkness would hide her furious blush. "Just hurry," she said. "I raised my brother alone. Seeing a man dress is nothing new to me."

It was only a half lie. She and Will had been decorously modest in their years together. Harriet had not seen her brother unclothed below the waist since his early childhood. And this gruff, looming man was definitely not her brother.

"Suit yourself." Turning away from her, he tossed the trousers on the bed and seized a set of long johns that lay over the back of a wooden chair. In a series of quick motions he thrust his feet into the legs and jerked them up beneath his nightshirt. Harriet felt her chilled flesh growing warm beneath her clothes. So far he had not given her so much as an indecent glimpse of his body. But the air of intimacy lay thick and heavy in the shadowed room, dizzying in its power. She fought the urge to avert her eyes, unmasking the falsehood she had told him, leaving herself exposed and vulnerable.

"Hurry," she whispered, and was startled by the husky timbre of her own voice.

The trousers came up next, then hastily donned wool stockings and a pair of heavy brogans before he stripped off the flannel nightshirt. For the space of a breath he stood bare above the waist, his skin glinting gold in the lamplight, his body spare and rock hard, as subtly powerful as a puma's. A crisp dusting of chestnut hair formed a dark inverted triangle between the mauve-brown beads of his nipples. Harriet battled the urge to let her eyes trace the shadowed line downward over his flat belly, to where it disappeared beneath the bunched long johns at his waist. Her mouth, she realized, had gone dry.

He moved swiftly, yanking the top portion of the long underwear onto his arms and over his shoulders.

With scarcely a pause, he bunched the discarded flannel nightshirt in his hand and flung it toward Harriet.

"Pull it on over your clothes," he said. "You'll need an extra layer of warmth, and there's not much in this house that will fit you." When she hesitated he added, "It was clean when I put it on tonight. This is no time to be fussy."

Ignoring the jibe, Harriet slipped out of Brandon's robe, found the hem of the nightshirt and pulled it over her head. The velvety flannel smelled of lye soap and clean male flesh. Lingering warmth from Brandon's body surrounded her as she pulled it downward over her frame. He was right about there being little to fit her in this house. Jenny was a fairy creature, as dainty as the dolls that decorated her room. And the length of Brandon's trousers would dwarf even Harriet's Amazonian height. As for their German housekeeper, whom Harriet had seen at church, she was as solid as an onion, no higher than Harriet's shoulder and almost as round as she was tall.

Brandon had flung on a thick woolen shirt and was tucking it into the waist of his pants. He glanced up from fastening his belt, his eyes troubled.

"I've thought on it," he said, "and I'm not taking you with me after all. It's a miserable night, and I'll make better time on my own."

Harriet slipped the robe on over his nightshirt, jerking the sash tight around her slim waist. "If you catch up with them, you'll need me there. Things could get out of hand—"

"Out of hand?" His black eyebrows slithered upward. "Don't be a silly goose! I'm a civilized man."

Turning away, he reached into the depths of the wardrobe and pulled out a cartridge belt with a long leather holster attached. Harriet felt the color drain from her face as he buckled the belt around his hips.

"No." The word emerged as a hoarse whisper.

"No?" He shot her a contemptuous look as he opened a hidden drawer in the nightstand and pulled out a hefty Colt revolver.

"You're not going after my brother with a gun!" she insisted, taking a step toward him. "I won't have it!"

"You think I'm going to shoot him?" Brandon swore under his breath. "After what he's done, your fool brother isn't worth the price of a bullet. All I want is to get my daughter back, safe and sound, so we can salvage the mess he's made of her life."

"And if Will has a gun, too?" Fear rose like cold black sludge in Harriet's throat. Her brother didn't own a firearm, but he had friends who did. It would be easy enough to borrow a weapon for the night.

Even now, the awful scenario took shape in her mind—the confrontation, the threats, one man drawing on the other, then a gunshot shattering the snowy night…

"No!" Harriet flung herself at him with a desperate fury she had not known she possessed. Her momentum struck his arm, knocking the pistol out of his hand and sending the weapon spinning across the floor. Her fists pummeled his chest in impotent rage, doing no more damage than the fluttering wings of a bird. "No! You can't—I won't let you—"

"Stop it!" He seized her wrists, his brute strength holding her at bay. His stormy cobalt eyes drilled into hers. "Damn it, Harriet, this isn't helping anything!"

His use of her given name startled and sobered her. She glared back at him, her face inches from his own. "Don't you see? This is a tragedy in the making. You with a gun, angry and upset—anything could happen out there. You've got to take me with you!"

"And if I refuse?"

"Then I'll rip my clothes and go to the sheriff." Harriet could scarcely believe her own wild words. "I'll tell him that I came here looking for my brother, and you dragged me up to your room and tried to have your way with me!"

"Oh, good Lord!" Brandon's hands released her wrists and dropped to his sides. A muscle twitched at the corner of his grimly drawn mouth. "You'd be a fool to try it. Nobody in his right mind would believe you."

The implication of his words was all too obvious. Only a depraved man would make indecent advances to a priggish old-maid schoolteacher like herself, and Brandon Calhoun was one of the town's most respected citizens. His arrogance stung Harriet like lye in a cut, but she masked the hurt with defiance.

"Wouldn't they?" She hurled the words, wanting to shock him, to hurt him. "Maybe the story wouldn't hold up in a court of law, but I have your nightshirt, and I can describe your bedroom down to the last detail. That should be enough to smear your precious reputation with mud."

Silence quivered between them like the hanging blade of a guillotine. Harriet's audacious threat, she sensed, had hit its mark. Brandon's livelihood depended on the trust and good will of the townspeople. Lose that and he might as well pack his bags and move away.

"You wouldn't dare!" he snapped.

"Wouldn't I?" Harriet's eyes narrowed in what she hoped was a menacing look. "You don't know me well enough to predict what I might do, Mr. Calhoun. Can you afford to take that chance?"

He groaned, looking as if he wanted to strangle her with his bare hands. "This is blackmail, Miss Harriet Smith. You know that, don't you?"

"Absolutely."

With a muttered curse, he snatched up the pistol from the floor and jammed it into the holster. "Let's get moving, then," he growled. "Come on, we're wasting time."

* * *

Brandon peered over the backs of the horses, into the stinging blizzard. The hood on the elegant black landau was fully raised, but the windblown snow peppered his face like buckshot. He could barely see the ears of the two sturdy bays, let alone the familiar road that wound north along the creek bed toward the county line.

Harriet huddled beside him on the seat, wrapped in his long woolen greatcoat. A thick shawl, belonging to Helga, swathed her head and shoulders. The shawl's edges were pulled forward, hiding her stoic profile from his view. And that was just as well, Brandon told himself. The less he saw of the insufferable woman, the better.

Had he gotten away alone, he would have saddled one of the horses and ridden through the storm. But Harriet was not dressed for riding. Moreover, after her performance in his bedroom, Brandon was ill-disposed to trust her. Put her on a horse and there'd be nothing to stop the fool woman from bolting after the runaways on her own. The landau was slower, but it would be safer—and as long as he held the reins, he would be the one in charge.

"How can we be certain they came this way?" She leaned toward him, raising her voice to be heard above the storm.

"We can't be certain. This is just a likely guess."

He shot her a sidelong glance and met the flash of her coppery eyes. Framed by the shawl, her pale, classic features reminded him of a Madonna's. A Madonna with the scruples of a whore and the disposition of a bobcat, Brandon reminded himself. And he had already felt her claws.

Would she have carried out her threat to ruin his reputation? Brandon huddled into his hip-length sheepskin coat, the pistol cold against his leg. Hellfire, he knew nothing about the woman—where she'd come from or what she was doing in a remote place like Dutchman's Creek. For all he knew, this show of concern for her brother could be an act. She could have encouraged the boy's relationship with Jenny, in the hope of snagging him a rich, pliant little wife that the two of them could control.

Whatever her plan, he swore it wasn't going to succeed. Once Jenny was safely home, he would get his lawyer to annul any marriage that might have taken place. Then he would go ahead with his plan to send the girl back east to have her baby.

Her baby.

The images hit him like a barrage of body blows. Jenny—his sweet, innocent Jenny, her body swelling with child; Jenny giving birth in agony, screaming, bleeding, maybe even dying in the process. Lord, she was so small. The birth was bound to be horrendously difficult for her.

And if Jenny died, Brandon vowed, God help

him, whatever the consequences, he would hunt Will Smith down and send him straight to hell where he belonged.

Chapter Four

Enter what the other boys are doing we do it in well, what I have known is hard and over think...

Chapter Five

Harriet sat with her fists thrust into the pockets of the thick woolen greatcoat Brandon had lent her. Falling snow danced hypnotically before her eyes as the road wound along the bank of the rushing creek. The wind that fronted the storm had lessened, its voice fading to a breathy moan. But even through the coat's luxuriant thickness, the cold still bit into her flesh, and worry rested its crushing weight on her shoulders.

Questions beat at her like black wings. Where were Will and Jenny? Were they safe? Was it too late to stop them from marrying?

Dear heaven, *should* they be stopped? Was it right that the baby who was her own flesh and blood, as well as Brandon's, be raised by strangers, without ever knowing its true family?

Early in their journey, before they'd run out of

civil things to say to each other, Brandon had told her about his plan to send Jenny back east to give birth. His sister, who'd evidently married well, would keep Jenny's condition a secret and turn the baby over to a church adoption agency. After a year or two of finishing school, the girl would be introduced to Baltimore society, where, in due time, she would choose a suitable husband from among her suitors.

Suitable. The word rankled like a burr. *Will* was suitable. He was honest and kind and hardworking, and he truly seemed to love pert little Jenny. Was it so wrong that they should marry and become a family?

Struck by a gust of icy wind, Harriet tightened the shawl around her head. What on earth was she thinking? If Brandon's plan succeeded, her brother would be free of any obligation. He could carry on as if nothing had happened—go to college, have a successful career, even travel abroad. In time he could marry a fine woman, one who'd be a helpmate and companion, not a spoiled little doll who would demand to be pampered and coddled every day of her life.

With the passing of years the hurt would heal, Harriet promised herself. Will would have other children, beautiful, happy children, to fill his life with love and laughter. Perhaps, in time, he would even come to forget that somewhere there was another child with his blood and his features. His firstborn.

The child he would never know.

Harriet blinked back a surge of scalding tears. All

her life, she had believed that there was a clear line between right and wrong, and that good, moral choices led to good consequences. But there was no good choice here—only the leaden weight of one heartache balanced against another.

Beside her, as immovable as a granite boulder, Brandon sat hunched on the seat of the heavy black landau. From the shadows of the shawl, Harriet studied him furtively. Cold anger lay in the taut line of his mouth, in the set of his jaw and the white-knuckled grip of his hands on the leathers.

He was as resolute as the march of time, she thought. Untroubled by the conflicts that tore at her, he was driven solely by the need to put things right— to avenge the ruination of his daughter and to erase the damage to her young life—if such a shattering event could ever be erased. Brandon wanted everything on his own terms, and he was a man accustomed to getting his way.

What would he do if he didn't get his way this time?

Straining to see into the darkness, Harriet brushed the snow from her cold-numbed face. Not far ahead the road entered a steep-sided narrows where the creek had gouged a deep cut through the foothills. Last summer, she recalled, she and Will had come this way in the preacher's wagon when they'd attended a church picnic at a popular canyon grove. Even in good weather the road along the creek was treacherous—prone to slides and cave-ins and so narrow that in many spots it was little more than a ledge. She could only imagine what it would be like in a winter snowstorm.

"There's no other way they might have gone?" She spoke more out of nervousness than doubt.

"Not if they planned to get married." Brandon's taut voice echoed faintly as they entered the narrows. The granite cliffs that rose on either side of them offered shelter from the wind and snow, but the cold was intense, the silence almost unearthly. "Since we're not seeing their tracks, they most likely left town ahead of this ungodly storm. They could already be in Johnson City by now. Or they could be stuck in the snow somewhere, unable to go on. I know it's miserable out here, and you're suffering, but it was your choice to come along. We can't turn back till we find them."

"I wasn't suggesting we turn back," Harriet retorted. "And I never said I was suffering. Have you heard one word of complaint from me, Mr. Calhoun?"

Brandon muttered something under his breath, but did not voice an answer. They were entering the narrowest part of the canyon now. On their left was a sheer rock face. On their right, a mere handbreadth from the wheel rims, was a five-foot drop-off to the rushing creek below.

Harriet held her breath as he guided the horses around a hairpin curve. A fist-size rock broke loose beneath one of the outer wheels. She swallowed a gasp as it skittered down the steep slope and splashed into the creek. Brandon would have had easier going alone, on horseback, she realized. But she had black-mailed him into bringing her along and, because she was in no condition to ride, he had hitched the team to the sturdy landau. If they slid off the road or broke an axle on this treacherous night, it would be, in part, her own fault.

The thought fluttered through her mind that she should apologize. But no, she had done the right thing. Whatever the risk, she needed to be there when Brandon caught up with Will and Jenny. Lives could depend on it.

As she remembered the pistol Brandon had loaded and buckled at his hip, a dark chill rippled through her veins. Even if she was there, she might not be able to stop a confrontation between Will and Brandon. With both of them roused to fury, it would be like trying to separate two charging bears. And with guns involved...

Harriet shuddered as the ghastly montage of events passed through her mind—Will's body bleeding in the snow, or perhaps Brandon lying dead and Will in handcuffs, or Jenny darting between them, her body stopping a hastily fired bullet.

Somehow she had to defuse the situation before tragedy struck. And the only way to do that, short of knocking Brandon out, was by careful persuasion.

"Have you given any thought to the baby?" Her voice echoed in the silence of the narrow canyon.

"What kind of a question is that?" His gaze remained focused on the road ahead, but his jaw tensed visibly.

"Jenny's baby will be your grandchild. Your own flesh and blood. How can you be so heartless as to pass it off like an unwanted puppy, to be raised by strangers?"

His eyes shifted toward her, narrow and cold as he weighed her question. "It's Jenny I'm thinking of," he said. "If she gives the baby up, she can still have the good life she deserves—a place in society and marriage to a respected man who'll provide well for her and her future children. If she keeps the baby, it's all over for her. She'll be branded a fallen woman, an outcast for the rest of her life."

"Not if she marries her child's father," Harriet responded with sudden conviction. "Lord knows, I've had dreams for Will, too, and I'm no happier about this mess than you are. But we have to do what's right for the baby!"

"My sister will see that the baby goes to a good home," Brandon snapped. "Now put it to rest. You're only making things harder."

"That's because you know I'm right! But you'll never admit that, will you, Mr. Calhoun? You've too much stubborn pride to see anyone's point of view except your own!" Harriet was trembling now, her plan of a calm reasonable approach shattered. "Those two poor, foolish children ran off in the night because neither of us was willing to listen to them! Neither of us could face the fact that Will and Jenny are the only ones who have the right to decide their future and their baby's future! We drove them to this desperate act, and if something terrible happens tonight, I'll never forgive myself—or you!"

You...you...you. Harriet's last word echoed off the rocky ledges as Brandon glared at her through the falling snow. The landau was inching along the narrowest part of the road now. Its outer wheels crunched through the soft snow along its edge, sending small showers of gravel rattling down into the creek. A horse snorted nervously in the darkness.

"Who made you an expert on life, Miss Smith?" Brandon's voice was as brittle as thin ice. "Lord, do you even understand what your brother had to *do* to my poor, innocent little girl to get her with child?"

Harriet's face blazed. "I won't even dignify that question with an answer," she snapped.

"For that alone, I could rip him to pieces with my bare hands. But no, I'm a civilized man. If my so-called heartless plan is carried out, he'll be as free as a bird! He can go on with his education, and his life, as if nothing had happened! Isn't that what you told me you wanted?"

"Yes." Harriet stared straight ahead into the swirling snow. "I just don't know if... *Look out!*"

The huge, tawny cat shape that flashed across the road and bounded into the rocks was gone in the blink of an eye. But that brief glimpse was enough to send the horses into a rearing, plunging frenzy of terror.

"Whoa…easy there…" Brandon pulled steadily on the reins and spoke with masterful calm, but it was too late. The landau had already lurched to the right and was tilting perilously over the creek bed. Gravel clattered down the slope as the wheels bit into the crumbling bank.

"Get to the left and lean out!" Brandon shouted at Harriet. "If she starts to fall, jump!"

Harriet did not need to be told a second time. She flung herself to the left side of the buggy, pushing behind Brandon to add her weight above the two stable wheels. But even when she leaned outward, as far over the side as she dared, it was not enough. With the horses bucking and the bank caving in, the heavy landau was canting farther and farther toward the creek.

"Hang on!" Brandon slapped the reins down with all his strength, using them as whips in a desperate effort to get the horses moving forward. But even as the sturdy bays pushed into their collars, the edge of the road caved in and the carriage tumbled sideways, toward the rushing water.

"Jump!" Brandon yelled. "Damn it, *jump!*"

Harriet clambered over the left side of the carriage. She caught a glimpse of Brandon still struggling with the reins as she gathered her strength and flung herself into the darkness.

The scream of horses filled her ears as she hit the road with a force that knocked the wind out of her. For a terrifying moment she lay still on the snowy ground, listening to the sound of splintering wood and the crash of the landau falling into the river.

Brandon! Her mind shrilled his name but she could not breathe deeply enough to shout. As she crawled toward the road's caved-in edge, she could hear the horses screaming and thrashing.

She was all right, Harriet realized as each of her limbs responded to her will. The snow on the road and the thickness of Brandon's coat had combined to cushion her landing. But where was Brandon? Had he gone into the water? Her gaze darted up and down the road. She could see no sign of him in either direction. That could only mean one thing.

Growing more and more frantic, she clambered shakily to her knees and stared down the slope. Through a swirling veil of snowflakes, she could see the broken, overturned landau, lying wheels-up in the creek. One horse was on its feet. The other lay on its side, its head raised above water. She could not see Brandon at all.

Sliding on snow and gravel, she skidded down to the water's edge. The creek was not deep, but an unconscious man with his face under water could drown in no time. If she didn't hurry, Brandon could be dead by the time she got to him.

"Brandon!" She found her voice. "Can you hear me?"

"Yes." His voice came from somewhere under the

chassis, muffled by the sound of the creek. "Don't worry about me. See to the horses."

"Are you all right?"

"Yes, damn it! Just something on my leg." He seemed to be biting back pain. "You've got to take care of the horses! There's a pocketknife in that coat you're wearing. Use it to cut them loose. Can you do that?"

"I'll try." Harriet found the knife in one of the pockets and managed to get it open.

"Listen to me." Brandon's voice sounded fainter than before. "I just honed that blade last week, so it should be sharp enough to slice through the leathers. From what I can see, Captain looks all right. Cut him loose first and get him out of the way. Then you can go to work on Duchess. If she can't get up, I'll hand you the gun and you'll have to shoot her. Do you understand?"

Harriet stared at the downed animal, her heart plummeting. If the horse couldn't get out of the water, it would drown or freeze. Better to put it out of its misery, she knew. Still...

"Harriet?"

"Yes, I understand," she said. "Hold on. I'll do everything I can."

Gathering her courage, she waded into the water and hacked at the twisted lines that fastened the standing horse to the landau. Seconds crawled by at the pace of hours as she sliced into the tough leather, but at last the big gelding was free. It snorted, shook its wet coat and lurched up the bank, onto the road.

The mare had been twisted onto her side by the momentum of the overturning buggy. Only the angle of her straining neck kept her head out of the water, and she was weakening fast. Clearly terrified, she laid back her ears and rolled her eyes as Harriet approached. "Easy, girl…easy, there," she murmured, praying with all her heart that she wouldn't have to shoot the poor animal.

This time the cutting was even more difficult. The leathers were twisted and soaked with water, and the icy cold numbed Harriet's hands, making them slow and clumsy.

"How much longer?" Brandon's voice grated with impatience, concern and pain. Glancing toward the overturned carriage, she could just make out his dark outline beneath the chassis. He was leaning back against a boulder, the lower half of his body pinned beneath the icy water. Even though he was in no danger of drowning, Harriet knew it was urgent that she free him and get him onto the bank. Over her protests, however, he had insisted she take care of the horses first.

What a stubborn, proud, irritating, impossible man he was!

"Harriet, I asked you how much longer."

"I'm working as fast as I can," she said, wishing he'd just be quiet. "I should have her loose in a few minutes."

"How's she doing?"

"Hard to say—" Harriet winced as the blade slipped and jabbed her thumb, leaving a dark bead of blood. "Her head's still up. We'll soon know the rest."

"Fine," he said. "Just hurry."

Harriet felt the sudden give as the knife sliced through the last of the harness that held the mare. Her heart hammered as she lifted the sodden collar from around the straining neck. "Come on, girl," she coaxed. "Get up now."

The mare's legs worked furiously as she struggled to right herself. Harriet had tried earlier to determine whether any bones were broken, but with the darkness, the mare's thrashing legs and the icy, moving current, there was no way to be sure. Either way, Duchess had spent her strength. If she was too chilled and exhausted to get up, they were going to lose her.

"How's she doing? Can she get her feet under her?" Brandon's voice rasped with anxiety.

"Not…yet." Harriet moved through the knee-deep current and braced herself behind the struggling mare. Bracing against a rock, she pushed with all her strength against one massive, water-slicked shoulder. "Please, Duchess…" she murmured under her breath. "Please get up…"

She might as well have been trying to move the Rock of Gibraltar. The mare's legs kicked against the icy current, but the heavy mass of her body did not budge. Either she had broken a leg, or she was too chilled and exhausted to get on her feet.

From beneath the overturned landau, Harriet could hear Brandon cursing in helpless frustration. She could see the fumbling motion of one hand as he moved it under his coat. Her heart plummeted as she realized he was working the pistol out of its holster. She found herself praying silently that the gun would be too wet to fire.

"Take it," he growled. "Put her out of her misery."

Harriet paused for breath, her arms supporting the mare's straining neck. "Oh, please," she begged, tears welling up in her eyes. "There has to be something more we can do! Let me help you get loose. Maybe then we can—"

"My leg's broken, Harriet," he said in a blade-thin voice. "I can't see it, but I can tell it's bad, and I don't think you're strong enough to lift this buggy off me. I'd take care of Duchess myself, but I can't get a clear shot from here, and I don't want to wound her. Now come get this damned pistol. Then, if you can't get her up, do what you have to!"

Harriet could not answer him. She was gazing down at the soft-eyed mare and choking on her own sobs. Brandon was right, she knew. If Duchess couldn't stand up, a bullet in the brain would give her a swifter, more merciful death than freezing or drowning. But the thought of pulling the trigger sickened her.

"Harriet, did you hear me?" Brandon's voice rasped with impatience, but Harriet detected an underlying thread of anguish. He cared for this beautiful mare, she realized; and he couldn't bear to watch a cherished animal suffer because a silly, weakhearted woman couldn't do what was required of her.

The mare's eyes were dark velvet pools.

"Harriet?"

Blinded by tears, Harriet flew at the mare, slapping the wet flanks, jabbing the massive rump with the toes of her boots. "Get up!" she shouted. "Get up, blast you to hell!"

To hell...to hell... The words bounced off the cliff and echoed down the narrows. The silence that followed was like a deep, shocked gasp, as if Harriet's language had stunned nature itself. For the space of a breath, everything seemed to freeze. Then, suddenly, the mare began to snort and thrash and roll. With a powerful lurch, she staggered to her feet and stood quivering in the water, all four legs braced solidly beneath her heaving body.

"Oh!" Harriet was beside herself. The tears spilled out of her eyes and flowed freely down her cheeks as she flung her arms around the mare's neck and pressed her face into the sleek, wet hide. "Brandon! Can you see her? She's up! She's all right!"

"I see her." Emotion roughened his voice. "Get her out of the water before she slips and falls again. Then come over here. I think I've figured out a way to get this damned buggy off my leg."

The mare needed no urging. She lunged up the bank to stand on the narrow road, next to the big gelding who was her harness mate. The two horses nuzzled each other, both of them nervous and agitated.

Wet and half-frozen, Harriet struggled through the swirling creek to reach the overturned buggy. In the beam of moonlight that penetrated the shadows beneath it, Brandon's face was as pale as marble. He was in worse condition than he'd let on, she realized.

"Here." He thrust a coil of waterlogged rope into her shivering fingers. "I managed to grab this before it floated away. Tie one end to the front axle—that's the one above my head. Is Captain still wearing any harness?"

"His collar." She glanced toward the road, where the two horses stood in the lee of an overhanging ledge.

"Fine. Use the collar to anchor the rope around his chest—be careful of the way you rig it, you don't want to choke him. Let me know when you're ready to pull. I can help lift and guide it from…here." A spasm of pain passed across his face. "Can you reach the axle?"

Harriet strained upward, grateful for her height. "Yes…I've got it." She looped one end of the rope around the buggy's stout front axle and tied it snugly. Then she slung the coil over her shoulder and staggered toward the rocky bank. With every step she prayed that the rope would be long enough to reach the road. Otherwise she would have to coax the gelding back into the creek and risk breaking its legs on the slippery rocks.

She reached the bank with rope to spare. Yes, it would be all right, she thought as she clambered up to the road. All she needed to do was to rig the rope to the gelding's collar and let the horse's strength move the buggy off Brandon's leg.

And then what? She had no medical training. If the break was a simple fracture, she might be able to splint it well enough to hold while she helped him out of the water, but if the break was as bad as she feared…

She would cross that bridge when she came to it, Harriet resolved. First catch the horse and attach the rope; then move the buggy; then do what she could to see that Brandon was safe and comfortable and, finally, get some help. Only when she broke the mountainous task into smaller steps did it all seem possible.

The hulking bay snorted and laid back its ears at her approach, warning her to be careful. "Easy, Captain," she murmured. "Easy, boy, I'm not going to hurt you."

Both horses seemed skittish. But then, they'd just survived a fearsome ordeal, Harriet reminded herself. It would take some time for them to settle down—time that, for Brandon's sake, she could not afford.

Slowly she uncoiled the remaining length of rope. If she could slip the end of it beneath the padded leather collar and tie it fast, the first step would be accomplished and she could get on to moving the buggy.

As she moved closer, the gelding snorted, stamped and backed against the cliff. Now she had the horse cornered. It would just be a matter of—

From the ledges above, a blood-chilling scream shattered the darkness. Harriet's heart dropped into her stomach as she realized what she was hearing. Merciful heaven, how could she have forgotten about that mountain lion?

Panic-stricken, the horses plunged this way and that. Whinnying in terror, the mare wheeled on her hind legs and bolted up the road. The gelding followed, its big body slamming Harriet hard against the cliff face.

As the sound of hoofbeats faded in the darkness, she slumped to the snowy road and lay still.

Chapter Six

Brandon twisted beneath the overturned landau, cursing like a mule skinner as the pain rocketed up his leg. The angle of the chassis hid his view of the road, but it didn't take a genius to figure out that something had gone horribly wrong.

He had heard the scream of the cat and the clamor of horses stampeding up the road. But from Harriet Smith he had heard nothing at all.

"Harriet!" he shouted with all his strength.

Harriet...Harriet... The name echoed down the canyon, mocking his efforts as he struggled to see past the side of the landau. Where in hell's name was the woman? And where was the cat? Cougars were shy animals and generally didn't attack humans, but if Harriet was hurt or unconscious, this one might see her as easy prey. The loaded Colt .45 was in his hand, but he couldn't shoot what he couldn't see. The only thing he could do was fire into the air and hope to frighten the beast off.

Praying that the Colt wouldn't be too wet to shoot, he thumbed back the hammer, pointed the pistol out the open side of the landau, aimed for the sky and squeezed the trigger.

The report thundered down the narrows, echoing and re-echoing off the cliffs. Brandon held his breath as the sound died away, straining to hear.

Nothing.

"Harriet!" he bellowed at the top of his lungs. "Are you all right? If you're out there, blast it, answer me!"

Still nothing. Nothing but the rushing sound of the creek, the mournful sigh of the wind and the utter silence of falling snow.

Lord, what had happened to the woman? Had the cougar finished her off? Was she lying in the snow, trampled by the horses? Had she slipped in the water and drowned on her way back to the road?

Brandon felt as if a leaden weight had settled into the pit of his stomach. True, he had never liked the prim schoolmarm, but he had to admit she'd shown admirable pluck in freeing the horses from the wrecked buggy. For all her prickly disposition, Harriet was a good woman, he sensed, resolute and strong of spirit. If anything had happened to her, his part in it would haunt him for the rest of his life.

But that didn't mean he'd ever forgive what her

brother had done to Jenny, let alone bless their union. Will Smith's offense was beyond forgiveness, and if Harriet had been killed or injured because of the boy's reckless action—

"Brandon?" The faint voice floated through the darkness from the direction of the road. Brandon's body went slack with relief as he realized it was truly Harriet and not some trick of his imagination.

"Are you all right?" His throat was so tight and raw he could barely speak.

"Yes…" She sounded shaky and uncertain, like a child just roused from sleep. "I don't remember what happened…must've been knocked out when—" She gave a sudden gasp. "Oh, no! The horses! They're gone!"

"They're gone, all right." Brandon forced a wry chuckle, trying to make light of the grim situation for her sake. "Judging from the way they lit out when they heard that cougar, I'd say they're probably halfway to Johnson City by now."

"But how are we going to get you out of the water without the horses?"

"Don't worry, we'll manage it," Brandon said, hoping she wouldn't ask how. In truth, he was fresh out of ideas, and his predicament was worsening with every minute that passed. "Is that cat still around, or did my shot scare it off?" he asked, deliberately changing the subject.

"You fired a shot?" She still sounded dazed. "I

don't remember hearing that. I was trying to rope the horse and the cougar screamed and… Sorry, I'm still a bit dizzy…got to sit down. How's your leg?"

"Can't feel a thing," Brandon lied through clenched teeth. Maybe it was a good thing he couldn't see how bad the leg really was. Growing up in Kentucky, he'd known a man who'd crushed his ankle in a bear trap. When blood poisoning had set in, a backwoods doctor had been forced to amputate the poor fellow's leg below the knee. Not a good thing to remember at a time like this.

"I could go for help," Harriet said. "Johnson City can't be all that far."

Brandon shifted against the rock that supported his weight. "We're about halfway between Dutchman's Creek and Johnson City, so either way it's about seven miles. But in your condition, you'd never make it, especially in this weather. Right now, the only smart thing you can do is find yourself a sheltered spot below the cliff and hunker down until somebody comes along who can help us."

"But you'll be in the creek all that time!" she argued, her words floating to him across the water. "You could freeze to death!"

"I'll be fine," he said, knowing it could well turn out to be a lie. "Go on, now! Find yourself a safe hollow before you catch your death of pneumonia!"

Harriet did not reply, but Brandon could sense her hesitation. "Go on!" he barked. "You can't do a blasted thing for me right now, so you might as well take care of yourself!"

The only answer was the banshee scream of the cougar.

Panic surged through Brandon's body. "Harriet!" he shouted. "Where the devil are you?"

"Here!" He heard her now, splashing through the creek toward him. "Let's just hope that big kitty doesn't like getting wet!"

"Did you see it?" He reached out and caught her hand, pulling her under the edge of the buggy. She was cold and trembling, her eyes huge in the darkness.

She shook her head in answer to his question. "I didn't take the time to look. But that cry—merciful heaven! He sounds like a giant version of the tom-cats I hear yowling in the cemetery at night." She managed a brave little laugh. "Who knows? Maybe he's just serenading a lady friend."

"I don't think this is the mating season for cougars," Brandon said. "Until we're certain he's gone, you'd better stay right here."

Opening his sheepskin coat, he pulled her close against the rock that was his anchor in the swift-moving current. He had never given a thought to embracing the maidenly Miss Smith, but holding her in his arms was the only way to make room for them both in the tight, dark space beneath the buggy. For a long moment her body was tense and resistant. Then, with a sigh, she sagged against him, curling

into the little warmth he had to offer. It was a matter
of survival, nothing more, Brandon told himself. It
would change nothing between them.

"How's your leg?" Her voice was an intimate,
husky whisper in the darkness.

"Water's pretty well numbed it," he muttered, his
head swimming with the fragrance of her damp hair
against his cheek. "Probably a good thing, keeping
it cold like this."

"I could try to look at it—or at least reach down
and feel it through the water."

"Don't bother. There's nothing you can do until
we get help. Meanwhile, I'd just as soon not know
how bad it is."

"I could try tipping the buggy off you. I might be
able to lift it from the open side."

Brandon exhaled shakily. "Tipping the buggy
might do more harm than good. Leave it be, Harriet.
God didn't appoint you to step in and fix everything
that's wrong in this world!"

She glanced up at him with a puzzled frown.
"Now where did *that* silly idea come from? You're
not going to pass out on me, are you?"

"I'm fine," Brandon snapped, although he did
seem to be feeling light-headed. What if the injury
to his leg had cut a vein or an artery and he was
bleeding into the water, too numb to feel what was
happening?

A shudder passed through his body as he realized

that, for now at least, there was nothing to be done. True, Harriet might be able to tip the buggy, but only from the open side, which would throw even more weight onto the crushed leg. To tilt the vehicle backward, lifting it free, would require the strength of several men or a horse. Meanwhile, a tourniquet around his thigh might stop the bleeding, but it could also cause the needless loss of his leg—a risk Brandon was not yet ready to take.

Come morning, there were bound to be travelers on the road. Dawn was hours away, but if he could just hold out until then, everything would be fine. Everything...

Harriet was watching him with anxious eyes, their long, black lashes beaded with moisture. She looked pretty against the softly falling snow, he thought. All damp and fresh and tousled, her face a mere handbreadth from his own.

Someone—for the life of him, he couldn't remember who—had once told him that all women were beautiful in the dark. But Harriet, he mused, would be at her most beautiful in dawn's rosy sunlight, her dark hair spreading over the pillow like a silken fan, her cheeks flushed with the memory of last night's loving...

Brandon jerked himself fully awake. Hellfire, what was he thinking? Harriet Smith, the sister of the no-account who'd destroyed his daughter's life, was the last woman whose face he would want to see on the pillow next to his own. She was the enemy—a prissy, irritating, mule-headed, blackmailing bundle of trouble!

So why did he find himself gripped by the totally insane desire to kiss her?

"How are we going to get out of this mess, Brandon?" Her voice, though strained, was a velvet whisper, warm and breathy against his ear.

"Right now, all we can do is wait." He spoke with effort, trying to make sure the words didn't sound slurred. "Sooner or later, somebody will come along, and even if they don't, the sun will come up. The cat will go home to bed, and it'll be safe for you to go for help."

She frowned up at him, creating a tiny furrow between her brows. "Maybe I should go now. You're hurt and cold and not getting any stronger."

"Too dangerous." His arm tightened around her shoulders, as if to keep her with him. "If something happened to you out there, we'd be even worse off than we are now."

"You're right, I suppose." She sighed and nestled closer against him, needing his human warmth as he needed hers. "Besides, how could I leave you here alone? You could pass out and fall over in the water."

"The rope." Brandon's vision blurred, then cleared again. "You could tie it under my arms and wrap it around the axle…" He could not put words together to finish the sentence. Lord, was he bleeding to death down there under the water? Would this be his last chance on earth to hold a beautiful woman in his arms?

"Brandon?" Her face was close to his, her lips soft

and ripe and inviting. "What's happening to you? Are you all right?"

From high in the ledges, the cry of the golden cat shattered the darkness. She shrank against him, instinctively seeking protection. All he had to do was tighten his arm and lean forward.

The kiss went through him like the first luscious jolt of warm peach brandy. He felt the flicker of resistance as he pulled her tight against his chest; but it was only a flicker. With a little half sob, she melted against him. Her arms found their trembling way around his neck. Her fingers tangled in his hair, pulling his head down to hers as her mouth softened beneath his like wild honeycomb, woman-sweet on the tip of his tongue. Her lips parted hungrily, wanting, demanding more. "Oh..." she murmured, straining against him. "Oh, Brandon..."

Those were the last words he heard as he tumbled into darkness. His last conscious thought was that this was indeed a lovely way to die.

Harriet caught his weight as he slumped forward, his eyes closed, his breathing shallow. Her pulse exploded into panic as she realized what must be happening to him. Why hadn't she realized he was losing blood down there, under the water? No wonder he'd looked so pale and drawn.

Laying him back against the rock, she plunged her arms into the creek and groped her way down his leg.

By the time she reached the trapped ankle, her chest was in the water, but her probing fingers found exactly what she'd been hoping *not* to find—the splintered sharpness of bone protruding through flesh just above the top of his boot. Only the numbing cold of the water and Brandon's own stubborn will had enabled him to stand the pain. But it hadn't stopped the bleeding.

Brandon been right about one thing. Tipping the buggy onto its side would have rolled the vehicle's full weight onto his trapped foot and ankle, crushing the bones. There was no way she could lift the buggy off him safely and no way she could leave him to go for help. All she could do was hold him, wait and pray that someone would come in time.

Sitting up again, she gathered him into her arms. He was deathly still, his face ashen, his breathing ragged and shallow. Only after Harriet had settled herself against the rock with his head cradled in the hollow between her breasts, did the impact of that soul-blistering kiss strike her with full force.

A shameful blush crept over her as she remembered the velvety rasp of his unshaven jaw against her skin and the soft roughness of his lips, bittersweet like new spring raspberries. She remembered the probing invasion of his tongue and how it had ignited a liquid blaze in the untouched depths of her body. Pure heaven—and absolute madness.

What on earth could have possessed her? Brandon

had been on the verge of fainting and could not be held responsible for his actions. All he had done was lean toward her, and she had done the rest. She had *wanted* to kiss him, Harriet conceded. But wanting was one thing. Doing was quite another. She had behaved like a shameless wanton. What was he going to think of her?

But what Brandon thought of her no longer mattered. His life was ebbing away drop by drop, and if help did not arrive soon he would never open his eyes again.

The storm had diminished to a few drifting flakes of snow. What time was it? she wondered. Surely it would be light soon. There would be travelers on the road, men with horses who would free Brandon's pinned leg and get him to a doctor.

Harriet's eyes scanned the ribbon of starlit sky above the canyon walls. Its color was an inky blue-black, with no sign of approaching dawn. Daylight, Harriet realized, could be hours away. And Brandon didn't have hours of life left in his body.

As she shifted his position to make him more comfortable, her hand brushed something hard and heavy beneath his coat. The pistol—he said he'd fired it to scare off the cougar. Could she use it now, to signal for help?

Reaching down, she pulled the hefty Colt revolver out of its holster. A quick check of the cylinder confirmed that there were four bullets left. The odds of anyone being on the road at this hour were slim, she knew. But she had to take a chance.

Aiming the pistol at the sky, she thumbed back the hammer and fired one shot, then another. The sound echoed off the sheer rock walls, sounding like a full-fledged gunfight. At least the noise should be enough to scare off the cougar, Harriet thought, forcing a grim smile to keep up her spirits. She would save the last two bullets in case she needed to signal again later. For now she could only wait and pray that someone had heard.

Holstering the gun, she strained her ears into the silence. The wind had died with the passing of the storm. Only the water, gurgling around the wrecked landau, broke the stillness.

Brandon groaned softly and shifted against her breast. "Be still," she whispered, holding him. "Rest and save your strength. Someone will find us, you'll see."

Exhausted now, she lay her cheek against his wet hair. The icy water had numbed her feet and legs, and the cold was creeping upward. It would feel so good to sleep, she thought. Just drift off here, under the buggy, with Brandon in her arms...

Two distant gunshots echoed down the canyon. The sound startled her, causing her body to jerk. Had she been asleep? How long?

Another shot! Yes, it had to be a signal! Someone was coming! Harriet fumbled for the pistol and fired an answering shot into the air. Brandon was breathing, but she could not rouse him. "Hold on!" she whispered, shaking his shoulders and rubbing his hands to warm them. "Just hold on!"

She could not see the road from beneath the buggy, but after what seemed like an eternity she heard the sound of horses on the road, coming from the direction of Johnson City. Closer and closer they came until, at last, Harriet heard them stop near the spot where the landau had careened into the creek.

"Papa?" A small, frightened voice floated out of the darkness. "Papa, where are you? Are you all right?"

The voice was Jenny's.

When Brandon opened his eyes, the first thing he saw was the familiar ceiling of his own bedroom. The second thing he saw was the elderly town doctor, Simon Tate, standing beside the bed, wiping his hands on a towel. Behind him, the shutters were closed. Slivers of bright sunlight slanted through the cracks to fall across the quilted coverlet.

"What...happened?" Brandon's mind felt as fuzzy as his throat. It was all he could do to piece two words together to make a question.

"You had a damned close call, that's what happened." The doctor took off his spectacles and cleaned them on the edge of the towel. His pale eyes were bloodshot with weariness. "Another half hour in that creek, bleeding the way you were, and you'd have been a dead man, or maybe lost the leg. As it is, you were lucky. You're going to be as sound as a dollar!"

The leg—Brandon's hand fumbled downward as the memories washed over him. The rolling buggy, the screaming horses, the awful, crushing weight, snapping bone and tearing flesh…and before that, Lord, yes, he'd been going after Jenny and that damn-fool boy, trying to stop them from making an even bigger mistake than they'd already made. Someone had been with him—he remembered big dark eyes in a pale face. Had it been the schoolmarm? His mind was like drifting fog.

"Don't worry, the leg's all there," the doctor said, noticing Brandon's alarmed expression. "I set it while you were unconscious. You'll be wearing the splint for a couple of months, and after that you may have a limp, as well as a touch of rheumatism over the years. But all in all, I'd say it's a miracle you're still in one piece."

The old man replaced the spectacles on his bulbous strawberry nose and busied himself with repacking his instruments. Brandon's heart dropped as he glimpsed the bone saw that had been close at hand but ultimately not needed.

"How…did I get here?" he asked.

"Well now, that's a long story. I'll let one of the people waiting downstairs tell it to you when I send them up. But don't overdo the visiting. You've lost a lot of blood and you're still not out of the woods. I've got a spare set of crutches I'll drop by in a couple of days, but meanwhile you need to rest. No gallivanting around, hear now?"

"The bank—" Brandon struggled to sit up, but the wave of dizziness that washed over him forced his head back onto the pillow.

"The bank will be there," the doctor said. "You have competent clerks who can handle the business just fine for a couple of weeks."

"Weeks—" Brandon pushed upward again, but this time it was the doctor's firm hand that pushed him back.

"It'll be even longer if you don't rest! You're only human, Brandon Calhoun, and if that boy hadn't come along and pulled you out of the water, you'd be lying on the undertaker's table, not in your own bed!"

"That boy…?"

The doctor's medical case snapped shut as if to cut off the conversation. "I'm going home and get some rest myself. It's been a long night. I'll send your daughter and the others up, but they're only to stay for a few minutes. After that, Helga has orders to give you some hot porridge and see that you're left alone to sleep."

Sleep. Sleep was the last thing he wanted right now, Brandon told himself as the old man walked out of the room and closed the door. He needed to find his daughter and the man who had ruined her sweet young life. He needed answers to his questions about what had happened. But he was already drifting into a gray fog that enfolded him like a soft blanket, and he was too weary to resist. As it closed around him, the last thing that floated through his memory was a pair of deep, copper-flecked eyes.

"Papa?" The voice, like the tinkling tone of a little silver bell, startled Brandon out of his slumber. How much time had passed since the doctor had left? Minutes? Hours?

"Papa, can you hear me?"

He blinked himself awake. Jenny stood next to the bed, gazing down at him with worried eyes. Her golden braids were pinned into a coil on the crown of her head, like a halo, he thought. His angel child. Why did she look older than he remembered? Why were there violet shadows beneath her eyes?

Brandon forced a drowsy smile. "The doctor tells me I'll be almost as good as new," he said. "And I will, now that you're here."

Jenny's gaze flickered nervously toward the open doorway. Looking past her, he caught sight of two people standing on the threshold—the last two people on earth he wanted to see.

Will Smith was rumpled and unshaven, dressed in clothes that looked as if he'd slept in them. His sister stood beside him, dressed in a faded gray twill gown that washed out her pale features. Her hair was skinned back into its usual tight bun and her eyes looked as if she'd been up grading papers all night for the past week.

"What are they doing here?" he muttered.

Jenny reached down and clasped Brandon's fist between her child-size hands. "Don't you remember? Will was the one who pulled the carriage off your leg and brought you back to town. And Harriet was with you the whole time, holding you in the water. When we got you to the road, she tore up her petticoat to bandage your leg. You owe them your life, Papa."

"Owe them my life, you say?" Brandon raised his head off the pillow, only to fall back again, overcome by a wave of dizziness. "What the devil do you think I was doing in the narrows at that hour, snipe hunting? If Miss Harriet Smith had kept a proper eye on that brother of hers, I would never have been there. And I wouldn't be lying here like a slab of beef with my leg in a splint! Owe them my life? I don't owe them a blasted thing!" He glared at the pair in the doorway, then cast a gentler gaze on his daughter. "Never mind. You're home now. Send them away and we'll get on with my plan to set things to right."

"No, Papa." There was a thread of steel in Jenny's girlish voice.

"No?" He stared up at her.

"When Will and I found you, we were on our way back from Johnson City. We were married there last night. It's done, Papa. So now I'm giving you a choice."

"A choice?" Brandon felt the walls of his world begin to crack and shatter.

"Will is my husband now," Jenny said. "The rest is up to you. Either you welcome him to the family as your new son-in-law, or so help me I will never set foot in this house again as long as I live!"

Chapter Seven

Time slowed to a crawl, each second punctuated by the sonorous tick of the grandfather clock in the entry downstairs. Harriet's gaze was fixed on Brandon's profile where he lay on the pillow, staring up at his daughter as if she had just plunged a knife into his chest.

Jenny's ultimatum had caught them all off guard. Who would have guessed that beneath the girl's doll-like prettiness lay a core of the same stubborn steel that ran through her father? This clash of two unbendable wills, Harriet feared, could only end one way—in heartbreak.

For the space of a breath she was tempted to leap in and do her best to smooth things over. But no, she swiftly realized, it was not her place to interfere in this deeply personal confrontation. Nor was it her brother's. She felt Will beside her, straining as if held back by invisible chains. Jenny was his wife now, and it was natural that he would want to stand beside her. But it was clear that she had warned him off. She had wanted to face her father alone, as an equal.

In the leaden silence Harriet's memory flew back over the events of the past hours. After their midnight wedding, Will and Jenny had planned to wait out the storm in Johnson City. But when, purely by chance, they had spotted and recognized the two loose horses wandering the main street of town, Jenny had realized her father was in trouble. Rounding up Captain and Duchess, they had tied the pair behind their rented buggy and headed back down the dangerous road into the narrows.

Will had been instrumental in rescuing Brandon out of the creek and easing him into the buggy, as well as getting him undressed and into his bed. Brandon had been semiconscious much of the time, moving his head and muttering incoherently; but now that he was awake, it appeared that he remembered almost nothing that had happened after the accident.

Including that earth-shaking kiss.

"Choose, Papa." Jenny stood beside the bed, looking every inch her father's daughter with her jaw firmly set, her spine ramrod-straight. "Will is here waiting to shake your hand, but we won't beg you to accept us. If your answer is no, we're prepared to have a perfectly good life without you."

Brandon's angry gaze flickered toward Will, then back to Jenny. "I'd just as soon shake hands with the devil!" he snapped. "Don't you know it's your money he wants, girl? I tried to buy them off—that boy and his schoolmarm sister. But no, that wasn't enough. They wanted everything—you and your whole inheritance. Well, by heaven, they're not going to get it. You walk out of this house, Jenny Calhoun, and the first person I'll send for is my lawyer. You and your new so-called family will never get a cent from me!"

The color had drained from Jenny's face, but she stood her ground. "My name is Jenny Smith," she said, "and my husband is quite able to provide for me and our baby."

"Is he?" Brandon's hands had clenched into fists. "You have no idea what it's like to be poor. You don't know how a woman can suffer when there's not enough money to pay for the roof over her children's heads or even to put a decent meal on the table. But you'll find out. And when it happens, don't come begging to me. I gave you a choice, and you're the one who made it."

Harriet watched, heartsick, as Jenny drew herself up to her full five-foot height. The girl was clearly on the verge of tears, but not one drop escaped to trickle down her face. "You had a choice, too, Papa," she said. "And someday that choice is going to make you a lonely, bitter old man."

Jenny's body was rigid as she turned away from the bed and walked toward the door. Brandon did not watch her go. When Harriet glanced back at him, she saw that he had turned his face toward the wall.

They descended the stairs in silence, like mourners at a funeral.

Will opened the front door and the three of them passed out of the dim hallway into the blinding afternoon sunlight. Dazzled by the glare, they crossed the porch and made their way down the front steps of the imposing brick house. Last night's storm had passed and today's warm sunshine had melted much of the snow. Water filled the wagon ruts, turning the road into a quagmire of fallen leaves and sticky brown mud. Sparrows flocked around a puddle, grateful for this last reprieve from winter cold.

Harriet tried not to think of Brandon, alone and helpless in his bed, with only the dour Helga to look after his needs. The man had thrown away his daughter's love for the sake of his own stubborn pride. For that, she told herself, he deserved to be miserable the rest of his days!

Still, as she stole an upward glance at the shuttered window, she could not help feeling the anguish of the man who lay in that shadowy room. No one could doubt that he loved his pretty child. But loving a person wasn't the same as owning them. That was a lesson Brandon had yet to learn—and Harriet could only pray that time would grant him the wisdom to learn it.

As she tore her gaze away from the house, the scathing memory of last night's kiss swept over her. How many times over the past hours had she relived the thrill of his lips closing on hers, the heady taste of him, the dizzying rush of sensations from the wet, quivering core of her body?

What would it take to purge that memory from her mind? How could she stop herself from feeding it, nourishing it, dreaming of it?

The careless moment that had passed between them last night meant nothing to Brandon. *She* meant nothing to him. She was only the schoolmarm, the sister of the enemy who had taken his daughter. He had all but ignored her today, and she wanted to hate him for it, to shake her fist and curse his name to the sky. But right now she was simply too tired. Hatred was like a bonfire, demanding fuel, and she had nothing left to feed it.

Because of Jenny and the coming baby, she was bound to have future dealings with Brandon. She would do her best to be civil to the man. But she knew better than to let down her guard with him. He had humiliated her once. She would not give him the chance to do it again.

Only after they had climbed into the rented buggy and pulled away from the house did Jenny's self-control begin to crumble. She stared straight ahead at the road, her chin quivering and her breath coming in tiny hiccups. Will handed the reins to Harriet and gathered his little girl-wife into his arms, where she broke down and began to sob.

"It's all right, sweetheart," he murmured, cradling

her head against his shoulder. "We'll be fine. Lots of families start out with no more than we've got."

She looked up at him, her eyes overflowing with tears. "It isn't the m-money, Will. It's my father. You saved his life and he didn't even thank you! I never knew he could be so hateful! The thought of living in the same town with him, passing him on the street and not even speaking—" She pressed her face against his damp coat in a paroxysm of grief. "How can we stay here?" she sobbed. "Surely you can get a good job in Johnson City. We can buy a nice little house there, with a big tree in the yard where you can put up a swing for the baby…"

Will sighed and stroked her shoulders. His young face was already etched with care. "I know you'd like to get away from your father. So would I, darlin'. But winter's almost here, and we don't know anybody in Johnson City. I've got a good job right here in Dutchman's Creek and I can't afford to walk away from it. As for buying a house, that's going to cost a lot of money. We'll need to save for a few years, maybe pick up some cheap land and build on it. But you'll have just what you want one day, I promise. I'll work my fingers to the bone to get it for you."

Jenny frowned, her forehead wrinkling prettily. "We need someplace to live right now, Will. I don't have any money of my own, and I know you spent most of yours on renting this horse and buggy—and on my ring, of course." She fingered the tiny gold band on her finger as if it were the greatest treasure on earth. "What are we going to do? We can't sleep in the street."

Harriet had kept herself out of the conversation, leaving the two young people to deal with the realities of their new life. But now she sensed an impasse. It was time to step in and offer them the only solution that made sense.

"Why don't you stay with me for the winter?" she suggested. "I could move into your room, Will, and give you two my bigger bed. True, we'd be crowded, but we could manage all right. Instead of paying rent somewhere else, you could save your money. Then come next spring, after the baby's born, you could find a little place of your own."

Will looked as if the weight of the world had been lifted from his shoulders. But Harriet could sense Jenny's hesitation. Sharing an ugly little house with her new sister-in-law could hardly be what Brandon Calhoun's spoiled daughter had expected of married life. But that couldn't be helped. Will was eighteen years old. He was a hard worker, but he had not come far enough in the world to provide a home for his bride and baby.

Harriet's thoughts flickered briefly to the money in the Denver bank—the money she had saved for Will's education. It would be more than enough to buy the newlyweds a nice little home and some things for the baby. But no, the voice of wisdom whispered. That money was for the future. Offer it to them now, and they would burn through it in a few months. Then the money would be gone and, with it, the hope that Will would ever have the means to make something of himself.

Taking a deep breath, she reached across the seat and squeezed Jenny's small, cold hand. "I know this isn't what you'd hoped for," she said. "But I'd be happy for your company over the winter. And you're going to need some help when the baby comes. It's not a good time for a woman to be alone."

Jenny had pulled away from Will and sat with downcast eyes. Her fingers, their nails bitten to the quick, toyed with her wedding band, twisting it one way, then the other. The girl had been through a wrenching night, Harriet reminded herself. The elopement, the wedding, the hours of waiting while her father lingered between life and death, followed by their final, shattering confrontation, had all taken their toll on her. She was emotionally and physically drained. A rational decision at a time like this might be too much to expect from her.

"Of course, you don't have to make up your mind right this minute," Harriet said, feeling awkward. "We can talk about it after we've all had something to eat and a good night's rest. Or it can wait a few days. Goodness knows, I don't want to push you to a decision you won't be happy with."

"No, that's all right." Jenny raised her eyes and her

shy smile was like the first glimpse of sunlight on a gloomy day. "We'd be happy to stay with you, Harriet, if you think it's for the best. I can help you with the cleaning and the washing, and when you and Will come home from your work, I'll have supper on the table. I don't know much about cooking and keeping house, but I'm willing to learn, if you'll teach me." She reached out and timidly touched Harriet's arm. "I've always wanted a big sister. Now I have one."

Caught off guard, Harriet blinked back a freshet of tears. She had said some spiteful things about this girl, both to Will and to Brandon. Only now did she realize how judgmental she had been. She owed Jenny an open mind, if nothing else. Maybe time would prove that her brother hadn't chosen so badly after all.

She could only hope, for all their sakes, that time would do as much for Brandon's feelings toward Will.

She was in his arms, her skin warm, living satin to the touch. Her aroma floated through his senses, stirring waves of fevered desire. Brandon moaned beneath the quilt as he felt himself rise and harden. He needed her so much—needed her strength and passion, needed to be inside her ripe woman's body, feeling her moist heat tighten around his shaft, hearing her little love cries as he thrust deeper, deeper into the sweetest heaven a man can know.

She hovered above him, secrets as old as time

*dancing in her copper-flecked eyes. A smile teased
her mouth as he reached up and pulled the pins from
the teacherly coil of her dark mahogany hair, setting
the fragrant mass free to tumble over him in a long
silken cascade. Her breasts hung free as she leaned
over him, their nipples brushing his chest. He caressed them, kissed them...*

*Now, he thought, he had to have her now or he
would burst.*

*Sensing his need, she shifted above him and glided
downward to capture him in the place where he
wanted to be. He thrust upward, deeper, harder...
feeling the delicious, shattering surge—*

A sharp rap on his bedroom door jarred Brandon
like a dash of icy water. The afternoon sunlight was
pouring into the room. Receipts and ledger books
were scattered across the coverlet, one page blotched
with ink where the pen had fallen when he'd dozed off.

A sticky wetness on the part of the sheet that covered his hips told the story of what had just happened to him. Brandon cursed as the rap on the door
sounded again.

"*Herr* Calhoun?" The familiar voice was Helga's.
"Are you awake?"

"I am now," he muttered, although the question
was not unreasonable at three in the afternoon. When
was the doctor going to bring those damned crutches
by so he could be up and about his business? After
three days in bed, he was sick of this mollycoddling,

sick of making work for himself to pass the time. Most of all, he was sick of the silence in this big, lonely house.

"What is it, Helga?" he asked, attempting a more civil tone.

"You have a visitor. It's *Fraulein* Smith, the schoolteacher."

Brandon groaned. Harriet Smith was the last person he wanted to see, especially in his present condition. "Tell Miss Smith that I'm…indisposed," he snapped.

"But *Herr* Calhoun, she knows that—"

"Tell her I'm dead, then. Tell her anything you want. Just get rid of her."

"I heard that, Brandon Calhoun." The door swung open. Harriet strode past the protesting Helga, into the room. She appeared to have just finished her day's teaching, for she was primly dressed in one of her drab gingham frocks, this one navy blue with a plain white collar. Her hair was pulled back into its schoolmarm bun and there was a smudge of chalk dust on her cheek. "You look very much alive to me," she said crisply.

"Do you always make a habit of storming into men's bedrooms without an invitation?" he asked, conscious of his unshaven face, his uncombed hair and the rumpled condition of the bedclothes.

"If I waited for an invitation, I'd never get in, would I?"

"Why don't you try it and see?" He was still a bit muzzy from the dream and the tone of his voice lent a none-too-subtle innuendo to the words. Her copper-flecked eyes widened, contrasting nicely with the warm pink blush that crept into her cheeks. He ought to try embarrassing her more often, Brandon mused.

His memory of that stormy night in the narrows was spotty at best. But something, Brandon sensed, had happened between himself and the proper Miss Harriet Smith. If only he could remember what it was....

"How can I help you, Harriet?" he asked with forced politeness.

She took a sharp breath. "I've come for some of Jenny's clothes. The girl has nothing to wear except for what's on her back, and I was hoping—"

"Take anything you like," Brandon cut in gruffly. "I have no use for anything of hers."

"Not even her child?"

"Don't." He glared at her. "Don't even start on me. You came for the clothes. They're in her old room. Go ahead and take them."

"Don't you even want to know how your daughter is doing?"

"Helga told me she'd moved in with you. I'm assuming she must be all right or you'd have told me right away."

She sighed. "Jenny's fine, except for the morning sickness, and that's to be expected. But she was devastated by what happened between the two of you.

She loves you, Brandon. And nothing would make her happier than to heal this breach that's opened up in your lives."

"Fine. All she has to do is come home—without her husband."

Harriet stared at him as if he'd struck her across the face. "You don't know what you're asking!" she exclaimed. "Jenny and Will love each other! For all their poor circumstances, they're so happy together and so excited about the baby, it's a joy to be around them!"

"But for how long?" Brandon felt the old bitterness welling up inside him, like the festering of a wound that had never healed. "How long will it be before your brother begins to feel trapped—before he starts to dream of all the things he's missed by being saddled with a family at eighteen? How long before he begins to resent his dependent little wife— maybe even to hate her? How long before Jenny discovers how he feels?"

The color had faded from Harriet's face. Her hand crept to her throat. "Is that what this is about?" she asked in a strangled voice. "Are you judging my brother by your own measure? How dare you? You don't even know him!"

Brandon leaned back into the pillows, studying her through narrowed eyelids. "Maybe not. But I know how life plays out when two people have to get married. And I won't have any man putting Jenny through the hell that her mother went through with me."

The silence in the room was absolute, as if the air itself had frozen. Harriet's fingers trickled down the front of her dress as if her hand had lost the strength to control them. Brandon had not meant to tell her so much, and he certainly had no plans to tell her the rest of the story. But he wasn't sorry for what he'd said. Maybe now, at least, she would understand his objection to the marriage.

"Does Jenny know?" she asked softly.

He shook his head. "Jenny thinks she was born prematurely. You aren't going to tell her the truth, are you?"

"No." She looked uncertain. "No, of course not. But maybe you should tell her yourself, now that she's grown."

"Why? It wouldn't change anything, and it would only cause her pain. She'll have enough of that without my adding more."

"More than you've already given her, you mean?" Harriet's voice had sharpened.

Brandon exhaled and picked up the ledger book that lay open on the bed. Harriet Smith had collected her pound of flesh for the day. He'd be damned if he was going to give her his blood, as well. "As you see, I have work to do," he said. "Help yourself to Jenny's clothes. You know where her room is." He glanced up as a thought struck him. "Did you come here on foot?"

"Yes, I came straight from school."

"Then you won't be able to carry much away, will you?" Brandon made a show of focusing his attention on the ledger. "Go ahead and choose a few things to take with you today. I'll have Helga box up the rest and send them over in the wagon by the end of the week."

Had he sounded uncaring enough? Brandon wondered. Had he managed to hide the fact that even thinking about Jenny's empty room triggered a gnawing sensation in his gut that never quite went away? Well, fine. If he could convince Harriet Smith he was nothing but an unfeeling monster, maybe she'd stop coming around and sticking nails into his flesh.

And maybe she'd even stop haunting him like a succubus in those maddening dreams.

He dipped the pen into the inkwell, aware that she was still standing beside his bed, an oddly knowing expression on her face.

"As I mentioned, I've got work to do," he said brusquely.

"So I see. And is it always your custom, Mr. Calhoun, to work with your ledger upside down?"

Brandon glanced down at his lap, cursing under his breath as the inverted numbers swam into focus. She had just humiliated him soundly, and he wanted to snap back with something that would cut her to ribbons. But his sleep-drugged mind was not up to clever retorts today, which was just as well since Miss Harriet Smith had turned on her heel and walked calmly out of the room.

Brandon lay back against the pillows, his face burning as the brisk cadence of her footsteps died away down the hall. Under most circumstances he was a self-contained and rational man. So what was it about the drab, plainspoken schoolteacher that turned him into a blithering beast whenever the two of them were alone together?

It was certainly not her allure, although she was passably good-looking. As for wit, she possessed far more than her share. Brandon liked intelligence in a woman, but in Harriet's case she used her sharpness to irritate, not to charm.

So why wasn't he simply indifferent to her? Why did she have the power to rouse him to a froth of helpless fury? And why was it *her* eyes, *her* face he saw in those erotic dreams that had tormented him since the night of the accident?

What was it about that night? About her?

Methodically, like a detective laying out clues, Brandon pieced together the events that had led to this debacle—Harriet's disheveled appearance on his doorstep; their desperate midnight foray into the storm; the narrows, the crumbling bank and the crushing weight on his shattered ankle; the fleeing horses and the scream of the cougar that had sent her plunging through the water to huddle beside him under the overturned buggy.

Suddenly it all came back to him.

Lord help him, he had kissed the woman. And if

her ardent response was any indication, she had liked it.

The devil of it was, he had liked it, too.

Chapter Eight

Will dipped a spoon into his bowl of beans and raised it to his mouth. Jenny sat across the table in the flickering lamplight, watching his expression as he chewed, swallowed, then sighed.

"Jenny, darlin'," he said gently, "these are right tender beans, but they'd be a mite tastier if you'd remembered to salt them before you put them on to boil."

Jenny's dainty features fell. Taking a taste of the beans in her own bowl, she wrinkled her nose. "Oh, dear, you're absolutely right!" she exclaimed, putting down her spoon. "They have no taste at all! I never knew cooking could be so complicated! Oh, Will, what a useless little ninny you married!"

"Useless? I wouldn't call growing a pretty little baby useless." Will doused his beans liberally with ketchup, took another mouthful and nodded. "There, that's better."

"A cat can grow pretty little babies. In fact, she can grow four or five of them at a time. But a woman should know how to cook and sew and run a house. And she should know how to make a living if she needs to, or if she chooses to, shouldn't she, Harriet?" Jenny cast an adoring glance at her sister-in-law.

"You'll learn all those things, Jenny. It just takes a little time." Harriet buttered a slice of the bricklike bread Jenny had baked that morning. The girl's need for an older woman's affection and approval was almost staggering. What a shame Brandon had never remarried, she thought. Helga had clearly lacked the disposition to mother his lonely little girl. Perhaps that was why Jenny, on the brink of womanhood, had turned to a boy for the love she craved so deeply.

Brandon again—Harriet suppressed a sigh. She had resolved to stop thinking about the wretched man, but his rumpled and unshaven image still surfaced in her mind at every unguarded moment. Nearly a month had passed since the day she'd confronted him in his bedroom, and apart from the promised delivery of Jenny's clothes, he'd had no contact with her or with his daughter. But Harriet had glimpsed him a few times on Main Street, going in and out of the bank on his crutches. Every time she saw him, or even thought about him, their last meeting came crashing in on her with the impact of a tidal wave.

Brandon's candor about his own marriage had

shaken the very floor beneath her feet. It came as no surprise that his wedding to Jenny's mother had been a hurry-up affair—he had obviously married very young, perhaps even younger than Will. But his brutal honesty about the relationship had left her in turmoil. Why would he tell her such a thing? Had he wanted to shock her? To repel her after that shattering kiss beneath the buggy? Or had he simply wanted to explain his vehement objection to Jenny and Will's marriage?

Never mind, Harriet told herself, taking a bite of Jenny's rock-hard bread. Brandon Calhoun was a puzzle better left unsolved. If he wanted to steep in his own misery, that was his problem. She had her own life to live, and right now that life was as cluttered as the space inside this crowded little house.

"How beautifully you've set the table, Jenny!" she exclaimed, watching the girl's eyes light up at her sincere praise. With the burdens of teaching school and raising an active boy, Harriet had never taken the time to fuss over the appearance of the meals she cooked. Jenny, however, had covered the scarred wooden table with a red-checked cloth she'd unearthed from the depths of an old chest. She'd added prettily folded white napkins and had even ventured out into the November snow to gather a little bouquet of evergreen sprigs and bright red berries, which she'd arranged in a plain white mug in the center of the table. The mismatched plates, glasses and cutlery had been polished until they gleamed in the lamp-light. The effect lent a cheery glow to the drab little house.

Jenny blushed modestly. "Making dinner look nice is easy. Making it taste good, that's harder."

Harriet reached around the table and squeezed the girl's thickening waist. "Wait until Saturday. While Will's at work, we can make some meat pies together. Maybe we'll both learn a few things."

They finished the meal in casual conversation about the day's happenings. Then, insisting that Jenny get off her feet and rest, Harriet washed the dishes while Will went outside to chop some firewood.

By the time she'd finished in the kitchen, Harriet was worn out and ready for an early bedtime. Closing the door of the small room that had once been Will's, she began to undress. Her sleep had suffered from the none-too-subtle sounds of two newlyweds through the thin wall until, just three nights ago, she had pulled wads of cotton batting from an old quilt and stuffed them into her ears. Since then she had slumbered in relative peace, disturbed only by occasional dreams of rushing water, screaming cougars and Brandon's rough, seeking lips on hers.

Being kissed was not exactly a new experience for Harriet. At the time of her parents' death, she had been engaged to a promising young lawyer named Jonathan Millsap. The relationship, though chaste and somewhat formal, had not been without physical affection. But when Harriet had insisted on keeping and raising her young brother, Jonathan had walked away. That was the last time she had allowed herself to be physically close to a man—until the moment Brandon had drawn her into his arms beneath the overturned landau.

It was a moment Brandon had clearly chosen to forget.

Harriet hung her dress in the wardrobe, unfastened her corset and yanked the high-necked flannel nightgown over her head. She had buttoned the collar to her throat and had just sat down at the makeshift dresser to unpin and brush her hair when she heard a timid knock at the door.

"Come in." Harriet turned, poised with the brush in her hand, as Jenny slipped into the room, leaving the door ajar behind her.

"Sorry, I know you're tired, Harriet, but there's something I need to ask you."

"Of course. Ask me anything you like." Harriet reached up with one hand and pulled the tortoiseshell pins from her hair. Its natural waves uncoiled from the tight bun that had imprisoned them, falling to her waist in a glossy cascade.

"Oh, what lovely hair you have!" Jenny exclaimed. "Would you let me brush it for you while we talk?"

Without waiting for a response, Jenny took the brush from Harriet's hand and began working it

through her hair. Harriet sighed as she felt the tightness easing away from her scalp, her neck, her shoulders. Only now did she realize how tense she had
been.

"You could do so much with hair like this!" Jenny
said, twisting the dark mass in one hand. "Would you
let me pin it up for you tomorrow morning? It'll only
take a few minutes, I promise! Please say yes!"

Harriet hesitated, wondering how her students
might react to an overly fancy hairstyle. Then she
laughed as the truth struck home. In the eyes of the
youngsters, she was just the teacher, hardly a real
woman at all. They wouldn't care how she looked.
They probably wouldn't even notice.

"All right," she said, wanting to please Jenny. "Just
be certain you don't make me late for school."

"I promise. And if you don't like what I do with
your hair, I'll never bother you about it again."

Jenny brushed away in silence, until Harriet began
to wonder if she should remind the girl about the un-
asked question that had brought her here. Her pretty
face wore a troubled look. Harriet could only hope
it didn't have something to do with Will.

"What was it you wanted to talk to me about?"
Harriet asked gently.

"It's…my father," Jenny said, and Harriet felt her
heart lurch.

"Has something happened, Jenny?"

"Not really. But today before I went outside to

look for the red berries, I put on the dark blue coat
he'd sent over with the rest of my clothes. As I was
buttoning up the front, I felt something heavy in the
pocket. When I reached inside, this is what I found."

Jenny put the brush down on the dresser, reached
beneath her apron and held out her hand. In her palm
was a gold coin—a twenty-dollar double eagle.

Oh, Brandon, Harriet thought.

"After I came back in the house, I went through the
rest of the clothes Papa had sent over. I found nine more
of these in the pockets. Two hundred dollars in all."

Harriet felt her knees go watery. Was Brandon
taking the first step toward reconciliation with Will
and Jenny? Was he trying to buy her back? Or did he
just want to make sure his daughter was not in need?

"Does Will know about this?" she asked.

Jenny nodded. "We talked it over. As long as Papa
refuses to accept Will into the family we don't want
his charity. But two hundred dollars is a lot of money,
Harriet, and we know how hard you've worked to
help us. That's why we want you to have it."

Jenny slipped her hand into her apron pocket and
pulled out the rest of the coins. She thrust the handful of money toward Harriet. "Take these. Otherwise
I'll take them outside and throw them into the creek."

Looking up at those blazing blue eyes and determinedly thrust chin, Harriet had no doubt that Jenny
would carry out her threat. How like her father she
was, neither of them willing to yield an inch.

With a sigh she took the coins from Jenny's hand and laid them on the dresser, concealing them beneath a well-worn copy of *Shakespeare's Complete Works*. "I'll take the money," she said, "but there's only one thing I intend to do with it—give it back to your father."

"That's your choice." Jenny picked up the brush and, before Harriet could rise, began brushing her hair again. "At least we can say we offered it. We do appreciate your letting us live here, Harriet, and all the other things you've done."

"Having you here has been a joy," Harriet said, and realized it was true. Then, because the moment seemed right, she found herself asking the question that had been on her mind since her last clash with Brandon.

"Jenny, what was your mother like?"

The stillness in the room was broken only by the muffled thud of Will's ax in the backyard and by the crackle of the brush as it glided through her hair.

"I loved my mother," Jenny said at last. "And in her own way, I think she must have loved me. But she was the unhappiest woman you can imagine. Nothing I did could make her smile. Nothing Papa did could make her smile. All she wanted was enough brandy to get her to sleep at night."

Too dismayed to speak, Harriet reached up and squeezed the girl's thin arm.

"I used to think it was my fault," Jenny said. "I

thought if I could just be a better girl, maybe she'd stop drinking. But Papa told me I wasn't to blame, and I tried to believe him."

The brush kept stroking, stroking, as Jenny collected her thoughts. "I was eleven when she died. It was after dinner. Papa was helping me with my schoolwork at the dining room table and Helga was in the kitchen. Mama had been drinking in her room. I heard her come to the top of the landing, shouting something at Papa. Then she screamed and we heard the sound of something falling down the stairs. When we ran to the entry hall, she was lying there…"

Jenny's unsteady hand laid the brush on the dresser. "She was only twenty-nine, Harriet, and still so pretty. As far as anyone could tell, she just lost her balance and tumbled down the stairs. But Papa blamed himself, I think, because he hadn't been able to make her stop drinking."

"So he tried to make it up to you." Harriet thought of the exquisite pink bedroom, the canopied bed, the dolls, the beautiful dresses in the wardrobe.

"Papa spoiled me," Jenny said with startling candor. "He wanted to make a perfect life for me. But I'm not his little girl anymore. I have the right to choose my own life. When he accepts that—if he ever does—maybe we'll be able to talk to each other again."

"But, Jenny, dear, if you won't give him a chance—"

The sound of the back door opening cut off Harriet's argument. A draught of cold evening wind blasted through the house, blowing the bedroom door back against the wall as Will staggered into the kitchen, carrying a small mountain of firewood in his arms.

With a little cry, Jenny flew into the kitchen to shut the door behind him. Harriet could hear the two of them laughing together as she got up to close her bedroom door against the noise and the cold. Her conversation with Jenny was over for the night, but the problems the girl had raised were bound to go on and on. Jenny clearly loved her father, and it was just as evident that he loved her. But this stubborn clash of wills over her marriage had opened up a chasm that could keep them apart for a lifetime. Something had to be done—and only she, Miss Harriet Smith, cared enough to try.

Tomorrow after school she would stop by the bank and return the two hundred dollars to Brandon in his private office. She could only hope he would give her a chance to plead for reconciliation. She would tell him how kind and patient Will was with his bride. She would tell him how happy the two youngsters seemed together. Brandon would have to listen. She would *make* him listen. After all, he could hardly throw a respectable woman out of the bank with so many townspeople looking on.

Overcome by weariness, she turned down the narrow bed, plumped up the pillow, slid between the sheets and pulled the covers up to her chin. As she closed her eyes, Brandon's words flashed through her memory with the heat of summer lightning.

I know how life plays out when two people have to get married. And I won't have any man putting Jenny through the hell that her mother went through with me.

Jenny's story had given Harriet a glimpse of what lay behind Brandon's bitter words. But Jenny's childish eyes had only seen the surface of what had happened. The whole truth had to be darker and deeper than an eleven-year-old girl could begin to imagine. Darker and deeper than even Harriet wanted to know.

Brandon faced the two men across the polished walnut surface of his desk. This, he thought, was the worst part of being a banker, the part he absolutely hated.

The stocky, unkempt pair who sat opposite him, slumped in their chairs, were twin brothers who owned a small ranch south of town. Last spring they had mortgaged their property for five thousand dollars to buy cattle, which were to be sold at a profit in the fall, when the mortgage was due. Brandon could only guess at what Harvey and Marlin Keetch had done with the five thousand, but no one had seen so much as a heifer on their land, and now it was time to pay the money back to the bank with interest.

"'Tweren't our fault Ma died of the flux," Marlin whined. "We needed money for the undertaker and the coffin and for the spot in the graveyard. After that, by the time we got up to Laramie, there wasn't no cows left to buy."

"I see." Anyone who knew Marlin and Harvey could have guessed the rest of the story. The brothers had blown most of the mortgage money on drinking, gambling and whores. Brandon had approved the loan in the first place because the widowed Martha Keetch had been an honest woman with a sound head for business. But any good influence she'd had on her sons had evaporated with her death.

"I'm sorry, but you leave me no choice," Brandon said. "As of today, your ranch is in foreclosure. You have ninety days to repay the loan in full, with interest. Otherwise the property will have to be put up for sale."

"That ain't fair!" Harvey, always the surly one of the twins, rose out of his chair and leaned across the desk. His breath smelled of chewing tobacco and rotgut whiskey. "We come to ask you for more time on the loan 'cause Ma died, and you tell us you're gonna take our land, our home, what our folks built up from nothin'! Filthy stinkin' rich banker! You could pay the five thousand outta yore own pocket and not even miss it! Hell, you don't need our ranch! What's it to you?"

"Sit down, Harvey." Brandon deliberately stayed in his seat, using his voice and manner to dominate the man. "Sit down and hear what I have to say."

Still bristling, Harvey lowered himself back onto the straight-backed chair. His little pig eyes blazed pure hatred.

"It wasn't my money you borrowed," Brandon explained calmly. "It belongs to the people who've deposited their savings in this bank, and it's my job to see that they get back every cent they put in, and more. If you can't get the money to repay the loan, my advice would be to sell the ranch yourselves. There are people in Dutchman's Creek who'd likely buy it if the price was right. The five thousand would come off the top and you could keep the rest of the cash for yourselves."

"The hell you say!" Harvey Keetch was on his feet, his stocky, muscular body quivering like a prize-fighter's. "Well, you ain't takin' our ranch, you tight-fisted buzzard! We're stayin' on that land if we have to shoot every man, woman and child what sets foot through the gate. You hear that, Banker? You ain't takin' our home, and that's that!"

"I think we've said enough, gentlemen." Brandon rose out of his massive leather chair. He was a full head taller than the twins and disliked using his size to intimidate, but sometimes it was called for. "You have ninety days to pay off the mortgage or lose your property. Now, I trust you can find your own way to the door."

The two men backed away like cowering dogs. "That ain't fair!" Marlin whined. "It weren't our fault that Ma got sick and died."

"We'll git you for this, Banker!" Harvey snarled. "You lay one greedy finger on our land, an' you'll wish you hadn't. We'll make you curse the day you was born!"

For all their bluster—and it was just that, Brandon thought—the two men left meekly enough. He didn't relish the thought of taking their property, especially since their parents had been good, hardworking people. But the money the twins had borrowed was gone, with nothing to show for it, and he had a responsibility to his depositors. There would be more unpleasantness ahead, more scenes like the one that had just occurred, before this ugly business was finished.

Maneuvering his splinted leg beneath the desk, Brandon settled back into his chair. A glance at the clock told him the bank would be closing in fifteen minutes. Not enough time, he reckoned, for one more disaster in a day that had started with Helga's news that she was returning to her family home in Bremerhaven, and had gone steadily downhill from there. The confrontation with the Keetch brothers had been the capper. He was ready for a bracing walk home, a good shot of whiskey and a nap in front of the fire, with his throbbing leg propped on a footstool.

But no, fate was not going to let him off so easily. Striding through the doorway was the one person capable of shattering his hard-won composure and turning him into a snapping, snarling, subhuman beast—the one and only Miss Harriet Smith.

"Hello, Harriet," he said, forcing politeness. "Please have a seat."

"Who on earth were those horrible men?" She closed the door behind her, then lowered herself onto one of the chairs that faced Brandon's desk.

"They're customers," he replied curtly, "and since it's not my practice to discuss other people's business, what can I do for you?"

Her copper-flecked eyes flashed and he knew that his brusqueness had piqued her. She glared at him across the desk, her dark hair framing her face in soft, feminine waves. Gazing at her, Brandon found it impossible to forget that he had held this woman in his arms and kissed her passionately. What would it be like to do it again? he wondered. How would it feel to unbutton the front of her ugly gray dress and free those luscious breasts to tumble into his hands like sweet, ripe melons?

The fantasy, brief as it was, triggered a rush of heat to Brandon's loins. Color stole into his face as he felt the sudden swelling and realized he was aching to touch her.

This was crazy, he thought. If he wanted the woman so much, why did he take such pains to alienate her every time they met?

But why was he asking himself that question when he already knew the answer? Harriet was his worst enemy. She and her brother had taken Jenny away from him. They were holding her hostage to poverty and disgrace, pushing her toward a downward spiral that would turn her into an alcoholic wreck like her mother.

Jenny had always been a sensitive child. Brandon had recognized her vulnerability early on and he'd done all he'd could to cushion her from life's blows and to ensure her a happy future. But his best efforts had come to nothing—to *this*.

Now, gazing across the desk at Harriet's prim figure, he felt cold, helpless and plain, damned scared.

"Is Jenny all right?" he managed to ask.

"Jenny's fine. She's a lovely girl. I have to say you've raised her well."

"And?" he asked, still on guard.

A faint smile danced on her lips, showing him a flash of startling beauty. "It seems your daughter's inherited your pride," Harriet said. "She asked me to give you these."

Brandon sighed as she reached into her reticule and laid the handful of gold coins on the desk. He didn't need to count them to know that all ten of the double eagles he'd slipped into Jenny's pockets were there.

"I wish she'd kept them," he said. "I know I told Jenny she'd never get another cent from me, but she walked out of here with nothing but the clothes on her back. I couldn't stand the thought of her living on your charity."

"She's not living on anyone's charity," Harriet said. "Will is her husband, and he's working hard to provide for her. While they're staying with me, they're saving up for the down payment on a little home. They're so happy together, Brandon. Will is good to her, and she's learning how to cook and sew and manage a household."

In other words his precious Jenny had become a servant, Brandon observed, although he knew better than to voice that thought. Scowling, he leaned back in his chair, folded his arms and regarded her from beneath his stern-looking eyebrows. "Listen to yourself, Harriet Smith," he said. "The first time we talked, you claimed to be as dead set against the marriage as I was. You wanted your brother to go to college, not to be stuck in Dutchman's Creek with a spoiled little wife and a baby. What happened to make you change your mind?"

She leaned forward against the edge of the desk, her face heart-stopping in its earnestness. Whatever she'd done to her hair, it was damned becoming, Brandon thought. Why had he ever thought the woman plain?

"I haven't changed my mind," she said. "I've just learned that sometimes, when things don't turn out as we've planned, all we can do is accept what's happened and make the best of it. It's a lesson you'd do well to learn yourself."

"Stop lecturing me, Harriet," he said. "You sound like a schoolteacher."

"And you sound like a little boy who's sulking because he didn't get his own way!"

Brandon bit back a curse. He had just faced down the Keetch brothers without so much as a spark of temper. Why did this woman, of all people, have the power to goad him to fury with a look and a few softly spoken words?

"We're not talking about a toy or a lost turn at bat," he retorted icily. "We're talking about my daughter. I wanted her to have everything, to be happy—"

"She *is* happy. Just not on your terms."

"Then you've already turned her against me."

"Oh, Brandon!" Harriet's face paled and she looked genuinely shocked. "We would never do that! Jenny loves you! Truly she does!"

"Then why wouldn't she accept my help?" He made a frustrated gesture toward the scattered pile of gold coins that lay between them on the desk.

"There's only one thing Jenny wants from you, and you know what it is."

Brandon took a deep breath. "No," he said. "Your brother seduced my innocent girl and then ran off with her behind my back, hoping to get his hands on her inheritance. I won't forgive him, and I certainly won't accept him as my son-in-law."

"I don't think Will gave Jenny's inheritance a second thought!"

"Your brother clerks at the feed store and hasn't got a bean to his name! You wanted him to go to college, but getting an education is hard work. Marry a banker's daughter—that's the easy way to get ahead, isn't it?"

He had finally gotten a rise out of her. Harriet

faced him across the desk, pale and shaken, fighting for self-control.

"You're despicable, Brandon Calhoun!" she said in a strangled voice. "I came here in the spirit of peace, to offer you a plan to help Jenny without sacrificing her pride or yours. And all you can think of is slandering my brother!" She rose to her feet, trembling. "If I didn't care so much for those two sweet youngsters, I'd walk out of here and leave you alone with your big fancy desk and your gold. Jenny was right! If you can't come to terms with this situation, you're going to end up a lonely, bitter old man!"

Brandon met her furious gaze, knowing he'd pushed her too far, but not wanting to give her the satisfaction of an apology. Beyond the closed door of his office, the workday was ending. He could hear the faint, familiar sounds of closing drawers, sliding locks and departing feet. Minutes from now, if Harriet did not leave, he would be alone with her.

Was that what he wanted? Heaven help him, he didn't know. And he didn't know what he would do if she stayed. He only knew that right now the prospect of her walking out that door triggered a feeling as desolate as a storm-swept winter prairie.

He exhaled slowly. "Sit down, Harriet," he said. "You mentioned a plan to help Jenny. Tell me about it."

Chapter Nine

Features composed, spine ramrod-straight, Harriet lowered herself onto the edge of the chair. Brandon watched her every move as if he expected her to pull a pistol out of her reticule and use it to hold up the bank. His cobalt eyes glittered with arrogance.

She wanted to fly at the man, to rake his smug face with her nails and slap him senseless. But that would only make things worse. She had come here on a mission to help Jenny and Will. She could not allow her own feelings to interfere with that mission.

"Well?" he asked in a tone that raked her nerves like the sound of new chalk on a damp blackboard.

Harriet swallowed her annoyance and plunged ahead. "The idea came to me today, as the children were leaving to go home. I haven't had time to think it all out, but since I needed to see you anyway, to give back the money—" She broke off, realizing that she was talking too fast, explaining too much.

The stillness on the far side of the door crept in on her senses. Her eyes flickered to the large pendulum clock on the wall and she realized that by this time the customers and employees would have gone, leaving Brandon to close the building. Her heart sank. She had come here deliberately, hoping to avoid a painful exchange like the one that had taken place in his bedroom. Too late, she realized she had set up the same kind of trap and walked right into it.

"Take your time, Harriet. I'm listening." His voice, though gentler now, carried a mocking undertone. The man would jump at any chance to make her look like a fool, Harriet realized. But she could not back off now, with so much to be gained.

Once more, she plunged ahead. "Here's what I'm thinking. There are twenty-four students in my class, when none of them are absent. Their ages range from six to sixteen, and giving them all a good education is a real challenge. The younger ones need practice with letters and numbers. The older ones need to learn history and science and algebra—and they're all there at the same time. If I had an assistant, someone who could take the little ones aside and help them with the basics of reading and writing and arithmetic—"

She stopped for breath, dismayed by the frown on his rugged face. Then, as she watched, two small flames seemed to ignite in his eyes.

"You're talking about Jenny?" he asked.

"Why not? She's a bright girl—too bright to spend all of her days cooking and scrubbing in the house. She'd be wonderful with the children, and it would give her a chance to earn a little money of her own before the baby comes."

He winced at her last words. Plainly, he had not yet come to terms with his daughter's condition. "Have you spoken with Jenny about this?" he asked.

"Not yet. For one thing, I just thought of the idea. For another, I don't want to disappoint her if it can't be done."

"Do you think she's physically strong enough to handle a job like this?"

"Dr. Tate's examined her and says she's in good health. And being at school shouldn't be any more strenuous than being at home." Harriet held her breath, hoping he'd be pleased, even excited. But Brandon's only response was a skeptical frown.

"The money for your salary comes out of the school fund, which is controlled by the mayor and the town council. That fund is stretched to the limit now. I can't imagine they'd agree to paying another salary, even for a few months."

"They wouldn't have to!" Harriet moved the ten gold pieces into a single neat stack and shoved it toward him. "Not if you fattened the school fund with this."

He stared at her, stunned by her audacity.

"Listen to me, Brandon!" She reached across the

desk and seized his wrist. "Don't you see how many people this plan would help? Jenny could earn money doing something she enjoyed. You'd have a way of helping her without hurting her pride. I'd have the help I need in the classroom, and the children of Dutchman's Creek would have a better education! How could we go wrong?"

Still he hesitated, maddeningly. "We'd be lying to Jenny," he said, "and presumably to your brother, as well."

"But it would be such a small lie, such a white lie. And I'd be the one telling it, not you."

"I'd have to be truthful with the mayor."

"Of course you would. But Hans Peterson's a good man. He'll understand and he'll keep it to himself."

"And if he insists on running it by the town council?"

Harriet let go of his wrist and sank back into her chair. There were indeed members of the town council who considered themselves the self-appointed moral guardians of Dutchman's Creek. But she was not about to back down in the face of their criticism.

"Brandon, this is a small town. By now, there's not a soul who doesn't know what happened with Jenny and Will and why they're living under my roof. As scandals go, it's old news. As long as council members are willing to keep quiet about where the money came from, there shouldn't be a problem."

"Unless one of those old hens on the council objects to having a fallen woman teach the children."

Harriet sprang to her feet, incensed. "I can't believe you'd say such a thing about your own daughter, Brandon Calhoun! Jenny's a married woman. Her baby will have a name and a father. And if the truth be told, I'd wager that at least a third of the families in Dutchman's Creek started out the same way!" She spun toward the door, then turned back to face him. "Why in heaven's name can't you put this business behind you? Everyone else has!"

"Harriet, wait—" He had risen and was moving awkwardly around the desk.

"Never mind showing me out!" she stormed. "I came here with a wonderful idea. But I should have known you wouldn't listen to me. All you can think about is what would go wrong! You're the most tight-fisted, hard-hearted man I've ever met, Brandon Calhoun. Why don't you just change your name to Ebenezer Scrooge and be done with it?"

Her hand was on the doorknob when he caught up with her and seized her by the wrist. Brandon had intended only to stop her from leaving, but as she jerked away from him, her resistance triggered enough momentum to swing her backward toward the wall. Supported by only one leg, he lost his balance and crashed into her, pinning her against the wood panel with his own weight.

"Ebenezer Scrooge?" His mocking blue eyes

drilled into hers. "Is that what you think of me, Harriet?"

Her coppery eyes blazed up at him, mere inches from his own. Her mouth was full and ripe in the light that slanted through the shuttered window. "Let... me...go," she breathed, quivering against him.

And that, Brandon thought, was exactly what he ought to do. But the feel of those full, firm breasts thrusting against his chest and the exquisitely light pressure of her hips against his swelling groin held him like a magnet. Under threat of death, he could not have moved away from her.

"Brandon—"

"No, hear me out first." His voice was thick and husky. "I wasn't arguing against your idea. It's a good one. But I don't want Jenny hurt, damn it. I don't want her held up to the scrutiny of people who'll say cruel things behind her back, or even to her face. Before I agree to help you, I need to be sure that isn't going to happen."

"You can't be sure." She strained against him, setting off heat waves where their bodies touched. Brandon couldn't tell whether she was struggling to get free or driven by the same sensations that were shooting liquid fire through his veins. Whatever was happening, he could not bring himself to step away and let her go.

"You can't be sure of...anything." Her voice was breathy, her words tangled skeins of logic. "You can't just bend life to your will, Brandon. Things happen, and sometimes you have to let them. You bet and you lose...you love and you get hurt, or you hurt others..."

"Since when did you become so wise, School-marm?" His lips brushed the soft hair at her temple as he spoke. "You don't strike me as a lady who's done a lot of living."

Or a lot of loving, he thought. Lord, the lessons he would teach this woman if things were different between them. He would smother her with intimate caresses, kiss her, stroke her, drive her half-mad with wanting him. He would thrust himself into that lovely, innocent body and pleasure her until she begged for mercy.

"Maybe not a lot of living," she murmured, stirring against him, making him ache. "But I've done a lot of reading. That should count for something."

Brandon chuckled under his breath, suddenly more relaxed than he had felt all day. How long had it been since a woman made him want to laugh? He had almost forgotten what it was like.

But this was crazy—worse than crazy because it was all wrong. Harriet Smith was the creature of his nightmares, not the sensual angel of his dreams. Any moment now she would turn on him with a remark that would leave him grinding his teeth in frustration. And even if she didn't, there was the bigger picture. Harriet's support of Jenny's marriage had shattered his hopes for the girl's promising future. Harriet had defied his wishes and turned his own daughter against him. Take her in his arms and he might as well be embracing a rattlesnake.

She gazed up at him, her moist, ripe lips all but begging to be kissed. "Please talk to the mayor, Brandon," she implored. "You have influence. I know you can make this happen. Do it for Jenny and the children at school. Do it for yourself."

This was the moment, Brandon thought. Kiss her and he would tumble over the precipice. He would lose everything—his pride, his integrity, even his soul. He had to distance himself now, before the temptation grew strong enough to sweep him away.

Steeling his resolve, he dropped his arms and backed away from the wall where he had pinned her. His splinted leg made it hard to retreat with dignity, but when he stumbled backward, he managed to keep his balance by catching a corner of the desk. Harriet stood where he had left her, looking flustered and confused.

"There's no need for you to use your wiles on me, Harriet," he said, fixing her with a black scowl. "I'm not prepared to pay the price for what you're offering."

"What I'm offering?" Her cheeks flamed. Her eyes widened. "What I'm *offering?*" She took a step toward him, her fists clenched, her body quivering.

"I could slap your face for that, Brandon Calhoun!" She spoke slowly, as if drawing each word from a well of fury. "The only thing I'm offering you is a way to help your daughter! Anything else you perceive to be on the table exists only in your arrogant male imagination!"

She flung the door open, then turned back abruptly. "You think you're such a fine catch, with your looks and your big house and your gold, don't you? Oh, I've heard the stories—how every unmarried woman in town has thrown herself at you at one time or another. Well, I'm not one of those women! I don't know if I'll ever marry, but if I do, it will be to a kind and gentle man with a forgiving heart—and I won't care what he looks like or how much money he has in the bank! So good afternoon to you, Mr. Calhoun—and goodbye!"

As the door slammed behind her, Brandon sagged against the desk. Harriet had not laid a hand on him, but his insides felt as if he'd been kicked by a mule. He had deliberately set out to insult her, wanting to push her so far away that he would no longer be tempted to act out those feverish dreams. The strategy had worked all too well—except for one problem.

He wanted her—wanted her with a hot, raw hunger that made his whole body burn. The fact that she had flung her anger in his face and walked out only heightened his desire. Lord, what was he going to do?

Forget her, that was the only answer, he told himself. He was old enough to know that a man who took everything he wanted was a man out of control. Brandon had been in perfect control—until the day he'd walked into Harriet's classroom and tried to bend her to his will. That was the day when his life had begun to fall apart.

It was time to pick up the pieces and move on, he resolved. With Jenny gone and Helga leaving shortly to care for her aging parents in Germany, he would be alone in the house. This might be the proper time to look for a second wife—not a pushy, irritating creature like Harriet Smith, who would keep his life in constant turmoil, but a gracious, submissive, quietly capable woman who would run his household smoothly and welcome him with a smile and a hot meal when he returned from work at night.

He even knew such a woman—a comely widow he had met at a reception in Denver a few months ago. As soon as his leg was free of this damned splint, he would pay her a call and renew their acquaintance. Maybe something good would come of it. And even if it didn't, at least it might prove a distraction from the miserable mess his life had become in the past few weeks.

Why don't you just change your name to Ebenezer Scrooge and be done with it?

The words mocked him as he took a small leather pouch from the desk drawer and scooped the ten gold coins into it. Was that how Harriet saw him— as a mean-spirited, miserly curmudgeon? Was that what he was becoming?

The idea of paying Jenny to help in the classroom was a stroke of brilliance—Brandon had realized that at once. But it irked him that Harriet hadn't given him the benefit of the doubt. When he'd questioned what could go wrong—always a wise thing at the start of a new venture—she'd become defensive. In the end she'd completely misread him.

But what did it matter? If Harriet Smith wanted to be impossible, that was her problem. He was happy for the chance to help Jenny, but he would rather tangle with a wounded wildcat than deal with the prickly schoolmarm again.

Brandon jammed the coins into his pocket and reached for his crutches. If he hurried, he might be able to catch the mayor before he left his office for the day. With luck, Hans Peterson would be willing to set up an account to pay for Jenny's work without the formality of going through the council. That would make everything easier.

As he opened the door of his office, the memory of Harriet's presence crept over him like a lingering aura. The thrust of her breasts against him, the warm, womanly aroma of her skin, the trembling softness of her lips swept over him, filling his senses with thoughts of what he could not—must not—allow himself to have. Brandon bit back a groan as the pain of need sank deeper. Thinking of her like this was the worst thing he could do. He was finished with the woman—had to be. For good.

Brandon forced her memory to the back of his mind. Then, still aching, he locked the doors of the bank and hurried off on his crutches to find the mayor.

* * *

Harriet stepped off the boarded sidewalk that fronted Main Street and headed down the alley that separated the hotel and the dry-goods store. If she cut behind the livery stable, she would emerge partway down the cemetery road, which led to her little house.

There would be no funerals taking place this late in the day. Harriet was grateful for that small boon, at least. She had a reputation to maintain in the community, and she could not afford to let curious eyes see the state she was in.

As she skirted the back of the hotel, picking her way past bins of refuse and heaps of discarded furniture, the stinging November wind made her eyes water. She dabbed at the wetness with her tattered handkerchief, telling herself it couldn't possibly be tears that were trickling down her cheeks. There was no way a man like Brandon Calhoun could make her cry. It was only the weather, nothing more.

But what a fool she had made of herself, thinking she could expect decent treatment from such a man. He had belittled her plan and her motives. Then he had caught her wrist, spun her into a corner and almost crushed her against the wall before he backed away and accused her of throwing herself at him.

Her face flamed as she recalled the solid male heat of his body against hers, that sensually chiseled mouth, a mere handbreadth from her own and moving closer. Merciful heaven, she had actually been fool enough to think he was going to kiss her! Worse, she'd been ready to kiss him back, ready to feel all the wild, glorious sensations that had flooded her body when his lips had captured hers beneath the wrecked buggy. Then, in a heartbeat, everything had changed. He had pulled away, glared down his nose at her and declared in a self-righteous tone that he was not prepared to pay the price she was offering.

A gasp of rage that was not quite a sob forced its way out of Harriet's throat as she tripped over an old bed spring and almost fell into the half-frozen mud. Brandon had scalded her with humiliation. She had wanted to punch him with all her strength, to bloody his cheek with her knuckles, maybe loosen a couple of teeth in that smug, arrogant mouth. Oh, why hadn't she done it? It would have felt so good!

Blinking back tears, she trudged toward the rear of the livery stable, where the road cut back toward the cemetery. The cold wind jabbed icy fingers through her shawl and plucked tendrils from the hairstyle Jenny had arranged so carefully that morning. The air had the damp feel of an approaching blizzard. She would be lucky to make it home before the storm struck full force, pelting her with sleet and freezing her to the bone.

She had almost reached the road when two squat, burly figures in sheepskin coats stepped directly into her path.

"Not so fast, teacher lady," a nasal voice growled. "Me and my brother want to have a little talk with you."

Harriet's heart crept into her throat as she looked into two identical faces and recognized them as the pair she'd seen with Brandon in the bank.

"I think you've mistaken me for someone else," she said, trying to push past them. "I don't even know you."

"Aw, but we know you," the second man whined. "You was there outside the bank office when we was leavin'. Looked to us like you was waitin' for the place to close up so you and that bastard banker could have yourselves a little quickie! How was it, eh?"

Harriet drew herself up. "Let me pass. You don't know what you're talking about."

"Don't we?" The first man grinned, showing a missing front tooth. "You was in there alone with the son of a bitch for as long as it takes. We wasn't born yesterday y'know."

"We have nothing to talk about. Let me pass before I start screaming." Harriet tried to sidestep the two men but one of them seized her wrist. The other hooked her neck with his arm and clamped a smelly hand over her mouth. His breath reeked of bad teeth and bad whiskey.

"You give that boyfriend of yours a message for us," he snarled in her ear. "Tell him that if he lays one greedy finger on our ranch, he's gonna be one sorry man. After we git done with you, you might not look so pretty!"

Harriet tore herself away as he loosened his grip. "You don't know what you're talking about!" She spat out the words, half-hysterical with rage and fear. "Brandon Calhoun isn't my boyfriend. And he wouldn't care if you cut me up in pieces and threw me to the coyotes! You'd only waste your time and risk getting yourselves thrown in prison. Now leave me alone! Take your problems somewhere else!"

The men sidled away, as if they knew they had little to fear from her. The one who'd grabbed her neck gave her a leering grin. "You tell the bastard what we said, hear?"

Harriet stood quivering and disheveled as the two men vanished into the livery stable. Her heart was slamming so hard against her ribs that she felt as if it might crack her bones.

Her first impulse was to run back to the bank, find Brandon and warn him. But after what had happened between them, she was loathe to face him again. Besides, it was her own safety, not his, that the pair had threatened. And, now that she thought of it, they looked like a couple of buffoons—all bluff and bluster. Surely they could not pose any serious danger, especially to a man like Brandon. As for warning him, there was no need. The two men had already threatened him in the bank. Brandon would be very much aware of any danger they posed.

Lifting her chin and lengthening her stride, Harriet made her way along the cemetery road. The wind howled around her. Snowflakes whirled through the air as the storm's first blast struck her solitary figure. She fought her way homeward, feeling lost and alone in the vast whiteness. Now, through the flying flakes, she could see the house. She could see the smoke curling from the chimney and she knew that Jenny had made a warm fire to welcome her. There would be hot tea brewing on the stove and conversation to cheer her while she rested from her ordeal. What a blessed angel Will's little bride had turned out to be!

How much should she tell Jenny about the afternoon's horrific events? Nothing, she swiftly decided. In her delicate condition, the last thing Jenny needed was disturbing news. But another idea occurred to Harriet as she paused on the stoop to stomp the snow off her feet. Maybe Jenny would be interested in helping with the class as a volunteer. There wouldn't be any money in it, but she might enjoy working with the children. And if she did a good job, there was always a chance that the mayor could be talked into paying her a small salary.

Yes, Harriet thought, as long as Jenny was interested, the plan could be made to work. If Brandon was too proud and self-absorbed to help, so be it. They would manage without him.

Harriet opened the door. Only then did she smell the acrid gray smoke that was pouring out of the iron cookstove.

Chapter Ten

Flinging the door wide open, Harriet rushed into the house. Smoke was pouring from the kitchen stove, curling from beneath the burner covers, fanning from around the oven door and forming a ghostly ring around the black pipe that served as a chimney. Thick gray layers hung below the ceiling, blanketing everything in the house.

"Jenny!" Choking on the bitter air, she rushed into the bedroom. The wide bed was empty, as was the bed in her own small room. Before leaving, she wrenched the window sash upward. A cross draught of icy wind from the front door swept through the house.

"Jenny! Where are you?" She dashed into the sitting alcove and found the girl at last, curled like a sleeping kitten on the settee beneath the rose afghan that Brandon had sent with her clothes. Her eyes were closed, her breathing deep and even, but her face was pale.

"Wake up, Jenny!" Harriet seized the thin shoulders and shook them hard. Jenny moaned faintly but did not open her eyes.

"Wake up!" Harriet slapped the pale cheeks, softly, then hard enough to leave stinging red marks. "Jenny, wake up!"

"What are you doing?" Will burst in through the open doorway.

"The smoke—I can't wake her—"

"No!" Will bent over the back of the settee and swept his wife's unconscious body up in his arms. "Come on, we've got to get her outside!"

Together they plunged out into the storm. As he cradled Jenny against him, Harriet could see Will's lips moving in silent prayer. Harriet prayed with him. *Please, oh, please, let her wake up.*

Shocked by the cold, fresh wind, and the feel of snowflakes on her face, Jenny coughed and opened her eyes. "What…?" She stared up at Will in confusion. Then she turned her head. Her gaze darted toward the house, where smoke was still pouring out of the open door. "Oh, no!" she groaned. "What's happened now?"

"It doesn't matter, darlin'." Will caught her close, and buried his face in her hair. Harriet caught the glint of a tear in his eye. "But did you do anything special to that stove?"

Her lovely cornflower eyes stared up at him. "Why—I gave it a good dusting this afternoon, right up to the top of the stovepipe. Then I put more wood on the fire and lay down to take a little nap…that's all I remember. Did I do something wrong, Will?"

"Not that I—" He frowned. "The damper! You must've bumped the handle that closes it! Stay here!" Lowering her feet to the ground, he passed her to Harriet's waiting arms and dashed back into the house.

"Will—" she called after him, but her voice was too feeble to carry above the storm.

Harriet wrapped the shivering girl in her thick wool shawl and cradled her against her breast. "He'll be all right," she soothed. "Take some deep breaths. You need to clear the smoke out of your lungs."

Jenny gulped the stormy air. "Oh, Harriet, I could've burned the house down, and everything you own with it! As it is, we'll have to air all the clothes and bedding to get rid of the awful smell! Oh, why do I have to be such a silly goose?"

"Hush." Harriet rocked her like the child she was. "You couldn't have known about the damper—no one told you. And the damage is nothing that a little fresh air and washing won't cure. You're all right, that's the important thing. You could have died in there!"

Jenny's face paled. "Why, yes, I suppose I—oh!" Tearing herself away from Harriet, she began to retch. Her body shook with heaves, as she bent over, clutching at her stomach. "Oh, no!" she gasped.

"Oh, Harriet, what if I've done something to hurt the baby?"

Will came out of the house, his arms loaded with blankets. "It was the damper, all right, closed as tight as a drum. But the rod that held it open had corroded through. What happened wasn't your fault, Jenny. It was that rusty old stove. The landlord should've replaced it years ago!"

He studied his wife's ashen face, then thrust the blankets toward Harriet. "You two bundle up in these and get under the shed till the smoke clears out of the house. I'm going to fetch Dr. Tate."

Neither Jenny nor Harriet were of a mind to argue. They staggered toward the rickety toolshed while Will set off for town as fast as his long legs could carry him.

Jenny continued to feel nauseous, and Harriet grew more and more concerned as the minutes passed. Without a doctor's examination, there was no way of knowing whether Jenny had breathed in enough smoke to harm herself or the baby. Dr. Tate's home office was no more than a fifteen-minute run for Will, but if the old man was out on a house call, he might not be back for hours.

Bundled in blankets, Jenny rested her damp head against Harriet's shoulder. "My baby's got to be all right," she whispered. "I love him so much—I'd rather die than have anything go wrong!"

"Him?" Harriet laughed, masking her worry. "Have you had a revelation?"

Jenny sighed. "Of course not. I just have a feeling it's a little boy."

"And if it's a girl?"

"Oh, that will be fine with me, and with Will, too. We just want a healthy, happy baby."

Harriet's arm tightened around Jenny's shoulders. If only Brandon could hear his daughter's words, she thought. If only he could hear the love in her voice, he would realize how wrong he'd been about everything.

"Harriet?"

"Yes?"

"Today when I was lying down I think I felt something inside me, almost like a little fluttery fish moving right under my hand. Do you think that could've been him? Is that how a baby is supposed to feel?"

"That's something I've never experienced," Harriet replied softly. "You should talk with a woman who's had babies, Jenny."

"Oh, but you know everything!" Jenny exclaimed. "You're so wise, Harriet!"

"No, dear, I may have memorized a lot of facts, but in other ways I'm not wise at all, especially where babies are concerned."

Harriet watched the snowflakes flying past the eave of the shed, thinking that she would probably never feel that miraculous first flutter of a child growing in her body. That part of her life would be forever missing, like the lost piece of a broken toy. She would spend her life teaching other people's children, watching them learn and grow, but the closest she would come to holding a baby of her own would be when she helped care for this precious child of Will and Jenny's. She would savor every minute of that time, she promised herself. She would make it a sweet time, with no room for envy or self-pity.

"I always wished Papa had married again after Mama died," Jenny said. "Our house was so big and lonely and quiet. I had friends over sometimes, of course, but I would have loved some little brothers and sisters to play with."

"Why didn't your father remarry?" Harriet could have kicked herself for asking.

"I guess twelve years with Mama would sour any man on marriage. Heaven knows, plenty of ladies have set their caps for him, and he's even seemed interested in a few, but—" She broke off as a dark, distant object caught her eye through the whirling mist of snow. "There's Dr. Tate!" she cried. "And Will is with him. Oh, thank goodness!"

By the time the doctor's buggy pulled up to the house, most of the smoke had cleared from the rooms. While Will braced the damper open and put fresh wood on the fire, Dr. Tate examined Jenny in the chilly sitting room. Frowning behind his thick spectacles, he listened to her heart and lungs, peered into her eyes and pulled up the eyelids to examine the whites.

"How do you feel, Jenny?" he asked her.

"Better—but what about my baby?" Jenny's eyes were wide with fear.

"I think both you and the baby are going to be fine," he said, taking off his stethoscope and folding it into his black bag. "But I want you to lie down and keep warm for the rest of the day, hear?"

"I'll see that she rests," Harriet said. "Would you like some hot coffee, Doctor? It won't take a minute."

"Thanks, but I'd better head Bessie for the barn," he said. "The longer I delay, the more snow there'll be on the road, and she's getting to be an old horse. Like me." He shot her a sidelong glance. "Would you walk out to the buggy with me, Harriet? It's a mite slippery for these old legs."

"Certainly." Harriet felt a jab of concern as she reached for her shawl, tossed it around her shoulders, and picked up her reticule. Despite some rheumatism, Simon Tate was a fit and agile man for his seventy years. She had never known him to need help walking through ankle-deep snow.

All the same, she guided him to the door and offered him her arm as they stepped outside. Feigning unsteady balance, he linked his elbow through hers.

"What is it?" she asked as the front door closed behind them. "Is something wrong?"

"Nothing right now, but I do have some concerns I need to share. I don't want to frighten Jenny or worry the boy, so that leaves you."

"Tell me." Harriet spoke through the knot of fear that had jerked tight in her throat.

"It's the birth I'm worried about," he said. "She's a delicate little thing with very narrow hips. Unless the child is small and perfectly positioned, she's likely to have problems—and those problems could kill both her and the baby."

Oh, no… Harriet's mind formed the words, but her mouth could not utter them. *Not this! Anything but this!*

"My advice would be to get her to a specialist in Denver and leave her under his care for the last few weeks of the pregnancy. When that girl goes into labor, it's going to take more expert hands than mine to get her through it safely."

"I'll see that it's done," Harriet said, thinking of the money set aside for Will's education. How unimportant that seemed now. She would spend every cent of it, and more, if need be, to see that Jenny and her child survived the birth.

"How much do we owe you, Doctor?" She reached into her reticule, hoping she had enough cash to pay the old man.

"Nothing. It's taken care of." He gave her a wink as he climbed into the buggy.

"But you came all the way out here in the snow!

You performed a medical examination on Jenny! Certainly we can't expect you to do all that for nothing!"

"I didn't say I was doing it for nothing, I said it was taken care of." The doctor grinned down at Harriet from the wagon seat. "The last time I saw Brandon he told me to see that Jenny got all the medical attention she needed and to send the bills to him— but Jenny's not to know, understand?"

Brandon again. Harriet sighed. She was grateful for Brandon's help, especially in view of the doctor's concerns for Jenny. But why did he have to be so high-handed about it? Why couldn't he give his daughter the one thing she wanted and accept Will into his family? What a terrible, foolish thing pride was!

"Does Brandon know what you just told me about Jenny?" Harriet asked.

"He does. And he's ready to pay for her confinement with a specialist in Denver. Again, Jenny's not to know."

"He doesn't have to do this," Harriet said. "We aren't charity cases. We can pay."

The doctor hunched into his ample black coat and picked up the reins. "Brandon would never stand for that. Beneath that blustery nature he shows the world, he's a very kindhearted man."

"Well, he's certainly done a good job of fooling me!" Harriet shouted into the wind, but the doctor had already turned his buggy down the road and was vanishing into the storm.

* * *

The Holiday Social was the biggest event of the season. By tradition, it was held in the town hall on the second Saturday evening in December, and all the respectable citizens of Dutchman's Creek were expected to attend.

Jenny, who was growing rounder by the day, had declared that she wasn't feeling well enough to go. Her real reason, Harriet suspected, was that she had no wish to see her father, who, as a member of the city council, would certainly be there.

Will, of course, had chosen to stay home and keep his wife company. Harriet would gladly have done the same. Unfortunately, as the town's only teacher, she was expected to take charge of the bake sale, the traditional fund-raiser for the school. She had been dreading the event for weeks, especially the dancing, which was sure to be an exercise in humiliation. When it came time to choose partners, the bachelors would ignore her in favor of the younger women; and if a married man asked her to dance, even once, his wife would look daggers at her for the rest of the night.

Whatever happened, the whole evening was bound to be an ordeal, especially with Brandon there. Maybe if she hid behind the baked-goods table no one would notice her. Surely she had a dress that would match the color of the wall behind her, allowing her to blend in and simply disappear.

Jenny, however, had very different plans for her.

"Just pretend you're Cinderella and I'm your fairy godmother!" she laughed, twirling Harriet's long tresses around her fingers and pinning them into place. "You're going to the ball, and it's my job to see that you look beautiful!"

"You might as well try making a silk purse out of a sow's ear," Harriet said ruefully. "Really, Jenny, I'm only going to tend the bake table."

"Oh, no! You're going to dance with the prince and he's going to fall wildly in love with you!" Jenny twirled to the wardrobe in high spirits, which seemed to droop as she opened the doors and pawed through Harriet's sad collection of gray, brown and navy blue dresses.

"Don't you have anything else?" she asked with a sigh.

"I haven't had much need for pretty gowns over the years, let alone the money to buy them," Harriet said. "Just grab one for me. It doesn't matter what I wear tonight."

Jenny was still shuffling through the dresses. "What a shame you can't wear my clothes," she mused. "Maybe...yes!" She seized a dark brown wool twill with an ample shawl collar of ecru lace. "Heavens, this one must make you look just like Martha Washington! But we can fix that. I have just the thing!"

Her small fingers began pulling at the lace collar, ripping away the stitches that held it in place.

"What are you doing?" Harriet cried. "That dress needs the collar to cover the bodice! Without it, I'll be liable to get arrested for indecent exposure!"

"Don't worry." Jenny grinned impishly. "I have something better. Wait till you see it!"

She dashed into the other room and Harriet could hear the sounds of her rummaging through her trunk. Moments later she returned with a triangular shawl of exquisite silk brocade, patterned in a rich design of forest green, burgundy and amber leaves. It was edged with silk fringe and trimmed in tiny amber beads.

"My aunt Ellen bought it from a Hungarian woman," Jenny said. "It doesn't suit me at all, but on you it would be perfect."

Harriet put out her hand. The fabric was as soft and delicate as the skin of a new baby. "It's beautiful," she murmured. "Much too beautiful for me to wear."

"Nonsense," Jenny said. "Put on your brown dress. Then sit down in front of the mirror."

Harriet did as the girl had asked. Without the lace collar to soften it, the brown dress looked stark and showed far too much of her shoulders and breasts. Jenny moved behind her, holding the Hungarian shawl. "Close your eyes," she said. "Don't open them until I tell you."

Harriet closed her eyes, trying not to squirm as Jenny draped, tucked, clipped and pinned the sensuous fabric around her shoulders and over the bodice of her dress. An exotic, musky aroma lingered in the folds of the shawl, as if its former owner had drenched herself in perfume, perhaps for a lover.

The Hungarian shawl began to cast its spell even before Harriet opened her eyes. When, at Jenny's signal, she looked at herself in the mirror, she almost forgot to breathe.

The woman gazing back at her was as radiant as a sunset. The colors in the shawl, which Jenny had fastened artfully over the bodice of the dress, brought out the subtle rose glow in her ivory cheeks and turned the copper flecks in her eyes to dancing dots of fire. Her hair, which framed her face in gleaming waves, was caught up and pinned at the back of her head in a loose knot of curls.

"One more thing." Jenny dashed back into her room again and came back with a small green-velvet box. Opening it with a flourish, she pulled out a pair of dangling gold filigree earrings set with faceted carnelian beads that glimmered in the lamplight, reflecting a myriad of tiny flames.

"Aren't they perfect?" Jenny gushed happily. "I just happened to notice you had pierced ears." She bent close, blocking the mirror and causing Harriet to wince as she worked the wires into place. "You need to wear earrings more often, Harriet. These little holes have almost closed up."

"Most days it's not worth the bother."

"Well, it's definitely worth the bother tonight. Look at you!"

Jenny whirled away from the mirror, giving Harriet a full view of her reflection. The baubles that dangled from her earlobes provided the crowning touch to the transformation. The gold filigree contrasted richly with her mahogany hair, and each facet of the deep red carnelian beads reflected a warm dot of lamplight on her face. She looked…intriguing, like a mysterious woman from a romantic novel.

"Oh!" Harriet murmured, staring at the mirror. "Oh, my goodness, who is that person?"

"That person is you, and you're just stunning!" Jenny clapped her hands, beside herself with delight. "Now, go to the ball, Cinderella. Dance with the prince. But be sure to come home before midnight!"

"Silly, I'm just going to tend the bake-sale table," Harriet protested. "And they'll be needing me there any minute, so I'd best get moving."

Flinging on her cloak, she hurried out through the kitchen. On her way, she passed the shiny new black-and-chrome Red Oak stove that their landlord had installed the day after the smoke problem. Since the landlord was a tight man with a dollar and seldom fixed anything around the place, Harriet suspected Brandon's hand in the matter. After Jenny's near disaster, she could only be grateful for his help.

The night was mild and clear, the walk to the church an easy distance through well-tracked snow.

Harriet arrived early enough to arrange the cakes, pies and cookies the women had brought in earlier, post the price list and put some change in the cigar box that served as a till. By the time the crowds started arriving she was seated primly behind the table, braced for the night's ordeal. A few parents stopped by, and she sold four plates of cookies, but no one mentioned her appearance except one ten-year-old girl who stared at her across the table for a long moment before piping in a loud voice, "Oh, Miss Smith, you look just like the queen of the Gypsies!"

Harriet shrank a little lower in her chair. Yes, she did look like a Gypsy, she realized, with her dark hair and eyes, the exotic Hungarian shawl and the glittering earrings. But it was too late to do anything about it now. Removing the shawl would expose the ugly bodice of her dress, to say nothing of her breasts and shoulders. And the earrings were surely valuable. To take them off would be to risk losing them. Worst of all, she could not leave the hall. The queen of the Gypsies was stuck right here, on open display, for the entire evening.

Her heart lurched as Brandon's tall figure loomed in the doorway. Harriet pretended to count the change in the cigar box as she watched him covertly through the screen of her lowered eyelashes. Dressed in an immaculate white shirt and dark blue suit, he was walking with a cane instead of his crutches. It appeared that the doctor had removed the heavy splint and replaced it with a light brace that barely showed under his well-fitted trousers.

He looked fit and elegant and meltingly handsome. Just seeing him made Harriet want to slink under the table and hide. She held her breath until he took his seat on the front row, with the other members of the town council, then sighed with relief. So far, at least, he had not appeared to notice her.

The festivities started with a flag ceremony and an opening prayer, followed by an enactment of the Christmas story by the children in the town, under the direction of the minister's wife. After that, a good half hour was devoted to the singing of Christmas carols. Finally, after peppermint sticks had been passed out among the children, the chairs were moved to the walls, clearing the floor for dancing.

Men and women scurried to find their partners as the fiddler took his place next to the piano and struck up a lively polka. Harriet was pretending to count the change in the cigar box when a long-fingered brown hand thrust into view and a deep, masculine voice with a hint of Texas drawl said, "May I have the honor of this dance, Miss Smith?"

It wasn't Brandon. Harriet knew that at once, and her heart sank a little. But as her eyes shifted upward to the clean-cut features and twinkling brown eyes of Sheriff Matthew Langtry, she told herself she could do far worse. The sheriff was a few years her junior, and several of the older girls in her classroom had teenage crushes on him. It was easy enough to see why.

"I'm afraid I can't leave—" she started to say, but an elderly woman inspecting the pies interrupted her.

"Oh, go ahead and dance, dearie! I'll watch the till for you. You're much too young and pretty to hide behind a table all night!"

With a polite murmur of thanks, Harriet allowed the sheriff to lead her onto the dance floor. He was almost as tall as Brandon but more slender and athletic. He was an excellent dancer and, although she felt awkward for the first moment, he soon had her flying around the floor.

"Is this the way they dance in Texas?" She laughed up at him, out of breath.

"Oh, no, ma'am." His expressive eyes smiled down at her as if they were seeing an attractive woman, definitely not the queen of the Gypsies. "In Texas we do the Spanish fandango and the Texas two-step. I'd be right pleased to teach you those dances sometime."

"I just may take you up on that, Sheriff." She flashed him a bubbly smile that did not seem like her at all. Among the blurred faces at the edge of the dance floor, she caught a glimpse of Brandon's familiar scowl. He was watching her, probably thinking that she was making a silly fool of herself. Well, let him think whatever he pleased! She was having a good time.

No sooner had the polka ended than Enoch Farley, the town undertaker, claimed her for a reel. Enoch was a widower nearing fifty and rather shy. Harriet did her best to put him at ease, but it was a relief when the dance ended and she found herself in the arms of Hans Peterson, Dutchman Creek's plump, affable mayor.

"You're quite the belle tonight, Miss Harriet Smith." His grin showed the gleam of a gold front tooth. "The only a way a man can get a word with you, it seems, is to ask you to dance."

"You wanted a word with me?" Harriet's breath caught as he swung her out of the path of a whirling couple.

"That's right. But my feet and my mouth don't work very well at the same time. What do you say we get something to drink?"

Harriet allowed the mayor to lead her to the refreshment table where he dipped her a cup of cold apple cider from a cut-glass bowl. "Brandon spoke with me about your having Jenny help with the little ones at school for a few months. As long as the girl is strong enough, I think it's a fine idea. The money's in place. Let me know when you want her to start."

Harriet gazed at him in happy astonishment. Brandon had come through, after all. "Jenny's not to know the money came from her father," she cautioned.

The mayor gave her a sly wink. "Since the money's now part of the school budget, that shouldn't be a problem."

"And no one on the town council objected?"

"It wasn't the council's decision. It was mine."

"Thank you." Harriet seized his big ham of a hand in her own. "I can hardly wait to tell her! She'll be so excited."

"It's Brandon you should thank," the mayor said. "And since he's standing right behind you, I'll just wander back to my wife and leave you to do that."

Harriet stifled a gasp as she turned around and saw Brandon looming above her. His face wore a polite smile but his eyes were like a panther's, smoldering with ferocity.

The fiddler had begun to play a slow, sweet waltz. Keeping his gaze locked with hers, Brandon balanced his cane against the end of the table. "You might have to hold me up, but I think I can manage this dance if you'll do me the honor," he said.

Harriet glided into his arms, aware that she was trembling. He moved well, even on his injured leg, but the silence between them was awkward. She'd been glib and flirtatious with the young sheriff. But now her tongue seemed to have taken leave.

"I'm…glad to see your leg's getting better," she stammered. "Did the bones knit well?"

"As well as could be expected. I won't be winning any footraces, but I should be able to get around all right." He was looking at her in an odd way, as if there were something about her he disliked, yet couldn't tear his eyes away from.

"How is Jenny?" he asked as if he'd waited all evening to find out.

"Resting tonight, but she's healthy and happy, thank heaven, with no ill effects from the smoke. She'll enjoy helping with the children at school. Thank you for following my suggestion. I—I'm sorry for calling you Ebenezer Scrooge."

"You didn't call me Ebenezer Scrooge, you just suggested I change my name." His smile was a bit cold, and he seemed slightly ill at ease.

"Forgive me, but I need to say this." Harriet plunged ahead impulsively, knowing she might not have another chance. "Christmas is just two weeks away, Brandon. It's a terrible time for people to be estranged. I know how many ways you've tried to help Jenny. Can't you just—"

"No." The word was spoken with the finality of a slamming door. "Let it go, Harriet. You're just wasting your breath."

"But—" The protest died on her lips as she saw the reflected glimmer in his eyes and realized what he'd been looking at all along.

Heaven help her, it was those accursed gold-and-carnelian earrings!

Chapter Eleven

Until a moment ago Harriet had loved the beautiful earrings Jenny had lent her. She had loved the weight of them, their faint musical tinkle as she danced, and the warmth of red-gold light that burned in the depths of each faceted carnelian bead. Until a moment ago, they had possessed an aura of pure magic.

But not now.

"Oh," she whispered, gazing up at Brandon with stricken eyes. "Oh, Brandon, I'm so sorry! It was Jenny's idea to lend me these earrings. I'm sure she only meant to be kind, but I should have realized where they came from—" Her fumbling fingers reached up for the wires, but she swiftly realized that removing the earrings would only rouse people's curiosity. It would be more discreet to leave them in place.

"Jenny inherited her mother's jewelry," Brandon

said stiffly. "The pieces are hers, and she has the right to do whatever she pleases with them."

"But for me to wear them here, to flaunt them in front of you and all these people—"

"Harriet, you didn't know." He sighed wearily. "Now let's just finish our dance before people start looking at us."

They moved like marionettes as the waltz played out to its end. Harriet stared fixedly at Brandon's neatly tied cravat, acutely conscious of the pressure of his hand against the small of her back and the clamminess of her fingers where they rested in his palm. He held her as lightly as he might have held one of Jenny's porcelain dolls, and with no more emotion. Oh, why hadn't she stayed behind the baked-goods table where she belonged? She should have known what a terrible mess she'd make of the whole evening.

The music swelled to a crescendo and crashed into silence as the fiddler lowered his bow. Harriet shot Brandon a farewell glance and made a break for her table—only to be swept back into the maelstrom of dancers by the handsome young sheriff. "You're a popular lady!" he said, grinning down at her. "I've been waiting to get another dance with you!" With that he caught her waist and whirled her into the bounding rhythm of another polka.

"Hang on to your hairpins, Miss Harriet!" he laughed. "Here's how we do this dance in Texas!"

* * *

Brandon watched from the corner of the hall as Harriet flew around the floor with Matt Langtry. Flushed and laughing, with the Hungarian shawl bringing out the color in her face, she looked downright seductive, he thought—but then, he had long since concluded she was a beautiful woman. Tonight other men were clearly thinking the same thing.

The young sheriff, known to be a ladies' man, was probably just having a good time. All the same, Brandon's fists were quietly clenching with the urge to storm the dance floor, punch him in the jaw and reclaim Harriet for himself.

All evening, from the moment he saw her, Brandon had ached to have her in his arms. That ache had driven him to brave the waltz on his still-injured leg. But all his good intentions had been doomed the instant he recognized those cursed earrings she was wearing.

He had given the earrings to Ada for their fifth wedding anniversary, the first year he'd had the money to buy her something of value. She had worn them to a dinner party that night, where she'd begun sneaking liquor behind his back almost as soon as they'd arrived. By the time he'd gotten her home she'd been reeling drunk and he had been sick with frustration.

Behind their closed bedroom door, they'd had a terrible argument. It had followed the same course as other battles they'd had over the years, but with one devastating difference. Brandon would spend the rest of his life trying to blot out the words his wife had said to him that night.

Now, as Harriet spun around the dance floor in another man's arms, the earrings caught the light, flashing the message of those killing words into his brain. He struggled to ignore them. After all, what difference did it make? Ada was dead, and Jenny had gone her own way. None of it mattered anymore.

But his head had begun to ache and his lungs cried out for fresh air. The dancers and the music and the laughter swirled around him, enclosing him in a fog of light and sound and movement. In recent years Brandon had almost never suffered from the blinding headaches that had plagued him during the years of his marriage, but he felt a humdinger coming on now. There was no remedy for it, he knew, except to go home, go to bed and try to sleep it off.

Gripping his cane, he edged around the hall and stepped out into the blessed cold stillness of the December night. Snow crunched under his shoes as he made his way down the steps. Behind him, the music blared as Harriet polkaed around the floor in the young sheriff's arms. Never mind her, Brandon told himself. There were other women in the world—sweet, pliant, predictable women who would not try his patience and turn him into a raging madman. For instance…

What was the name of that attractive widow he'd

met in Denver? The one he was going to visit after his leg healed?

Lord help him, in his present condition, he couldn't even recall.

"How many now? Let's count them together! One, two, three, four..." Jenny was helping the youngest children string popcorn kernels for the little Christmas tree that stood in one corner of the crowded schoolroom. It had been her own idea to turn the activity into an arithmetic lesson. Harriet could not have been more pleased.

"Now let's add three more. One...two...three! How many do we have now?"

The children wriggled excitedly and raised their hands, all of them eager to answer. Smiling, Jenny called on a shy little boy in patched overalls who seldom spoke up in class. The girl was a natural teacher, Harriet thought. What a pity she'd ended her schooling here in Dutchman's Creek. But at least, with her gift for reaching children, Jenny would be a wonderful mother.

Will was a bigger worry, so bright and promising, and still breaking his back at the feed store. How would he get the education he needed, with a wife and baby to support? The money she'd put aside was enough to pay for school, but not nearly enough for a growing family to live on while he attended classes. Would he be doomed to a life of hard labor, spending the strength of his body while his fine mind lay fallow?

She sighed as she walked quietly between the rows of desks, where the older students labored over their American history examinations. Jenny and the coming baby had blessed her life in surprising ways. But few blessings tumbled pure and unmixed from heaven. Everything had its price—and no one could know what that final price would be.

Outside, a fresh winter storm rattled the windows, pelting the glass panes with huge, wet flakes of snow. With only a week remaining until Christmas, the children were so excited they could barely sit still. Even the boys and girls from the poorest families could look forward to a gift—the town council saw to that with the help of several businessmen including, she suspected, Brandon. No one could ever say that the people of Dutchman's Creek did not take care of their own.

Harriet herself was looking forward to celebrating the day with Jenny and Will. There wouldn't be much in the way of presents, but they would enjoy a fine dinner of baked ham and potatoes, with hot rolls and mince pie for dessert. There would be games and carols, laughter and warmth and love.

It would be the perfect time for reconciliation between Jenny and her father.

The idea had come to Harriet weeks ago, and she had been bolstering her resolve ever since. After their last encounter, it would take all the courage she possessed to face Brandon and invite him to share their humble Christmas, but she would do it in the true spirit of the season. She would do it for Jenny, whom she had come to love. After all, Brandon was family now. And it was senseless, even tragic, for a father and daughter who cared so deeply for each other to be kept apart by their own stubborn pride.

Brandon had slammed the door on the whole idea when she'd brought it up at the dance. But then, she'd been wearing his late wife's earrings at the time. She might as well have waved a red flag in front of a bull. No wonder he'd closed his mind and refused to listen.

She would not make that mistake again, Harriet promised herself. She would call on him looking as sedate as a nun. And she would not push him to forgive his daughter or to welcome Will into his family—that would be asking too much. She would simply invite him to Christmas dinner as a neighborly gesture. If she could persuade him to take that one small step, love and human nature would surely accomplish the rest.

But first she would need to get Jenny's cooperation.

Her chance came after school, as the two of them walked down the path through the falling snow. The maple branches were bare above their heads, the ground slippery beneath their boots. Harriet gripped Jenny's arm to steady her on the uneven slope as the flakes swirled around them, soft and white and cold.

"You're doing a wonderful job with the little ones, Jenny," Harriet said. "Your father would be so proud of you."

Jenny's body stiffened warily. "I love working with the children. But that has nothing to do with my father. Why are you bringing him up now, Harriet?"

"I was just thinking about him, alone in that big house, with Christmas coming. It's going to be a sad time for him."

"It's his own choice, you know," Jenny said in a taut voice. "If Papa doesn't like being alone at Christmastime, we both know what he can do about it."

"I know, but he's a very proud man." Harriet's arm tightened around her young sister-in-law. She wished she dared tell Jenny about the things Brandon had secretly done for her. But the girl's obstinance was equal to her father's. She would most likely rebel at having to accept his help.

"Sometimes pride needs a nudge in the right direction, Jenny," she said. "Inviting your father to share our Christmas could provide that nudge."

"It could," Jenny replied pensively. "Or it could put everyone on edge and end up in a big, ugly fight like the ones Papa and Mama used to have. I don't want that to happen, Harriet. This will be my very first Christmas as Will's wife. I want it to be peaceful and happy, with no bad memories to spoil it. So please don't even think about inviting Papa to come to our house. I love him, but if he shows up, I promise you, I'll get a sick headache and go to bed."

Harriet sighed as her hopes crumbled away. Jenny was right. If Brandon were to come to the house, his presence would impose a strain on them all. But there had to be some other way, something she could do to make this Christmas a time of love and healing.

"I did make Papa a present," Jenny said. "Remember last month, when you taught me to knit and helped me make that little blanket for the baby?"

"I do remember, and you did a fine job." Harriet recalled how Jenny had labored over the soft blue blanket. The end result had been lopsided because of her uneven stitches, but it would be warm for the baby, which was all that really mattered.

"After I finished the blanket, I started working on a neck scarf for Papa. I knew he wouldn't want light blue baby wool, so I unraveled an old gray shawl of mine to get enough yarn. I'll have it done by Christmas day. Maybe—" She hesitated, glancing down at her bulging waistline. "Maybe you could take it to his house, Harriet. I don't think I'm quite up to seeing him, especially on Christmas day."

"Of course," Harriet heard herself saying. "And if we wait until after dinner, I can wrap up a basket of food for him. With Helga gone and no one hired to replace her, he'll probably appreciate a home-cooked meal."

"Thank you." Jenny squeezed her hand. "Maybe someday I'll be ready to face him again. But not yet. The wounds are still too raw."

"Those wounds will heal someday," Harriet said, "but you have to let them heal, Jenny. You can't just leave them to fester."

"Tell that to Papa," Jenny said. "He's the one who can't seem to forgive."

"Forgiveness takes two," Harriet replied, wishing she felt as wise as she sounded.

"I've made him a gift," Jenny said quietly. "That should be enough to let him know the door is open. But he's the one who has to walk through it. No one can force him, not even you."

"All right, I see your point," Harriet said contritely. How naive she'd been to think she could step in and forcefully close the rift between Brandon and his daughter. Jenny, in her sweet way, had shown her the truth. No amount of manipulation could change two stubborn hearts. Forgiveness could only take place when both of them were ready.

She would deliver Jenny's gift to Brandon and plan to hold her tongue, Harriet resolved. But if the man provided her with an opening, by heaven, she would not turn away. She would tell him exactly what was on her mind. It might not move him a hairbreadth toward reconciliation, but at least it might give him something to think about.

After all, what did she have to lose?

* * *

By Christmas day the snow had blanketed the town in drifts that lay as deep as a horse's belly. Daily plowing had kept the main street clear for business, but the school had closed three days early and the road to Johnson City was impassable. Dutchman's Creek was cut off from the world, like an island in a cold, white sea.

Brandon had planned a trip to Denver for the week, to visit a few friends and look into renewing his acquaintance with Helen Woodridge, the widow whose name he'd finally managed to remember. But the weather had kept him here, a solitary prisoner in this big, empty, miserable dungeon of a house.

Since Helga's departure, he'd adjusted fairly well to living alone. Keeping the place clean was a matter of not getting it dirty to begin with. His laundry was done by the Chinese family who lived through the block from the bank, and when he wanted more than a simple meal, he could order whatever he wished in the dining room at the hotel.

The loneliness, however, was another matter.

The gruff, aging German housekeeper had never provided him with much company. But at least hers had been another presence in the house. Until Helga's departure, Brandon had never realized how much he missed the sound of another person's footsteps in the hall, another person's voice from the kitchen, or the cheer of light and warmth when he returned home at the end of a long day.

But missing Helga was nothing compared to missing Jenny. Jenny's absence was a black pit in the depths of his soul—a pit he could stumble into anytime he dropped his guard. If she had been away at school or suitably married, he could have borne it. But the fact that she was just out of reach, right here in Dutchman's Creek, pregnant and wed to the man who'd defiled her, was more than he could stand, especially on Christmas day, when all the blackbirds of emotion and memory came home to roost.

He stood, now, at an upstairs window, watching the bloodred ball of the sun sink toward the western peaks. The day had been long and dreary, and he was grateful to see it coming to an end. Tomorrow he would be all right. The bank would be open. He would have people to see and work to occupy his thoughts. Christmas, curse the day, would be over for another year.

Why don't you just change your name to Ebenezer Scrooge and be done with it?

Harriet's angry words flashed through his mind as he lowered his gaze to the snowy road and saw a dark figure trudging along a wagon track, coming toward the house. Joy and dismay did battle for his heart as he recognized her slim, erect stature and blowing cloak. Without doubt, she had come to torment him. But at least she had come.

By the time she had climbed the front steps, stomped the snow off her boots and rapped the lion-headed brass knocker, he was waiting for her in the front hall. A strange giddiness swept over him as he opened the front door. Suddenly, inexplicably, it was Christmas, and he was no longer Ebenezer Scrooge.

"I thought you might appreciate a little holiday cheer," she said, holding out the covered basket she'd taken from beneath her cloak. "It's only leftovers from our Christmas dinner, but since the hotel restaurant is closed…"

The words trailed off as Brandon stepped behind her and lifted the cloak from her shoulders. She was dressed in one of those awful gray schoolmarm frocks of hers, with no jewelry to brighten its grim effect, but her hair waved softly around her face, framing her luminous eyes and cold-pinked cheeks. What did the woman want from him this time? he wondered. He knew better than to believe Harriet Smith would walk a mile through the snow to pay a social call on a man she despised.

But never mind, he would know soon enough. Meanwhile, he could savor the company of a female who, by turns, challenged, intrigued, aroused and maddened him. For better or for worse, Brandon realized, he had never spent a boring moment in her presence.

"Are you hungry?" she asked, as if groping for something to say. "There's ham and potatoes and fresh rolls in this basket. They were warm when I left the house, but I fear I couldn't walk fast enough to keep them that way."

"There's a fire in the stove," Brandon said, draping her cloak over a chair. "I can warm up the food in the oven, but I'll only take the trouble if you'll agree to stay and share Christmas dinner with me."

Her eyebrows arched above her stunning, copper-flecked eyes, but before she could protest, he spoke again.

"It's been a long, black day, Harriet. I realize you might not be hungry, but you can sit at the table and share the time. Afterward I'll drive you home in the buggy."

Still she looked uncertain. "You're alone now. The gossip—"

"Hang the gossip! It's the company I'm craving even more than the meal. Stay. Please."

Her breath eased out in a little sigh of resignation. "Very well. For a little while." She handed him the basket, pausing to take a small, wrapped package from beneath the gingham towel that covered it. "A gift," she said. "Let's put this dinner in the oven. Then you can open it."

"A gift?" Brandon was taken aback. "Blast it, I didn't—"

"Oh, it isn't from me," she said. "It's from your daughter."

For an instant Brandon felt himself teetering on the edge of the black pit. He wrenched himself back to a state of cold control. "I asked the boy at the dry-goods store to deliver a gift to Jenny," he said. "Did she get it?"

"The rose-colored shawl? Yes, she opened it this morning. The color is lovely on her. But there's only one gift Jenny wants from you."

Brandon felt the black pit yawning beneath him. "Don't start," he said, unable to keep the raw edge from his voice. "It's Christmas day and you're here to help me celebrate."

He found an iron baking pan in the cupboard and carefully scooped the ham, potatoes, gravy, yams and bread into it from the plate Harriet had brought. There was enough food for two meals, at least, with a generous slice of mince pie wrapped in a separate napkin. Rinsing off the plate and putting the pie on a saucer, he replaced Harriet's belongings in the basket. Then he slipped the pan of food into the hot oven. Harriet watched him from the doorway, looking ill at ease, as if she feared that invading a man's kitchen might be a breach of etiquette. Maybe asking her to stay had been a mistake.

"There, that's done," he said with forced cheerfulness. "Now, while that fine dinner warms, we can relax in the parlor."

She moved aside to let him pass into the dining room, then followed him to the parlor with the air of a condemned prisoner being led to the gallows. The tension between them was leaden. Maybe they would both have been better off if he'd just snatched the damned basket from her hands and sent her back the way she'd come. Or better yet, if he'd simply re-fused to answer the door.

But no, it was Christmas and he had been drown-ing in despair before she came. Prickly and defen-sive she might be, but he was grateful for her company and he would do his best to make her visit enjoyable for them both.

Since Jenny's departure he had rearranged the parlor to suit his own comfort. The two armchairs that had once flanked the fireplace had been moved back against the far wall. In their place, the long, comfortable leather couch had been pulled up before the fire, with a low mahogany table in front of it. On these solitary winter nights, it had become Brandon's accustomed place. He ate, worked and sometimes even slept here.

Pausing to lay a fresh log on the fire, he ushered her to a seat on the couch. She sank into the sump-tuous leather with a little sigh, savoring the soft warmth as Brandon walked to the sideboard, took out two small etched-crystal wine goblets and filled them with the aged Bordeaux he kept for his most impor-tant guests. He rarely drank unless he was entertain-ing, or being entertained, but this seemed a fitting occasion.

"Merry Christmas," he said, holding one goblet to-ward her.

Her full lips parted. "Oh, but I don't—"

"It's cold outside, and this lovely wine came all

the way from France to warm you up," he said lightly. "Every drop holds a season's worth of bright summer days. Try it."

She took a tentative sip. Her mouth puckered appealingly, recalling the memory of that lingering kiss beneath the wrecked landau. He would like to taste those lips again, Brandon thought—to mingle the taste of the wine with the taste of *her*, losing himself in the rich, heady, biting sweetness, to kiss her until she moaned beneath him and begged for more.

She took another small sip. "It's…rather good," she said, setting the goblet on the table and reaching into her pocket. "Now it's time to open your present."

Brandon felt his stomach contract as she handed him the small, soft package, which was wrapped in plain brown paper and tied with a bow of red yarn. He felt the black pit, created by his rift with Jenny, widening beneath him, threatening to pull him down.

"I'm sorry," he said, fighting for self-control. "I didn't expect—"

"I know," she whispered, her fingertips brushing his arm. "Open it, Brandon. It was made with love."

His hands, all thumbs now, fumbled with the simple bow. The edges of the paper parted to reveal a folded length of clumsily knitted gray wool, trimmed with knotted fringe at the ends.

"She made the scarf by herself," Harriet said. "It's not perfect because she was just learning to knit, but it will be warm this winter. Jenny didn't want to forget you at Christmastime."

Brandon checked the package for a note. To his mixed disappointment and relief there was none. But an aching lump had closed off his throat. He fought back the rising waves of emotion that threatened to drown him.

"It's…a fine gift," he said, fingering the lumpy, uneven stitches. "Tell her I'll wear it proudly. And please thank her for me."

"You could thank her yourself. Why don't you?" Harriet was leaning toward him, her eyes moist and shining in the firelight. Tendrils of dark hair had escaped their pins to curl softly against her cheeks. Her lips were parted, her full, firm breasts straining against the confines of the gray serge, showing the faint, shadowed outline of her nipples.

Brandon imagined burying his face between those breasts, losing his pain in the refuge of her womanly warmth. He imagined gathering her into his arms, stretching out on the couch and holding her close while his bitterness drifted away in a cloud of purest bliss. Miss Harriet Smith, his prim, straitlaced, sharp-tongued nemesis.

Lord, how he needed her.

Chapter Twelve

"Brandon?" Harriet spoke his name cautiously, as if awakening a sleepwalker. "You haven't answered my question. Why not thank Jenny face-to-face, or at least write her a note?"

He studied her a moment longer, then sighed and turned away to gaze into the fire. Placing the lumpy scarf on the table, he picked up the wine goblet and cradled it between his palms.

"I know you mean well, Harriet, but I don't want to thank Jenny for her gift in person, or even in writing. The scarf was a sweet gesture, but we've hurt each other enough already. Why open ourselves to more grief?"

"Jenny told me the same thing when I suggested inviting you to Christmas dinner." Harriet picked up her own glass and cupped it as he did. Backlit by the fire in its cut-crystal goblet, the wine glowed like faceted garnet between her fingers. She had enjoyed the way the first taste of it had burned a trail down her throat, but she was hesitant to drink more. Her self-control was frayed enough as it was.

"It's just as well you didn't invite me," he said. "I wouldn't have come. You can't fix what's happened, Harriet. Nobody can."

"Except you."

"Don't." He raised the glass, drained it and replaced it on the table with a click. "It's Christmas, and the last thing I need from you is one more argument."

"I see." Harriet took a nervous sip of the wine, cradling its mellow heat in her mouth while she groped for something intelligent to say to the man. Verbal sparring, she realized, had become their accustomed pattern. While attacking him or defending herself, she had never been at a loss for words. But now, in this state of truce, she found herself as fluttery and tongue-tied as a fourteen-year-old girl at her first dance.

Brandon leaned back into the leather cushions, his stormy cobalt eyes appraising her from head to toe. His skin was golden bronze against the stark white of his open collar, his silver-kissed hair rumpled, as if he'd combed it with his fingers. He looked as rakishly dangerous as a pirate.

"You're a beautiful woman, Harriet," he said. "Why is it you've never married?"

The color flamed in her cheeks. "I very nearly did marry once, years ago."

"May I ask what happened?"

"There were…complications on my part, things my fiancé didn't want to deal with." It wasn't a good time to mention Will, she thought. "In the end he walked away and married someone else."

"He was a fool." Brandon's vehemence startled her.

"No," Harriet said. "We weren't well suited. He was wise enough to see that."

"He was a fool." Brandon's voice had dropped to a throaty whisper. Their secret kiss blazed through her memory, rousing coils of liquid heat that tightened and shimmered in the deep core of her body. She found herself aching for the taste of his mouth on hers and the plundering thrust of his tongue that ignited a conflagration of need inside her.

The terror she'd felt that night had long since faded. But the memory of being in Brandon's arms remained tormentingly sharp and clear. In that moment when his warm lips had closed on hers, setting loose a rush of thrilling sensations, she had felt utterly, completely alive. The thought that she might never feel that way again was a dark, desperate weight in her soul.

Brandon had forgotten that kiss, or at least regretted it, she reminded herself. But her nature had become stronger than her sense of logic. Driven by yearning so deep she could not control it, Harriet parted her lips and leaned toward him.

His hand reached out and gently cupped her chin.

She felt her heart drop as his eyes burned into hers. "I do remember kissing you, Harriet," he said huskily. "And I remember you kissing me back."

His lips brushed hers in a foray of light, nibbling kisses that stirred a low moan in her throat. Her arms slid upward, hands catching his neck, tangling in his thick hair as the kisses grew deeper, and deeper still.

"Oh…" She arched against him, wanting only to be close, to feel his arms around her, the hard length of his body pressing hers. "Don't…"

"Don't what?" he murmured against the curve of her throat. "You'd better tell me now, Harriet, before it's too late."

"Don't…stop." She felt herself spinning out of control, wanting him, needing him, all of him.

His breath rasped as he fumbled with the buttons that fastened her high collar. She reached up to help him, frantic to feel his touch on her body. He uttered a mild curse as the last button popped loose, bounced to the floor and rolled under the sofa. Then she felt his kisses on the untouched skin of her breasts; oh, sweet, sweet heaven, she could have died from it.

"Damn it, I've wanted you, Harriet," he muttered, easing aside the tattered lace edge of her camisole. "Ever since that night, I've ached for the feel of you, the taste of you…"

Her heart seemed to stop as his tongue brushed her bare nipple. Gently he licked the sensitive nub of flesh, tasting, kissing, sucking, until she groaned. A flood of primitive sensations coursed through her body as she pushed upward against his hot, seeking mouth.

Brandon, I love you...I love you so much. The words quivered on her tongue, but Harriet knew better than to speak them out loud. Brandon had said nothing to her about love. He had not mentioned any kind of future together, not even something beyond this moment. She would be a fool not to slap his face, struggle off the couch and flee for the sake of her virtue. But the fire that surged through every vessel and fiber of her being was so exquisite that she had no will to resist. All she wanted was more of this deep, throbbing sweetness. More of him.

His exploring hand found her stockinged legs beneath her petticoats. "Tell me if you want me to stop," he whispered hoarsely. "Tell me now, or I might not be able to. I don't want to hurt you, Harriet. Only to pleasure you."

"You won't...hurt me." Her eyes were closed, her head flung back on the cushions. Her breath caught as his hand found the opening in her drawers and brushed her moisture-slicked thigh. She was about to become that most scandalous of creatures, a fallen woman. And in this heat of total abandon, there was nothing she wanted more.

They both sensed it at the same time—the bitter smell of smoke pouring out of the kitchen stove. Harriet gasped and went rigid. Brandon cursed roundly, vaulted off the couch and plunged toward the kitchen.

Crimson-faced, Harriet took a moment to rear-
range her clothing before rushing after him. She
found the kitchen filled with sooty black smoke.
Brandon, with a towel protecting his hand, had just
opened the oven, where the Christmas dinner they'd
put in earlier was burning down to cinders.

Seizing a pitcher of water from the counter, Harriet poured it over the burnt offering. Clouds of hiss-
ing steam billowed around her as Brandon rushed to
fling open the windows and doors to let in the fresh
air. A cold, snowy wind blasted through the house.

When he returned moments later to face her, his
features had once more assumed the impersonal
mask she knew so well. Harriet's stomach clenched
as he cleared the smoke from his throat with an im-
perious cough. Even before he spoke, she knew exactly what he was going to tell her.

"I don't know about you, but I'd say we were
saved from ourselves in the nick of time. Forgive me,
Harriet, I pride myself on being a gentleman. I don't
know what came over me. Maybe it was the wine."

Harriet clutched the white porcelain pitcher against
her body, aware that the steam had transformed her
hair into dank strings that hung woefully around her
soot-smeared face. "Yes," she said, willing her voice
not to tremble. "It must have been the wine. If I were
going to toss away my virtue and ruin my reputation,
it certainly wouldn't be with a man like you!"

"Oh?" One dark eyebrow slid upward. Merciful

heaven, he was going to prolong this miserable charade! "And for what sort of man would you toss away your precious virtue, Miss Harriet Smith? I'd be curious to know."

"A kind, gentle, decent man!" Harriet flung the words back at him. "A man who would value and respect me, a man who would never try to intimidate or bully me, or use me to get his way!"

"And?" His expression was like granite, his voice as sharp as a freshly stropped steel razor. "What else?"

"A humble, forgiving man! One who wouldn't be too hasty to judge others or let self-righteous pride cut him off from his own daughter—his own flesh and blood!"

The silence was broken only by the distant banging of a shutter and the whistle of wind through the open house. Brandon had not moved, but she could sense the rising tension in him, like floodwaters pounding behind a dike.

"Harriet," he said, in a low, tormented voice, "Jenny isn't my own flesh and blood."

The white porcelain pitcher slipped from Harriet's ice-cold hands to shatter on the tile floor. Neither Brandon nor Harriet made a move to pick up the pieces.

"Jenny doesn't know," he said. "Lord, I've never told this to anybody, and I don't know why I'm telling you now, except that I seem to end up telling you everything—" He exhaled raggedly and sank onto the edge of a chair.

"Ada, Jenny's mother, was two years older than I was, and a lot more experienced, although I didn't realize it at the time. I was barely eighteen when she lured me into one of the rooms of the hotel her father owned. A few weeks later she told me she was in a family way, and I did the honorable thing. Jenny was born less than eight months after the wedding, but when I saw her and held her for the first time, that tiny little scrap of life, I fell head over heels in love. I vowed to provide her with a good life if I had to work my fingers to the bone."

"And you did," Harriet said. "Jenny had everything a little girl could want."

"Except happy parents." He shifted on the chair, as if he were in physical pain. "We'd been married for five years when Ada told me. I don't think she'd ever planned for me to know, but she was drunk and we were in the middle of a ripping fight, and it just came out."

Numb with dismay, Harriet stood rooted to the floor with the shards of the broken pitcher scattered around her. Part of her ached to go to him. But Brandon, she knew, would not want to be touched or comforted. Not by her.

"She'd had an affair," he said. "The man was married and prominent in the town—she never would tell me his name, but it was easy enough to guess. Her monthly time was always regular, and when it didn't come, she went after the first randy young fool she could find. Me."

Harriet thought of Jenny—the stunning blue eyes, the mannerisms, the facial expressions, all the little ways in which she was so like Brandon. How could she not be his natural daughter? There had to be some mistake.

"Are you certain your wife was telling the truth?" she demanded. "She was drunk and angry. How do you know she wasn't just trying to hurt you?"

"You think I haven't asked myself that same question?" He shook his head. "No, it all adds up. The man in question was still living in the town. I knew we had to get away, so I took Ada and Jenny and moved here, to Dutchman's Creek. I could have divorced her—I certainly had legal grounds. But I didn't, and you know why."

"Yes, I know why," Harriet said, loving him in spite of the hurtful things he'd said to her. "The truth didn't matter. Jenny was your daughter in every way but one. She's still your daughter, Brandon."

"Don't preach to me, Harriet," he snapped. "You know how I feel about Jenny. You know how I've wanted to help her. I just can't stand the thought of seeing her life turn out like—" He bit off the rest of the sentence and stood. "Help me get the house closed up, and I'll drive you home."

Harriet stood her ground. "Like her mother's? Is that what you were going to say?"

He glared at her, his mouth set in the stubborn line she'd come to know so well.

"How dare you even think that, Brandon Calhoun?" She was suddenly furious, lashing out at him with all her strength of spirit. "Based on what I've heard about your wife, Jenny is nothing like her! She's open and loving and sweet-natured, without a devious bone in her little body! If she didn't get those qualities from her mother or from you, all I can say is that her real father must've passed on some excellent blood!"

She had gone too far. She realized it as soon as she saw the expression of horror and loathing on Brandon's face. If she'd been a man, she thought, he would likely have attacked her with his fists or challenged her to a gunfight. As it was, he could only take refuge in icy, exquisite politeness.

"It's time we were getting you home," he said. "I'll hitch the horse to the sleigh while you're putting on your cloak. Don't forget to take your basket."

Harriet drew herself up until her spine was ramrod-straight. "You needn't trouble yourself," she said. "It's a bit windy out, but the snow is well tracked. I'll be quite all right."

"A gentleman doesn't turn out a lady alone on a cold evening," he said. "You can wait in the parlor if you'd like. I'll only be a few minutes."

"No."

"No?" Again, that upward slithering of an eyebrow.

"The walk will do me good. And as for your being a gentleman…"

Leaving the rest of the sentence unspoken, she turned away and stalked toward the door.

She would have been wise to make that her final exit line, Harriet would reflect later. But as she stepped into the entry hall and reached for her cloak, the awful weight of the humiliation she'd just suffered came crashing in on her. She had been on the verge of giving her heart, soul and body to this man. Then he'd turned on her, treating her with a contempt so cold and stinging that he might as well have slapped her across the face.

Rage and hurt boiled up in her as she swung back toward him.

"How can you be so self-righteous, Brandon Calhoun? How can you judge your poor, unhappy wife, who only wanted to be loved, and then found herself trapped? She was a victim—the victim of a selfish man, bent on his own pleasure! A man no worse than *you!*"

A pale edge had formed around Brandon's mouth. He looked as if he wanted to lash back at her, but he stood in silence as Harriet plunged toward the end of her tirade.

"What a fool I was tonight! You would have ruined me, just the way he ruined her, and not given it a second thought!" She flung the words at him like poison-tipped daggers. "The next time you feel like judging someone, just look in the mirror. Look at yourself, you...you *hypocrite!*"

With that, she wheeled and fled out the front door, slamming it behind her. The cold wind, which had risen to a gale in the past hour, struck her at the foot of the steps, slamming her sideways and almost ripping the cloak from her hands. She struggled to get it around her shoulders as she reeled into the blowing snow. Home was a mile away and she would be chilled to the bone by the time she arrived. But even the risk of dying from pneumonia would be better than going back into that house and facing Brandon again.

What a fool she'd been—melting in his arms, then turning into a raging harridan when he'd changed his mind and spurned her. How could she ever face him again? How could she live in the same town, walk the same streets, knowing that he was close by?

A hunted animal's desperation threatened to close in on her. If only she could get away, pack her things and leave tomorrow, or even tonight—but that, she knew, would not be possible. Dutchman's Creek could be snowbound for weeks, and even if the roads were open, she could not leave the children without a teacher for the rest of the year. And she certainly couldn't leave Will and Jenny, not with a baby coming.

For now, she had no choice except to grit her teeth and stay. But come next spring, after the baby's arrival and the closing of school, she would make arrangements to leave Dutchman's Creek. Hopefully, Jenny, Will and the baby would leave with her, but that would have to be their choice. Either way, she would not remain in this wretched little town a day longer than she had to.

Stumbling through the snow-covered ruts in the road, she staggered forward against the blasts of icy wind. At least she had delivered Jenny's gift—the one bit of good she'd accomplished. But at such a price! Oh, why hadn't Brandon kept that awful story to himself? When would she be able to look at Jenny again without remembering? And Jenny was so tender, so vulnerable. Learning such a secret could destroy her.

Whatever happened in the future, Harriet vowed, Jenny must never, never know the truth.

Hunched in his sheepskin coat, Brandon retraced his path up the road. He had followed Harriet's narrow boot prints in the blowing snow, across town and out along the cemetery road, until they'd turned into her gate. Then, knowing she was all right, he'd headed for home. The last thing he wanted was to be seen by her, but he'd needed to make sure she'd made it safely home. Otherwise, he wouldn't be able to sleep tonight.

Not that he'd be able to sleep anyway. Hellfire, what a jackass he'd made of himself tonight! First he'd attacked Harriet like a depraved libertine, and then, as if that weren't enough, he'd given away the one secret he'd sworn to take to his grave.

What in God's name had he been thinking? What was it about being around Harriet Smith that made him want to open a vein and bleed all over her ugly shoes?

He would have given anything he owned to take back all he'd said and done tonight, but it was too late for that. All he could do was move on and try to forget what had happened. As for Harriet, he would be a grateful man if he never laid eyes on her again.

A full winter moon was rising above the eastern hills. Windblown clouds fluttered like veiled dancers across its face, their shadows causing the snowy landscape to float in and out of darkness. Taking his hand out of his pocket, Brandon fingered the knitted woolen scarf at his throat. Jenny's gift was soft and warm. The thought of her little hands plying the needles, looping each awkward stitch, raised an aching lump in his throat. He swallowed hard and trudged on through the blowing snow.

At least, he mused, he could trust Harriet not to tell Jenny what she'd learned tonight. Harriet was a kind person, and she appeared to truly care for the girl. He could not imagine her doing anything to cause Jenny pain. But then, again, who could say what might come out in a moment of hurt or anger? His recklessness had created a perilous situation, and the one at risk was his Jenny. If she learned the truth, he would never forgive Harriet—or himself.

Glancing back down the road, toward the cemetery, he could just see the lights that shone through the windows of the shabby little house. Inside, it was Christmas. There would be a tiny tree, trimmed with homemade decorations. There would be love and laughter and the smell of good food. There would be the daughter of his heart, and the woman he had very nearly made love to this evening.

If the disaster in the kitchen hadn't happened, would they have stopped themselves? Would they have drawn apart, horrified by the narrowness of their escape and repentant to the depths of their hidebound souls? Or would they be lying, even now, in each other's arms next to the crackling fire, warm and muzzy and deliciously sated?

Look at yourself, you hypocrite!

The words stung like pellets of ice as he remembered the feel of her in his arms, the ripe, willing lips, the sweet satin of her skin beneath his fingertips, the rushed, eager cadence of her breathing. He had never wanted a woman so much in his life. Even now he wanted her—for her untamed spirit as much as for her glorious body. Opinionated, irritating, maddening, Harriet, with the temper of a hornet, the passion of a goddess and the courage of a lion. He wanted her in his arms, in his bed, in his life.

Lord help him, he was in love with her.

He was in love with Harriet Smith, but it was too late to act on his feelings now. He had made such a tarnal mess of everything that she would never want to speak to him again.

All he could do was slink off with his tail between his legs and wait for cold reason to return. That, Brandon suspected, could take a very long time.

Chapter Thirteen

By late February, the first spring thaw had set in. The sun blazed in a dazzling sky, its warmth melting away the layers of ice and snow that had buried Dutchman's Creek all winter. Water dripped from the trees, drizzled from the eaves of the houses and ran in rivulets down the roads, turning them to troughs of liquid mud.

Harriet picked her way along the grassy edge of the cemetery road, holding up her skirts with one hand and clutching her schoolbag with the other. In the near distance, through the bare trees, she could see her house and yard. Jenny, a bright figure in her rose-colored shawl, was just coming out of the shed, teetering under the weight of the firewood she was carrying toward the house.

"Jenny!" Harriet broke into a run that carried her through the gate. "You shouldn't be doing that! Leave the wood to me or to Will!" She raced forward, seized the stacked logs from the girl's arms and put them down on the back porch.

Jenny sighed as she brushed the bark splinters from her sleeves. "Oh, Harriet, I'm fine! And it's such a beautiful day. I just had to get outside and do something!"

Will's bride had grown as round as a crab apple. She had curtailed her teaching at the school, but Harriet had left her the task of grading papers at home, so that she could continue to receive her small salary. Will was working overtime at the feed store to build up their savings before the baby's arrival. His absence left Jenny alone for too many hours of the day. With the birth scarcely a month off, Harriet worried constantly about her young sister-in-law's fragile condition.

Dr. Tate had written to the specialist in Denver to arrange for Jenny's confinement there. But the mail in and out of Dutchman's Creek was slow in the wintertime. As of this morning, no reply had come. Maybe now, with the snow melting off the canyon road, the letter would arrive.

"Oh!" Jenny's cornflower eyes—a more delicate shade than Brandon's, Harriet had come to realize— widened in wonder and joy. Her hands spread over her tightly swollen belly. "He's kicking me right here! Feel him, Harriet! Feel his little foot!"

She seized Harriet's hand and placed it over the moving spot. Something tightened around Harriet's heart as she felt the jab of a tiny heel against her palm. Once more, she prayed silently that Jenny's little one would enter the world without harm to itself or its mother.

As for herself—but to think of her own future would only throw her into turmoil for the rest of her day. Over the years, Harriet had learned to accept the likelihood that she would never have a family of her own. Now, once more, the chance was there. All she had to do was to say yes, and she would have it all—a husband, a comfortable home, a respected position in the town and as many children as heaven would allow.

But not with the man whose memory burned in her heart.

"Enoch stopped by on his way back from the cemetery," Jenny said with a sly wink. "He left some peppermints and asked me to remind you about the church supper Saturday night. He'll be picking you up at six o'clock sharp and he says he's hoping for an answer to his question." She giggled mischievously. "My, my, what could that question be…?"

Harriet suppressed a sigh. Enoch Farley, the widowed undertaker, had been calling on her since the first of the year. Twenty-one years her senior, with thinning gray hair, a narrow but pleasant face and a shy demeanor, Enoch was a good man and comfortably well-off. She could do worse, Harriet mused as she gathered an armful of kindling to carry into the kitchen. So why wasn't she champing at the bit to accept his proposal?

True, she wasn't in love with him. But if there was

kindness, sharing and mutual respect in a marriage, love would surely follow, wouldn't it? After all, how choosy could an old-maid schoolteacher afford to be? When did she think she was going to get another chance?

A woman in her situation would be foolish to turn down a proposal from a good man like Enoch. But how could she live here in Dutchman's Creek, longing for Brandon, straining for glimpses of him on the street or at town gatherings, when she was married to another man?

"For a woman with a serious beau, I can't say you look very excited about it," Jenny observed as she followed Harriet into the kitchen and began peeling potatoes for supper. "Would you be any happier if Matt Langtry had kept coming around?"

Harriet forced herself to laugh. "Matt's far too young for me. Besides, I don't imagine he'll be ready to settle down for a long time. He's got too much wildness in him yet, like an unbroken colt. The woman who lays a saddle on him will be in for a wild ride."

"But, oh, my goodness, just imagine that ride!" Jenny's eyes twinkled. Harriet smiled back at her. She and the young sheriff had enjoyed their brief flirtation, but neither of them had expected it to last. They had long since parted as friends and gone their separate ways.

Enoch Farley, however, had been widowed more than a year and was looking for a new wife. Harriet's gentle efforts to discourage him had had no more effect than waving a feather in the path of a millstone.

"Just think," Jenny said, practically bubbling. "If you marry Enoch, by this time next year, you could be expecting a cousin for this little mischief." She gave her bulge an affectionate pat. "Just think what fun they'd have as playmates!"

"Really, Jenny, it's a little soon to be making those kinds of plans," Harriet said, chopping at an onion from the root cellar. "I haven't agreed to marry Enoch yet. In fact, I'm not at all sure I want to marry at all!"

"But why not?" Jenny slipped the potatoes into the broth that simmered on the stove. "He's a very nice man, and not bad looking. I know that his being the undertaker takes a little getting used to, but he makes a very good living. Why, Enoch Farley is probably the wealthiest man in town, next to Papa—"

Jenny's words trailed off as she took in Harriet's stricken expression. Her eyes widened in sudden understanding.

"Oh, Harriet!" she murmured. "Dear Harriet, why didn't I see it before? You're in love with my father, aren't you?"

"Nonsense!" The vapors from the onion were making Harriet's eyes water. "Your father and I can barely stand each other! When we're together, all we do is argue! He's the most arrogant, stubborn, impossible man I've ever known in my life!"

"Christmas night, when you walked home in that

awful windstorm, I knew something had happened. But then, you didn't say anything, and I didn't want to pry. Harriet, if you married my father, then you'd be my stepmother! I would so love that! It would make everything all right again!"

"Don't wish for what can't be, Jenny." Harriet wiped her streaming eyes with the back of her hand, which made them water all the more. "The last time I saw your father, we said terrible things to each other, things that can never be taken back. I pray every night that you and Will might be reconciled with him, but as for myself—no, it's just not possible. Not now."

"So, are you going to marry Enoch?" Jenny's question was little more than a sigh.

"No," Harriet said, making the decision as she spoke. "I'm not going to marry anybody. I'm going to start writing letters and checking the newspaper advertisements, so that by the time school is out, I'll have a teaching position waiting in another town."

"What?" Jenny uttered a little gasp. "You'd leave Dutchman's Creek?"

Harriet scooped the chopped onion pieces into the pot. "You and Will and the baby would be welcome to come with me, of course. But I know Will likes his job here. If you decide to stay, I'll understand, and, of course, I'll plan to visit you as often as I'm able."

"But what will I do without you?" Jenny looked ready to cry. "You made it possible for Will and me to be a family. You taught me how to keep house and sew and knit, and how to be a teacher. I'll be lost without you, Harriet!"

Harriet gathered the distraught girl into her arms. "You'll be ready for a home of your own soon. And you won't need an old-maid sister-in-law to tell you how to manage things. You've grown up, Jenny. You're going to do fine."

A surge of tears flooded Harriet's eyes. She blinked them away. It was only the onion, she told herself. Just the silly old onion.

Brandon jabbed his pen into the inkwell and scrawled his name below the judge's signature at the bottom of the foreclosure notice. As he'd expected, the Keetch brothers had done nothing to repay the delinquent mortgage on their ranch. Now the foreclosure had been approved by the court. The matter would be turned over to the sheriff, who would serve the papers, evict the Keetches from the property, and have the place put up for public auction. Money from the sale would go to repay the debts on the ranch.

"I don't envy you this job," Brandon said as he passed the legal documents across his desk to Matt Langtry. "Harvey and Marlin may look like fools, but they've got a mean streak that runs bone-deep, and they're as cunning as a pair of weasels. Don't go out to the ranch alone."

"Thanks for the warning. I'll take along a couple of deputies to watch my back." Matt tucked the sheaf of folded papers into his vest. "Damned dirty work. But that's what we get paid for."

"Good luck." Brandon opened another file of reports as the young sheriff strode out of his office, closing the door behind him. The Keetch brothers wouldn't take kindly to being served with papers and ordered off the ranch. They were bound to be foul-mouthed and whiney, and they might even put up a fight. But Matthew T. Langtry was good at his job. Brandon felt confident that he would keep things under control and see that nobody got hurt.

Forcing the matter from his mind, Brandon tried to focus on checking the monthly reports from his bookkeepers. But the golden rays of sunlight, slanting through the high window above his desk, kept pulling his thoughts to the world outside his office— a world where the robins were singing, the wild violets were sprouting and the aspens were festooned with long brown catkins.

Spring had arrived in Dutchman's Creek, a time of hope and dread. Jenny's baby was due in less than three weeks' time. Simon Tate, who'd kept him appraised of her condition, had finalized the arrangements to transport her to Denver. The trip itself would be risky enough, but the thought of the birth ordeal and the things that could go wrong had Brandon worried sick.

He would not be going with her, of course. As things stood, he would not even be seeing her to the train in Johnson City. Will and the doctor would be making the trip with Jenny, and Harriet planned to join them a week later. That, Brandon told himself, was just as well. Harriet and Will were Jenny's family now, and the three of them appeared to be managing fine without him. Apart from the cost of Jenny's medical care, which he had secretly arranged to pay, there was no reason they should need him at all.

But if Jenny lost her precious young life bringing this baby into the world, Brandon vowed, Will Smith would pay for what he'd done to her. He would pay in this life, and he would pay in hell for the rest of eternity!

Releasing his anger in a long exhalation, Brandon bent to his paperwork once more. For a time he managed to concentrate, but after thirty or forty minutes the figures began to shift before his eyes, rearranging themselves in his mind to form the appearance of haunting brown eyes in a pale oval face, framed by soft wings of dark mahogany hair.

Ever since their soul-searing encounter on Christmas night, he had been struggling to rid his memory of Harriet. But the sight, smell, taste and feel of her had taken possession of his senses. He still awoke in the night, drenched and cursing from dreams in which she leaned over him like a succubus, the silky curtain of her hair hanging around him, her nipples brushing his eager mouth, her hips poised a finger breadth above his aching arousal as she teased and tormented him to a frustrating climax.

He had last seen her sitting beside Enoch Farley in the undertaker's shiny black barouche. Rumor had it that Enoch had proposed and had been gently refused, but clearly, he had not given up his pursuit. He was a tenacious sort, and he would keep pressing his quarry, plying her with gifts and outings, until she said yes.

Brandon glared down at the long, cramped columns of figures, struggling not to imagine Enoch making love to his bride. It would be like pairing a swan with a turkey, he thought. Or an elegant, wide-eyed doe with a moose.

Brandon shoved the file aside, shoved his chair away from the desk and strode to the window. From the prison that his office had become, he could see the open blue of the sky where a pair of red-tailed hawks soared on outspread wings, spiraling above the valley.

Maybe he ought to leave Dutchman's Creek, he thought. He could sell the house and his interest in the bank for enough money to live on the rest of his life. He could travel anywhere he chose, to London, Paris and Rome, to Greece, to Egypt. Why should he stay here, where the thought of Harriet in another man's arms would be like slow death?

With a weary sigh, he sat down again and took up his work. For now, at least, he was trapped right here. He had commitments and responsibilities. He had—

A sudden clamor from the bank lobby outside his

office wrenched Brandon's attention away from his own thoughts. He heard the sound of the door banging open and a man's gruff voice, strangely familiar, shouting orders. A woman screamed and something crashed to the floor.

Pulse slamming, Brandon reached into the back of the desk drawer and seized the loaded Navy Colt he had always kept there but never used until now. What he was hearing could only mean one thing. The bank was being robbed.

Cocking the pistol, he plunged toward the closed door, then froze. To come barreling into the lobby with a weapon would likely draw gunfire from the robbers. Innocent people could be hurt or killed. His first concern would have to be the safety of the employees and customers in the bank. Stopping the robbers and saving the money would be a distant second.

Moving along the wall, he touched a panel that opened into the small back room that housed the entrance to the vault. From there, another door opened into the space behind the counter. That door was slightly ajar.

Flattening himself alongside the doorframe, Brandon peered through the narrow crack. The first thing he saw was his two clerks. Both of them were standing behind the counter with their hands raised high. Beyond them, in the outer lobby, he could see the elderly man who waited tables at the hotel. His face was deathly white and his hands were in the air. Virginia

Wheaton, the wife of the livery-stable owner, stood a few feet behind him, protecting her four-year-old daughter who clung in terror to her mother's skirts. Mrs. Sims, the minister's wife, appeared to have fainted. She lay sprawled amid the ruins of a potted asparagus fern, which she'd most likely knocked off its stand when she fell.

From the narrow angle of his view, Brandon could not see the robbers. Only when he shifted his position did he get a clear look at the two men who stood just inside the front door, one holding an old army pistol, the other a double-barreled shotgun.

Brandon stifled a groan. Even with their pudgy faces masked by bandannas, there was no mistaking the squat, identical figures of Harvey and Marlin Keetch. The sight of them would have been laughable except for the deadly weapons in their hands. Few things could be more dangerous than stupid men with guns.

"You two boys better get out of here," Mrs. Wheaton declared in a quivering voice. "I just saw somebody run past the window, in the direction of the sheriff's office. Sheriff Langtry will be here any second and you'll be in serious trouble then."

The answering nasal guffaw was distinctly Marlin's. "In a pig's eye, he will, lady! Sheriff Langtry and his deputies is on the way to our ranch right now. Only they won't find us there, will they, Harvey?"

"Shut the hell up, Marlin," Harvey snarled. "There

ain't nobody comin' to help you folks, so you might as well do like we tell you to!" He shifted his gaze to the two young clerks. "Less'n you two want to see these good people hurt, you'll clean out the tills and put the money in this bag." He tossed a dirty feed sack on the counter. "Then we want all the cash what's in the vault. Go on, move!"

One clerk picked up the bag and started cleaning out the cash drawers. The other clerk cleared his throat and spoke, his voice tight with fear. "Excuse me, sir, but we can't open the vault. We don't have the combination. Only Mr. Calhoun does."

"Calhoun?" Harvey's voice rose to a yowl of hatred. "That's the son of a bitch we want! Where is the bastard?"

Brandon slipped the pistol into his vest and stepped through the doorway. "Right here, boys," he said quietly. "And your quarrel's with me, not with these good people. Why don't you let them walk out of here? Then we can talk in private, and I'll give you anything you want."

"What we really want is to carve you up like a stuck pig and listen to you squeal, Banker," Harvey jeered.

Brandon felt a bead of sweat ooze down his temple. "Understood," he said, "but you'd be crazy to do that in front of a half-dozen witnesses. Go on, send them on their way. Then you can deal with me man to man."

The two brothers glanced at each other. "Aw, let 'em go, Harv," Marlin wheezed. "I ain't got it in me to hurt women and kids and—"

"Shut up!" Harvey stormed. "Calhoun, you got about thirty seconds to open that vault and put the money in that sack afore I shoot one of these folks. Maybe I'll start with the kid." He glanced toward the little girl, whose mother clutched her even more protectively. The minister's wife had come to and was clambering to her feet. Her face was white with fear.

"All right." Brandon knew he could take no more chances. "Which one of you wants to come back to the vault with me?"

Harvey's bushy eyebrows knit in a scowl above the grease-splotched bandana. "You go," he said to his brother. "I'll stay here and make sure nobody tries no funny stuff."

Brandon walked back into the small room. Marlin followed him with the sack, using the muzzle of the shotgun to nudge him toward the door of the vault.

Brandon knew the combination from memory. His fingers ached with tension as he worked the dial on the heavy iron door, thinking of the helpless people in the lobby and the hair-trigger temper of the man who held them at gunpoint. If anything went wrong out there, he would blame himself for the rest of his life.

"If anybody dies in this robbery, you and your brother will hang, Marlin," he said. "You don't have to be part of this. You've always been the sensible one. Maybe you can talk some sense into Harvey now, before anybody gets hurt."

"Just shut up and open that vault," Marlin said. "Harvey and me, we had ourselves a talk. We's in this together all the way. Ain't neither of us backin' out now."

The tumblers clicked into place, releasing the lock on the vault. Brandon turned the heavy handle and the door swung open, revealing a brick-faced enclosure lined with narrow shelves, where bags of gold-and-silver coins and bundles of paper bills were stored.

Marlin thrust the feed sack into Brandon's hands. "We'll take the gold and silver first. Better'n paper where we're goin', Harvey says."

"Mexico?" Brandon began dropping bagged coins into the sack. He could only hope they would be heavy enough to slow the brothers down on their long ride south.

"Gonna buy ourselves a fine hacienda. Then we'll get us a couple of them purty black-haired *señoritas* and have ourselves a grand time."

"The only place you'll be going is to jail," Brandon said. "Think about it, Marlin. You're not a bad sort, but you'll pay a high price for letting Harvey get you into this mess."

Marlin scratched behind his ear with his free hand. Before he could speak, however, all hell broke loose outside in the lobby.

Everything happened in a flash, starting with a terrified wail from the little girl, followed by Harvey cursing and shouting at the mother to shut the brat up before he put a bullet in her. Then there was a scream, a crash and the sound of scuffling.

Catching Marlin off guard, Brandon grabbed his arm and, with a desperate jerk, pulled him into the vault and sent him crashing against the shelves. Before Marlin could recover, Brandon pushed past him, hurled himself out of the vault and swung the massive door shut behind him, locking the man in, shotgun and all.

Drawing his pistol, Brandon raced back into the lobby. The two young clerks had jumped Harvey and were trying to wrestle the old army pistol away from him, but they were no match for his brute strength and he still gripped the weapon in his hand. Brandon knew he had to stop them before the gun went off accidentally, wounding or killing one of the bystanders, who cowered against the walls.

"Get out of here!" he shouted at the two women and the old man. "Get out now!"

The three of them stumbled toward the front door, Mrs. Wheaton clutching her little girl in her arms. As soon as they were safely outside, Brandon pointed his pistol at the ceiling and fired. The sound echoed around the lobby, startling Harvey and the two clerks, who released their hold on him and staggered backward to a safe distance.

Brandon leveled the Navy Colt at Harvey's chest. "Drop that gun and put your hands up," he said. "It's all over, Harvey. Your brother's locked in the vault and isn't going anywhere. Give it up now, and the worst they'll charge you with is attempted robbery. I'll do my best to see that you get a fair trial."

Harvey Keetch had risen onto one knee. The bandana had been torn from his face, which was set in a paroxysm of pure animal hatred.

"Damn you all to hell!" he screamed, and raised his gun.

That was the last thing Brandon remembered before the world shattered in a burst of pain and died into blackness.

Chapter Fourteen

By the time school was out for the day, the news of the bank robbery was two hours' old and had spread from one end of Dutchman's Creek to the other. With each retelling the story had changed slightly, an embellishment added here, a detail omitted there. But everyone agreed on the basic facts—the Keetch brothers had held up the bank, the money was safe, Marlin Keetch was in jail, Harvey Keetch had escaped and was still at large, and Brandon Calhoun had been shot.

Harriet heard the story for the first time from a mother who'd come to get her two children after school. She listened with her heart in her throat, struggling to keep her emotions in check as the woman stood in the schoolroom doorway, chatting on and on about what had happened.

"They say that terrible man threatened to shoot

Virginia Wheaton's little Ellie. That's why I came to school today, to walk home with Betsy and Tim. With a madman like Harvey Keetch on the loose, one can't be too careful. Goodness me, what's this town coming to? It used to be such a peaceful place!"

"What have you heard about Brandon Calhoun?" Harriet asked, her nerves silently screaming. "How badly was he hurt?"

"Nobody seems to know. The doctor came, and they carried him to the buggy on a stretcher, with his head wrapped in bandages. Elvira Sims said he was unconscious. Oh, my, do you think anyone's told his daughter? Why, with her in a family way, and her time so close, there's no telling what the shock could do to her!" The woman glanced around for her children, who were playing in the schoolyard. "Tim! Betsy! You stay close now, hear? That awful man could be anywhere!"

"I've got to go." Harriet nudged the visitor off the stoop and locked the schoolhouse door. Her pulse was galloping and her skin felt as clammy as cold dough. She needed to find out what had happened to Brandon. And then she needed to get to Jenny.

Clutching at her shawl, she raced down the path to the road. Nightmare images flashed through her mind—Brandon falling to the polished slate floor as the bullet penetrated his skull, Brandon lying on the stretcher, bleeding and unconscious, his eyes closed, his head swathed in bandages. Sweet, merciful heaven, he could be dying right now. He could already be dead.

Where should she go first? To the doctor's office on Main Street, she resolved. It was on the way home, and someone there should have the most recent news.

Will worked on Main Street, so he would already know what had happened. By now, he would likely be with Jenny, giving her the comfort and support she needed. But there was no way to be certain of that. On this terrible day, Harriet could only be certain of one thing—she loved Brandon Calhoun with all her heart and soul. If he died, a warm and vital part of her would die with him. She would live on, but as something less than a whole person, too emotionally numb to feel the depths of pain or the heights of joy.

Why had the two of them been so foolish, letting pride lay waste to their time together? Why hadn't they realized that it was all the time they might ever have?

If Brandon lived, Harriet vowed, she would throw away her pride, go to him on her knees and beg him to forgive her. Then, if fate allowed them the blessing of starting over, she would thank heaven for each tick of the clock, each second and minute and hour of their time together.

A magpie scolded from its perch on a chokecherry bush. The harsh sound startled her, jerking her back to the ugly reality of the present. People rarely survived gunshot wounds to the head—or if they did, the injury left them so impaired that they needed nursing care to the end of their days. She needed to prepare herself for the worst possible news about Brandon; and no matter how bad it was, she could not allow herself to fall apart. She would need to be strong for Jenny's sake.

But where was her strength now? Her legs quivered as she stumbled down the path. Her stomach churned as her body reacted to the gut-wrenching fear. Her lips moved in silent prayer. *Please...please...*

She reached the main road, where the spring mud was drying into axle-deep ruts. Pausing to catch her breath, Harriet caught sight of something large and dark in the distance, moving rapidly toward her. A cry escaped her throat as she recognized the doctor's high-topped buggy.

She plunged down the road, running full tilt, heedless of her skirts and the treacherous ruts. By the time she reached the buggy, she was out of breath and had fallen twice. Her palms were skinned, her clothes smeared with dirt.

Dr. Tate leaned across the seat and offered a hand to pull her up beside him. He shook his head as his bespectacled eyes took in Harriet's condition. "I was just coming to find you," he said. "What the devil's the matter?"

"Brandon— I just heard—" She gasped out the words, gripping his arm with her muddy, bleeding hand. "Is he—?"

"Brandon's going to be fine," the doctor said. "But he gave us all a good scare. Bullet creased his scalp. Gave him a nasty gash and knocked him out for a good twenty minutes, but he's awake and resting now. Damned lucky man, I'd say."

Harriet felt light-headed, as if she were floating off the seat. She closed her eyes, too overcome to breathe, let alone talk.

"I wanted to keep him at my place, but he insisted on being taken home," the doctor said. "He promised me he'd go straight to bed. I hope I can trust him to do just that."

"Does Jenny know?" Harriet found her voice, but it sounded far away, as if she were hearing someone else ask the question.

"I gave her the news myself. Will had come home to be with her. She took it hard, but she'll be fine once the shock wears off."

"Thank heaven!" She sank back against the seat as the doctor turned his buggy around. She felt giddy and exhausted, like a child who'd just spent a long time spinning in circles. Brandon was all right. Jenny was all right. Her world had just slipped back into its orbit.

She remembered the surly twins who'd confronted Brandon at the bank and her own encounter with them later in the alley. The hatred emanating from the two of them had made her flesh crawl. "What about Harvey Keetch?" she asked. "Have they caught him yet?"

The doctor shook his head. "The sheriff's still out with the posse, but if I know Harvey, he'll take a heap of finding. His family prospected the back country west of town for years before they bought their ranch. He knows every rock and hollow, including the old mines. My guess is he'll lie low somewhere till the heat dies down, then he'll head for Mexico."

He clucked to his aging mare, easing the buggy forward, down the hill. "It'll be tough on him, alone out there, without his brother. Twins tend to be close, and those two have never been apart. Harvey was always the mean one and the leader. I've no doubt the robbery was his idea and poor Marlin just went along as usual. But a leader needs a follower. Harvey's going to be lost on his own."

"You think he'll try to break Marlin out of jail?"

"Maybe, although he'd be taking a big chance." The doctor chewed his lip thoughtfully. "I'd wager that's what the sheriff's hoping. Bait the trap and wait. That's what I'd do if I were Matt Langtry. It's easier to catch a rat in the kitchen than in the woodshed."

"Of course." Harriet had only half heard what the doctor was saying. Her thoughts were flying back to Brandon and the vow she'd made when she thought he might be dying. A promise was a promise, she reminded herself. She had sworn that if he survived, she would go to him and ask his forgiveness. Now that she knew his life had been spared, it was her turn to keep her word.

The buggy had reached the bottom of the hill and the doctor was turning the horse left, onto the cemetery road. Harriet reached out and touched his sleeve. "Could you just let me off here?" she asked. "I...have some thinking to do. It might help me to walk awhile."

He shot her a puzzled glance, but pulled the buggy to the side of the road, allowing her to climb to the ground. "You're sure you'll be all right? You don't seem quite yourself, Harriet."

"I'm...fine. Never better!" She waved him off with her thanks, then stood watching as the buggy swung back toward town and disappeared beyond a clump of poplars.

Fears and doubts lashed at her as she turned her steps toward Brandon's house. What if he refused to see her, or worse, welcomed her in, only to be icily polite? What if he tried to humiliate her, as he'd done before? Or—horrors—what if she were to walk in and discover that he wasn't alone?

Her courage almost failed her as she gazed up the road toward Brandon's tall, silent house. Her visit could wait, she told herself. Brandon would be resting, maybe asleep, and it wouldn't do to disturb him. Surely she could invent some pretext to visit him tomorrow, when he was feeling stronger.

But no, Harriet admonished herself. If she lost heart now, she would never find the courage to face him. This was the moment of truth, and it would never come again.

Half a league, half a league,
Half a league onward,
All in the valley of Death
Rode the six hundred.

The lines from Tennyson's poem, "The Charge of the Light Brigade," which she'd had her older students memorize that year, echoed in her head as she marched up the front steps.

Cannon to right of them,
Cannon to left of them,
Cannon in front of them
Volley'd and thunder'd;
Storm'd at with shot and shell,
Boldly they rode and well,
Into the jaws of Death,
Into the mouth of Hell
Rode the six hundred.

Holding her breath, she raised the lion's-head knocker, rapped it lightly and waited.

No one answered.

Cautiously she tried the latch. The door was unlocked. It swung quietly open at her touch, into the deserted entry. Only the sonorous tick of the tall grandfather clock disturbed the silence in the house.

Once more, Harriet almost turned tail. But she forced herself to mount the stairs, one step, then another. By the time she reached the landing at the top, her pulse was racing. What if Brandon's injury had gone deeper than the doctor suspected? What if he'd suffered a hemorrhage or a stroke and was sprawled somewhere in the house, unconscious or dead?

The door to his bedroom was slightly ajar. Harriet tiptoed forward and pushed it open.

Brandon lay in his massive four-poster bed, his head elevated on two pillows and the coverlet pulled up to his bare chest. His eyes were closed, his color natural, his breathing deep and even. The neat, white bandage wrapped around his head offered the only evidence of his close brush with death.

Harriet walked softly across the floor and stood gazing down at him. Her eyes traced the line of the bandage where it lay against his golden skin. His lashes were thick and dark, his firm lips relaxed in a little half smile, as if he were dreaming of something pleasant.

How she loved looking at him! Her gaze caressed every curl of his silver-kissed hair and traveled adoringly along every line and crease of his splendid patrician face. Her eyes measured the broadness of his smooth-muscled shoulders and traced the line of crisp, dark hair that tapered down from his chest to disappear beneath the sheet. His nipples were widely spaced and exquisitely small, like tiny shells from a secret beach.

He was as beautiful as a sleeping prince, Harriet thought. She ached to reach out and stroke his hair with her fingers, or to bend close and brush a kiss across his quiet lips. But her touch would undoubtedly rouse him from slumber. And Brandon awake was a very different creature from Brandon asleep.

A wave of cowardice swept over her and she was tempted once more to tiptoe out of the room and leave with her words unspoken and her dignity intact. But no, she had to do this. She had vowed to say what was in her heart. However…

Harriet sighed with relief as she realized she had left a loophole, albeit a silly one. She had committed herself to speaking to Brandon. But her vow didn't require him to be awake at the time.

At least it would be a way to start.

Sinking onto her knees beside the bed, she rested her head on the quilted coverlet, with her lips a few inches from his ear. "Brandon?" she whispered.

When he did not stir, she plunged ahead.

"I…don't quite know where to begin. When I heard you'd been shot, I was so afraid… Oh, Brandon, if that awful man had killed you, I don't know what I'd have done. I can't imagine my world without you."

Harriet paused for breath. She realized she had already said too much, but now that the words had broken loose, they spilled out of her in a torrent.

"That Christmas, the last time we were together, I wanted you so much. I would have thrown it all away—my reputation, my self-respect, everything— just to be loved by you. When you turned me away— for my own good, I realize now—I was hurt. I was so hurt that I wanted to hurt you back. I said some cruel things, half-truths, meant to wound you as deeply as you'd wounded me. Now I'd give anything to take them back. I'm sorry, so sorry…"

Harriet's eyes were welling with tears. She had said more than enough to fulfill her promise. But now the words wouldn't stop pouring out of her.

"I love you, Brandon…I think I started loving you the day you walked into my classroom and we had our first big fight. I've wanted to tell you how I feel, but I was always afraid of what you might think, what you might say." She inhaled a gulping breath. "It took this accident to make me realize that I needed to tell you now, today, before we lost any more time. If you don't feel the same, I'll understand, but if you do…"

Harriet suddenly found herself at a loss for words. Whatever came next depended on Brandon, and she could only speak for herself. She groped for words that would not come. Maybe it was time she left, while she could.

"Don't stop now, Harriet."

The deep male voice startled her. She pulled back with a little gasp as Brandon slowly opened one blue eye. His expression was sleepy, sensual and melting. "You were just getting to the interesting part," he said. "I'd really like to hear the rest."

"Ooh! You insufferable—"

She reeled to her feet, but he caught her by the waist and pulled her down on top of him. His mouth captured hers in a dizzying kiss that went on and on, until the taste and feel of him became like part of her own body. His heat flowed into her, through her, igniting currents of need. She felt the swelling, throbbing ache in the deep core of her womanhood. She knew what it meant and she was not afraid.

"Tell me the rest, Harriet," he whispered against her lips. "What would you do if you knew that I loved you? I need to know because I do love you…." He kissed her chin, her throat, stopping at the edge of her high collar. "I love every maddening, crazy, beautiful thing about you, and I never want to stop. So tell me what you'd do."

Harriet could feel her heart exploding like a burst of Independence Day fireworks. For the first time in her life, she felt desirable and wanton and mischievous. "You've just been shot," she teased. "I'm not sure you're strong enough for what I'd want to do with you."

"Try it and see," he murmured, nuzzling her earlobe. "If it's too much for me, I'll let you know."

"First," she said, pulling away from him, "I'd get up and lock this bedroom door." She flew across the room, closed the door and slid the bolt into place, then turned back to face him, her eyes sparkling. "Then I'd get out of these muddy boots and this ragged old horror of a dress."

Her unsteady fingers removed the boots and the

gown. She stood before him now in her camisole, corset and petticoat, her legs trembling beneath her.

His throat moved as she reached up and plucked the pins from her hair, freeing it to tumble to her waist in a cascade of dark waves.

"And then what would you do?" His voice was raw with arousal.

She moved toward him, loving his vulnerability and his undisguised need. "As a woman of limited experience," she murmured, "I would very wisely leave the rest to you."

She leaned over the bed, letting her hair fall around him like the walls of a silken tent. He groaned, pulled her close and buried his face in the yearning hollow between her breasts. Closing her eyes, she pressed her lips into his hair as he nuzzled her softness. The rough edge of the bandage brushed her skin, reminding her once more of how close she had come to losing him. Fear blended with sweetness in a surge of love that left her weak.

"Show me…" she whispered. "Show me what to do."

In answer he pulled her down to him, covering her breasts, throat and mouth in nibbling kisses. His tongue darted into her mouth like a butterfly's caress, then gently withdrew.

"More…more of that," she moaned, her lips parting.

"Why, you little wanton!" He gave her the full measure of what she'd asked for, his tongue thrusting deep, rippling over the sensitive surfaces of her mouth, touching off rivulets of sensation. When she repaid him in kind, his breathing roughened. His arms tightened around her, pulling her hips flat against his so that the long ridge of his maleness pressed her through the coverlet. She moved against the exquisite hardness, transfixed by the hot currents of need that the slightest motion aroused in her.

"So, how do you like these lessons, Teacher?" he muttered. "Are you ready for the next one?"

Her answer was a long, deep kiss that grew frantic as the desire that had smoldered for so long exploded into a burning conflagration. His hands molded her to him, pulling the camisole off her shoulders, baring her breasts to his touch. He cupped them, stroked them, licked them, rousing her to a frenzy of need. Her hands tore aside the coverlet and sheet that separated their bodies. Beneath it, he was naked, his body warm and golden and beautiful. Dear heaven, so beautiful…

"Touch me, Harriet." He guided her fingers gently downward. "Hold me."

Her breath caught in wonder as her hand closed around the hard, smooth shaft—like steel cloaked in living silk, she thought. He gasped as she began to stroke him, moving the skin lightly up and down along his swollen length.

"I…don't think you need any more lessons, you she-devil," he muttered, pulling her down beside him. "Lie still before you drive me to ruin!"

She was still clad in her corset, petticoat and open drawers. Without taking the time to remove them, he parted her willing legs and found the wet, pulsing center of her need. As he touched her, she exploded in shuddering waves, again and again, against his fingertips.

"Oh…" she murmured, her head rolling on the pillow. "Oh, Brandon, I've never…"

He raised up to look down at her. He was breathing hard, but his gaze was loving and tender. "We can stop," he said huskily. "I love you, Harriet, and I want you the way a drowning man wants air. But I won't take what you aren't ready to—"

Her kiss stopped his words. With it, she gave him her soul and her body and offered him her life.

He understood. A low groan escaped his throat as he shifted above her and entered in a single, gliding thrust that caused no more than a flicker of pain and yet, in that instant, was like dying and awakening again as someone else—someone warm and wise and unafraid to risk her heart to love. She opened herself to him, letting him fill her, letting him carry her on wild wings to places she had only dreamed of, her body one with his as they soared higher and higher, into the sun.

Afterward, spent and happy, they lay in each other's arms. He kissed her long and gently, then laughed down into her blissful face. "Something tells me we both need to get dressed, before someone comes and finds us like this."

"I did lock the bedroom door," she murmured, nuzzling his chest.

"Yes, but someone could come by to check on me. It wouldn't do for them to find you behind that locked door, especially in my bed, Miss Harriet Smith." He kissed her again, playfully this time. "I'll tell you what. There's a kettle of leftover soup in the kitchen. If you'll go downstairs ahead of me and put it on the stove to heat, I'll join you in a few minutes. That way, we can share a meal and talk in a safer setting. I'd like to get some things understood between us before I let you go."

"Things?" Her heart dropped. Was he going to tell her their lovemaking had been just a game to him, and she wasn't to set any store by it? Was he going to insult and humiliate her yet again? "What… 'things'?" she asked cautiously.

"Things like when and where to have the wedding. Do you want a big, formal affair with the whole town invited, or would you rather just go off somewhere and tie the knot quietly?" His face was a study in bland innocence.

"Brandon—" She stared at him in utter disbelief, fearful that she'd somehow misread his intentions and he was joking at her expense.

"Hurry and get your clothes on!" he said with a grin. "When we're both properly dressed, we can have this discussion in a more respectable setting. Otherwise, we're liable to end up back in bed!"

* * *

Fully clothed now, Harriet moved about the kitchen with an uneasy sort of lightness, as if she were walking on the rims of crystal goblets. She ought to be giddy with happiness, she thought. And she *was* happy. She loved Brandon deeply and completely. Their lovemaking had been pure heaven, and the thought of becoming his wife was like a dream come true.

What if it *was* a dream?

Was that what troubled her now, like a shadow hovering behind her, just out of sight? Things had fallen into place so swiftly and perfectly, like gifts she'd done nothing to deserve, let alone earn. Everything she'd longed for was there before her on an engraved silver platter. All she needed to do was to reach out and take it.

So why, then, did she feel as if the platter were about to be snatched away?

By the time Brandon walked into the kitchen, the soup was simmering on the stove. Looking fit and relaxed in his shirtsleeves, he moved behind Harriet where she stood stirring the pot, wrapped his arms around her waist and kissed the back of her neck.

"Don't plan on spending a lot of time in the kitchen after we're married," he murmured. "We can hire a housekeeper for that. I want to dress you like a queen and take you to all the grand places in the world. New York…Paris…Venice…" He nuzzled her ear between the names of places that made Harriet's head spin with dreams. She wrenched herself back to reality.

"Brandon, how can we make marriage plans with things still unresolved between you and Jenny?"

She felt him go rigid behind her. Her heart sank as he released her, turned away and walked toward the table.

"Things aren't unresolved," he said tautly. "Jenny and I have agreed not to be part of each other's lives. In any case, what does my relationship with Jenny have to do with you and me?"

"Why, everything!" Harriet suppressed the urge to fling the soup ladle at his head. "Your Jenny is married to my brother! I'd want to have them at our wedding, and I'd certainly want them and their baby to be part of our family afterward!"

"You could see them as often as you like," he retorted coldly. "You could even have them over to visit while I'm not here. But don't ask me to—"

"How can you be such a stubborn fool, Brandon?" Harriet flung the words at him, all the rage and frustration exploding out of her. "I know you have the capacity to forgive! You've managed to accept the fact that Jenny isn't your natural daughter. Why can't you accept her now, with a husband who loves her and a child on the way?"

"Because my wife's mistake wasn't Jenny's fault."

He faced her, standing, across the kitchen table, his eyes laced with raw pain. "The night Ada told me the truth, after she'd collapsed on the chaise in a drunken stupor, I went into the nursery and stood beside Jenny's bed, looking down at her while she slept. She was so sweet and so innocent—I knew I couldn't blame her for anything that had happened. And I couldn't love her any less for having been fathered by another man. She was my daughter in every sense but one, and after a while, even that didn't matter."

"So what's different now?" Harriet asked, aware of how much she loved him and how much she needed to break down this last barricade. "Why can't you forget and forgive? Is it because Jenny made the same kind of mistake her mother did, and then wouldn't let you try to undo it?"

He glared at her across the table, saying nothing.

"All she wanted was to keep her baby and give it a loving family. Is that so wrong, Brandon?"

"Harriet—" The undertone in his voice was a warning for her to stop, but she knew that if she and Brandon were to have any chance of lasting happiness, nothing could be held back now.

"Is it really Jenny you can't forgive?" She flung the challenge in his face. "Or is it your wife—or even yourself?"

In the silence that followed, one sound, so soft it was barely perceptible, struck their ears with the impact of a gunshot.

It was the quiet opening and closing of the front door.

Brandon's face blanched. Harriet flew to the kitchen door that opened into the dining room—the door that had stood ajar during their entire conversation.

No one was there, but as Harriet raced toward the front hall, her foot brushed something soft. A little cry escaped her throat as she bent and picked it up.

It was Jenny's rose-colored shawl.

Chapter Fifteen

Sick with dismay, Harriet turned around to face Brandon. At the sight of her stricken face and the shawl clutched in her hand, he crumpled as if he'd been gut-kicked. Pushing past her, he raced through the parlor to the front hall and flung the door open.

"Jenny!" he shouted, plunging out onto the porch. "Jenny, come back here!"

The only answer was the whisper of spring wind through the budding maples. There was no sign of Jenny at all.

Harriet had burst outside behind him. Realizing that he was about to rush off in search of his daughter, she caught his arm and swung herself into his path.

"Stay here and let me go after her, Brandon. She'll be in no state of mind to talk to you. Not if she heard what I think she heard."

She felt him resisting her, pressing forward

against her grip. Then, as the sense of her argument sank home, he exhaled raggedly, sagged into himself and nodded his acquiescence.

"Just find her and make sure she's all right," he muttered. "Lord, for her to hear something like that, and in her condition—" A spasm of anguish ripped through his body. "If she hates me forever, I'll deserve it, but that doesn't matter now. Just find her for me, Harriet. Hurry."

"Don't worry," Harriet said, struggling to reassure him. "She couldn't have gotten very far. I'll send word when I find her."

She might have reached out to comfort him, but he was clearly in no mood to be comforted. Turning away, she made for the road. Brandon *would* worry, of course. He would be frantic, as she was. She had to find Jenny before something unthinkable happened.

As she ran, her skirts flying, her ribs heaving beneath her corset, Harriet scanned the length of the tree-lined road. There was no sign of Jenny and no one in sight who might have seen her. Only moments had passed since the sound of the closing door had betrayed the girl's presence. Where could she have gone in such a flicker of time? And where was Will? He was supposed to be with her.

Maybe she and Brandon were wrong about what had happened, Harriet thought, grasping at straws. Jenny could have come to the house earlier, while they were in the bedroom. She could have surmised what was happening, decided to make a discreet exit and dropped her shawl on the way out. If, by chance, she'd left the front door ajar, the wind could have closed it later.

But that story had its own share of holes. The rose shawl had been found near the door between the dining room and the kitchen, where Jenny would have been drawn by the sound of their voices. And Harriet recalled that she had distinctly heard the front door open before it closed.

There was nothing to do but go home and check her own house. With luck, she would catch up with Jenny on the way. The poor girl was so heavy with child that walking more than a few steps had become a chore. How she could have made the mile-long trek to Brandon's home, then vanished so swiftly, was a fearful mystery.

By the time she reached the little house by the cemetery, Harriet was disheveled and out of breath. She found the place in perfect order, the outside doors locked, the rooms tidied but empty. There was no sign of Will or Jenny.

Choking on her own panic, she raced outside. By now the sun was setting in a crimson blaze above the mountains. In its light, a lone, lanky figure trudged homeward along the cemetery road. Harriet's heart dropped as she realized it was Will.

Harriet burst through the gate and raced toward

him. Seeing her, he broke into a long-legged sprint that brought them together in seconds.

"Where's Jenny?" she gasped. "The doctor told me you were with her!"

Startled, he blinked down at her. "I was. But she insisted that I go back to work. She said she was fine and didn't want me to lose the pay on her account." His young face paled in the fading light. "Isn't she here?"

Harriet shook her head. "As far as I know, she went to visit her father. But she left his house without seeing him—I was there with Brandon and we found her shawl. Now she seems to have vanished."

Will's groan was like a wounded animal's. "She said she was going to rest. I should've known she'd want to see her father after what happened at the bank! Why didn't she tell me? I'd have borrowed a buggy and driven her there myself!" In an explosion of panic, he pushed past Harriet and plunged toward the house. "Jenny!" he shouted at the top of his lungs. "Jenny!"

"She isn't here!" Harriet caught the tail of his jacket and jerked him to a halt. "We've no time to waste, Will. Do you know if the sheriff's still out with the posse?"

"They rode into town as I was leaving work. Somebody said they were going out again at first light to see if they could pick up Harvey's trail." His face went ashen. "Good Lord, you think he's got Jenny, don't you?"

"I don't know," Harriet said, struggling to stay calm. "But if he has, the sooner we go after her, the better. I'm going back to Brandon's house to see if he has any more news. You find the sheriff and bring him there. When we're together, we can decide what to do."

Will's face flashed ghostly pale as he wheeled away and made for the center of town at a dead run. Harriet caught up her skirts and raced back the way she'd come, toward Brandon's house.

Brandon paced the front porch, staring into the dusk. He had searched the yard, the stable and the sheds. Now there was nothing he could do except wait for word from Harriet. And waiting, he thought, was the hardest thing a man could do. Every instinct he possessed screamed at him to leap into action, to saddle a horse and gallop off in search of his daughter. But as things stood, all he could do was stand here while fear, worry and guilt chewed his guts out.

He'd behaved like a fool toward Jenny—insisting that she give up her baby, then disowning her when she defied him. Why hadn't he realized that the decision hadn't been his to make? Jenny was a woman. She was going to be a mother. She had the right to make her own choices.

In shutting Jenny out of his life, he had only succeeded in punishing himself. His stubborn pride had left him alone and miserable. It had even alienated Harriet, who had reawakened him to life and love. Now, it seemed that pride could cost him everything he treasured. If anything had happened to his daughter, he would never forgive himself.

As he peered through the twilight, Brandon could make out a slender, skirted figure moving up the road toward him. It was Harriet, he realized at once. And the fact that she was running hard likely meant bad news.

Striding down the steps, he broke into a sprint, meeting her in the road, fifty yards from the house. Harriet was out of breath. She clasped his hands, gulping air as she struggled to speak. But words were hardly necessary. Her face told him everything he needed to know.

"Jenny's missing, Brandon…. She's not at the house, not on the road. Will's gone for the sheriff. They'll be coming here. We're to…wait for them."

Wait. That damnable word. Brandon felt himself reel as if seized by a nightmare. Only the strong, solid grip of Harriet's hands seemed to anchor him to earth.

"Harvey Keetch." The name left a sickening taste in Brandon's mouth. "It has to be him. He's got her."

"We don't know that for sure."

"What else could've happened to her?" he snapped, wild with impatience. "And who else would have any reason to harm Jenny? He took her to get back at me! This whole miserable mess is my fault!"

Harriet's grip tightened. "Stop it, Brandon. It's nobody's fault, as far as we know. And casting blame isn't going to help us find Jenny."

Her gaze was earnest, almost tearful. He had made love to this woman and asked her to marry him, Brandon reminded himself. His feelings for her hadn't changed, but right now Jenny's safety had to come first. Every second counted, and they were wasting precious time.

"You're right." He swung back toward the house, pulling her with him. "Come on. We can't just stand around and wait. Let's get some lanterns, see what we can find before the sheriff gets here."

They emerged onto the porch minutes later, the light from their lanterns flickering around the yard. Their chances of finding tracks were slim at best, Brandon realized. The area around the house was landscaped in grass and shrubs, while the walks and drive had been graveled, at considerable expense, to cut down on mud. The property itself was well suited for a kidnapping. It was grandly set at the edge of town, on the side of a long, sloping hill. Stands of pine and aspen rose behind it, continuing all the way to the mountains. It would have been an easy matter for Harvey Keetch—assuming it was Harvey—to tether his horse in the trees, steal down to the house, crouch in the shrubbery and wait for someone vulnerable to appear. By chance or design, that someone had been Jenny.

"Brandon!" Harriet's urgent voice came from the side of the house. "Come here! I've found something!"

He raced around the corner of the house to find her crouched next to a low-spreading juniper bush. One hand held the lantern, shining its light on the damp earth beneath.

"Here," she said. "Look at these prints."

An ugly lump congealed in Brandon's throat as he stared down at the impressions in the dirt. Hands, knees and scuffed prints from the kind of hobnailed hunting boots that he'd seen both Keetch twins wearing. While the posse was combing the countryside for him, Harvey had been right here. He had crouched behind the corner of the house and waited for someone to come outside and start down the front walk, allowing him to creep up and attack from behind.

"He couldn't have known it would be Jenny." Harriet voiced Brandon's own thoughts.

"He was more than likely waiting for me," Brandon said.

"Or me, if he'd been there long enough to see me go in." Harriet told him about her encounter with the Keetch brothers in the alley behind the stable. "I wish it *had* been me! Why did it have to be Jenny, of all people? Think how terrified the poor girl must be!"

They gazed at each other in the flickering light, neither of them daring to voice their worst fear. Jenny was so fragile. With her baby nearly due, any kind of rough handling could start her labor early. If they failed to find her in time, she could die in agony, out there in the cruel darkness.

If Harvey Keetch didn't murder her first.

"Let's see what else we can find." Battling panic, Brandon raised his lantern and scanned the yard. The ground was still damp from snow melt.

Now that they had a better idea of where to look, they might be able to find more impressions, even in the grass.

Harriet moved forward in a line from the corner of the house. "He would have come this way," she muttered half to herself. "That would mean he'd have caught up with her about here and... Oh, Brandon!"

She shone her light higher, illuminating the clear trail of flattened grass where Jenny had been dragged behind the house. Brandon remembered the sound of the front door closing, then Harriet going into the parlor and returning to the kitchen with the rose shawl. After that, they had both dashed for the front door, missing Jenny by mere seconds. As he'd stood on the porch, shouting her name, his daughter had been close enough to hear but unable to answer.

Brandon had never wept in his adult life. But he was on the verge of tears now. He had come so close to finding Jenny in time—and he had failed her.

The sound of horses coming up the drive pulled him back from the edge of grief. Two riders reined up and dismounted in the circle of lantern light. One was Matt Langtry. The other was Will Smith.

Brandon met Will's gaze across the scant distance that separated them. This was the man who had defiled and stolen his precious daughter, the man he had cursed and hated for months.

Now, suddenly, none of it made a dime's worth of difference. They both loved Jenny and they were both desperate to save her and her unborn child. Nothing else mattered.

Harriet glanced from Brandon to her brother as if she expected them to go for each other's throats. As if to reassure her, Brandon turned around and shone his light on the strip of flattened grass. "Come over here," he said quietly. "Let me show you what we've found so far, and we'll take it from there."

Matt Langtry, who had the tracking instincts of a Comanche, had picked up the trail by lantern light. He'd found the place where Harvey Keetch had tied his horse and the four of them, on foot, had followed the hoofprints upward through the trees.

It was Harriet who'd found the most vital piece of evidence. Bringing up the rear, she'd snagged her skirt on the thorns of a wild rose that grew amid the tangled underbrush. In reaching down to tug herself free, she'd discovered a single thread of blue chambray. Its fresh color matched the dress Jenny had worn that day. Now their fear that Jenny had been kidnapped was a certainty.

"Chances are good she's still all right," Matt mused, examining the thread. "If Harvey had wanted to kill Jenny, he'd have done it near the house and left her for you to find. The fact that he's gone to the trouble of taking her with him means he plans to keep her alive, at least for now."

"But why?" Will's voice shook. "What would the

bastard want with Jenny? She's never lifted a finger to hurt him."

"My guess is that he plans to use her as a hostage," Matt said. "We've got Marlin locked in jail. Harvey wants his brother."

"Then give him his damned brother!" Brandon rasped. "As long as we get Jenny back unharmed, I'll throw in enough money for the two of them to live like kings in Mexico. And to sweeten the pot, maybe you can promise them a fair head start before you bring out the posse." He glanced imploringly at Matt.

"Agreed," the sheriff said. "Harvey and Marlin will dig their own graves in time, with or without our help. But we have to get Jenny back now, at any cost."

A full moon rose in the eastern sky as they wound their way up the hillside. Harriet walked behind Brandon, filling her eyes with the sight of his rumpled hair and broad shoulders. He moved with easy strides, the white bandage like a beacon in the darkness.

She fought the urge to reach out and catch his waist in a brief, comforting hug. Brandon would not welcome her comfort. His thoughts would be far away from her, as if their wild and tender loving had taken place in a different world.

If they lost Jenny, they would lose each other, as well, Harriet realized. There would be too much hurt between them, too many painful memories for them to go on. Brandon would withdraw so deeply into himself that she would never be able to reach him again.

Less than a mile from where they'd picked it up, the trail ended at the broad base of a rock slide. While Will held the lantern, Matt crouched to examine the rocks. After a long, tense moment he straightened and shook his head. "No use trying to trail him from here. He could've gone anywhere."

"Dr. Tate told me the Keetch brothers and their parents prospected these hills," Harriet said. "We could search for days, even weeks, without finding the place where Harvey's taking Jenny."

"We could…" Matt gazed pensively up at the slide. "But we won't have to. Harvey's smarter than I gave him credit for. He wants to be found. And he knows there's only one way we're going to find him."

"We'll take Marlin along with us. He's the only one who'll know where to find his brother." Brandon voiced the thought that had sprung into all of their minds. He glanced around the circle of faces and took charge.

"Let's go. Matt, while you're getting the little bugger out of jail, I'll withdraw five thousand cash from the bank. That should be enough. Will, I'll take your horse for now. You can saddle two more horses from my stable and meet us in town."

He glanced back over his shoulder, as if noticing Harriet for the first time. "Harriet, can you round up enough food and water for four men, maybe some blankets and medical supplies, and send them with Will?"

"Certainly. But I'll be going with you."

The three men stared at her. "It'll be a rough ride,

and likely dangerous, Harriet," Matt said. "There's no reason for a lady to come along."

"Oh?" She glared up at them. "And what if Jenny goes into labor? Which one of you is going to deliver her baby? Answer me that or saddle me a horse!"

An hour later they rode out of town. The moon shone like a silver coin in a cloudless sky, casting long streamers of shadow behind them as they cleared Main Street and swung their mounts toward the foothills.

Matt Langtry led the way with the handcuffed Marlin Keetch riding close beside him. Marlin sat hunched in the saddle, looking as peevish as a trapped wolverine. His eyes shifted again and again toward the heavy Colt .45 that hung at the sheriff's hip, as if he were wondering how to get his hands on the weapon. But no one expected any real trouble from Marlin. He had been told, in good faith, that if he led the small party to Harvey's mountain hideout, he would be exchanged for Brandon's daughter. With the promise of freedom so close, he'd be a fool to try anything reckless.

Will, Harriet and Brandon rode behind them, stringing out single file as the trail narrowed. They said little. Between the tension-charged air and Marlin's surly presence, no one felt much like talking.

Riding behind her brother, Harriet was acutely conscious of Brandon's gaze on her back. But he wasn't really seeing her, she knew. His thoughts would be fixed on his daughter's safety and on his own guilt. If the worst happened, he would suffer the torments of hell. It would haunt him all his days that he had let Jenny go without making peace between them.

Jenny's loss would affect them all. Will would be prostrate with a young husband's grief, and even Matt would blame himself for not having found Harvey in time to prevent the kidnapping.

But she would turn her thoughts away from tragedy, Harriet resolved. She would think of the love and sweetness that Jenny had brought into all their lives and she would look ahead to the joy they would feel when she was safe.

They would find her in time. They had to.

The moon rose to the peak of the sky as they wound their way into the foothills. Groves of aspen mottled the foothills, their trunks bone-white against the darkness. Higher up, velvety forests of pine and spruce rose to the timberline, ending below jagged granite peaks whose hollows still cradled pockets of snow.

The lower slopes of these mountains were honeycombed with old mines, where an earlier generation had dug for phantom fortunes in gold and silver. A man who knew this country, as Harvey Keetch did, could hide in this network of pits and tunnels as long as his supplies held out or even longer if he knew how to live off the land. Only Marlin Keetch would know where to find his brother—and Jenny. Brutish and unpredictable, Marlin held Jenny's life in the palm of his grubby hand.

Harriet's horse lurched as the trail zigzagged up the side of a wash. Glancing down, she tugged at her skirt to cover one exposed knee. There'd been no time to change into riding clothes. She'd been too busy rounding up food, water and the other things they would need for the long ride. She had also spent twenty minutes with Dr. Tate while he'd instructed her on what to do if Jenny's labor started. There'd been no question of the old man's going with them. The trail would be too rough for a buggy or wagon, and his rheumatism would not allow him to mount a horse.

He had given Harriet a kit that contained some sheeting, towels, a baby blanket, a stethoscope, a knife, scissors, a ball of string, a flask of whiskey and some evil-looking forceps that Harriet could only hope she wouldn't need to use. Her grandmother had been a midwife and, as a young girl, Harriet had gone along with the old woman to deliver a few babies. But the births had been easy ones and she'd had little more to do than fetch and carry. This time could be very different. She could only pray that, if called upon, her hands and mind would be equal to the task.

"How soon will we get there?" Will's strained voice broke the silence. "We've been riding for hours. It's got to be past midnight."

"Marlin told me we'd be there before first light," Matt answered. "That's as much as I know."

"And what if Jenny isn't there?" Will demanded. "What'll we do then?"

Matt sighed. "We'll cross that bridge when we come to it. For now, this is our best shot. And Marlin won't steer us wrong, because he knows that if he does, he'll be spending the next fifteen years at hard labor with a ball and chain clamped onto his leg. Isn't that right, Marlin?" He gave his prisoner a none-too-gentle nudge.

"I gotta take a piss!" Marlin whined. "'Tain't fair, makin' me ride all night without even stoppin' to do my business."

"May I remind you, Marlin, that there's a lady— a *real* lady—riding behind you?" Matt's voice was blade thin. "Watch your mouth. And you can do anything you blamed well please when we have Jenny Calhoun Smith back safe and sound. But for now, you'll stay on your horse."

"'Tain't fair!" Marlin's whine had become a blubbering wail. "First Ma dies, then that bastard banker takes our ranch, then Harvey makes me help with the holdup and I'm the one that gits caught! And now you're bein' mean to me! 'Tain't fair!"

"Stop griping, Marlin," Matt snapped. "Life isn't fair. I learned that early on. At least you had good parents who loved you and tried to raise you decently. And at least you've got a brother who seems to care about you—though I'd argue with his way of showing it. That's more family than I've got."

Marlin slumped in the saddle, muttering under his breath, but Will's interest had been piqued. "I thought your family was in Texas, Matt," he said. "I never knew you had no family at all."

The sheriff stiffened slightly, then shrugged his shoulders, as if realizing that Will needed the brief distraction from his worries. "My mother died when I was seven," he said. "I never knew my father—they weren't married—but she said he was a good man and she'd loved him. She promised to tell me the whole story when I was older, but she never got the chance to keep that promise. She was killed by a stray bullet in a drunken gunfight and I spent the next eleven years in an orphanage."

"And you never tried to find your father's family?" Will asked.

Matt shook his head. "I wouldn't know where to start looking. And even if I did find them, why should they want anything to do with me? Some things are better left alone."

"But didn't your mother leave you any clues at all?" Will persisted.

Matt sighed. "Only one. Langtry was my mother's last name. But my middle name isn't the sort she'd have plucked out of thin air, so I've always thought it might have been my father's."

"What is it?" Will asked.

"It's Tolliver." Matt nudged his horse forward to keep a closer eye on his prisoner. "Matthew Tolliver Langtry." His chuckle carried a raw edge. "Now, that's a mouthful, even in Texas!"

* * *

As the conversation faded into silence, Brandon shifted his weight in the saddle and unholstered the heavy revolver at his hip. Taking care to point the muzzle at the sky, he cocked and uncocked the hammer and checked the cylinder to make sure it was fully loaded. He had never shot a man and he hoped he wouldn't have to do it tonight. But if need be, to save Jenny or to protect Harriet, he would blast his way through the gates of hell.

He'd been too distracted to pay close attention to the exchange between Will and Matt, but the young sheriff's remark that he had no family had struck a deep blow into Brandon's heart. Family was always something he'd taken for granted until last fall when Jenny had eloped and left him alone, marooned in the ocean of his own pride. For the past six months he, too, had been without a family. It was the loneliest feeling in the world.

Now, like a vision in his mind's eye, Brandon saw everything that might have been his....

He saw himself, a few years older and infinitely wiser than now, seated at the head of a long table, spread for a holiday banquet. Around that table were the people he loved—his beautiful Harriet and the children she had given him. And Jenny was there, too—not only Jenny but her husband Will and their own babies, everyone talking, laughing, singing in a cacophony of pure happiness.

Brandon could not hold the vision. It faded as swiftly as it had come, giving him only a glimpse of his lost future. Why had he turned them away? Why had it taken this calamity to show him what he had done to all their lives?

Pulling his thoughts back to the present, Brandon eased the pistol back into its holster. The night was chilly, the sky dotted with the diamond pinpoints of a million stars. Harriet rode ahead of him, her figure slender and erect in the darkness. The argument that had followed their passionate lovemaking came back to haunt him now.

He ached to gather her in his arms, to bury his face in her sweet hair and tell her what a fool he'd been. She was his salvation, the love of his life, everything he had ever wanted in a woman. Why hadn't he told her that? Why hadn't he opened his heart to her and laid it bare?

His proposal of marriage had been so flippant that, in retrospect, it had sounded almost like a joke. At the time, he'd been dizzy with love and bubbling over with hubris. He had glossed over the words she'd needed to hear and hadn't even given her the chance to refuse. It was a wonder she hadn't stalked out of the room and gone straight back to Enoch Farley.

Would he ever have the chance to make things right? Or would the outcome of this night be so shattering that there could be no hope of going forward?

Nothing could be resolved until Jenny was safe. And she *would* be safe, he assured himself desperately. He would see to it himself or he would die trying.

Chapter Sixteen

Brandon was beginning to drift when something shocked his senses to full alert. It was not a sound or a touch, but a scent, faint but unmistakable on the cool night breeze. He inhaled deeply to make sure. Yes, it had to be fresh coffee, brewing over an open fire.

Matt had halted his horse below the crest of a low, rocky ridge. "Smells damned good, doesn't it?" he commented as Brandon moved his mount past Harriet and Will and came up alongside him. "You'd almost think our friend Harvey was expecting company."

"How can you be sure it's Harvey?" Brandon asked in a hushed voice.

"Marlin told me his family's old silver mine is down in the hollow, below this ridge. Judging from the signs, I'd say he's led us to the right place, and somebody's home."

"Now what?" Will had moved up beside them. "How can we make sure he's got Jenny?"

"Should be easy enough," Matt said, easing out of the saddle and swinging to the ground. "I'll just sneak down there and talk to him. With luck, we can make the trade and be on our way in no time at all."

With luck. A cold chill passed through Brandon's body as he thought of all the things that could go wrong. Jenny could be hurt or dead, or Harvey could refuse to give her up. Or it was possible they wouldn't find her here at all. Anything could happen down there in the darkness.

Harriet had dismounted a short distance away. She stood beside her horse, massaging the soreness from her back. Her eyes, brimming with fear and love, met his in the moonlight. Brandon ached to go to her, to take her in his arms and assure her that everything was going to be all right. But he could not make such a promise, least of all to himself.

"I'll need someone to watch my back," Matt said. "Brandon, you come along and cover me. Will, you stay here and keep an eye on our friend Marlin. If he tries anything, shoot him someplace where it'll hurt a lot."

"I gotta take a piss," Marlin whined. "You said I could."

"Shut up, Marlin," Matt snapped. "You can piss a whole damned river when we're done with this business."

Will had drawn his borrowed pistol and moved up

next to the prisoner. It was clear that the young man hadn't done a lot of shooting. He handled the gun awkwardly, holding it up to look as he cocked the hammer. But Will would be all right, Brandon told himself. Marlin would be a fool to try anything when he was about to be set free.

"Ready?" Matt glanced at Brandon, who had dismounted and drawn his pistol.

"Lead the way." Brandon thumbed back the hammer and followed the sheriff through a narrow opening between the rocks. They wound their way downward until they emerged on an open, brushy slope. For the rest of the way, darkness would be their only protection.

A hundred yards below, on a fan of tailings above a dry streambed, a small campfire flickered. Its light illuminated the timbered opening of an old mine tunnel. Near its entrance a stout figure huddled, poking at the fire with a stick and tending a pot of coffee. Brandon's pulse broke into a gallop as he recognized Harvey Keetch. But where was Jenny?

Brandon peered into the deep shadows, his heart twisting into a knot of anguish. His daughter was nowhere to be seen.

By now they were within shouting distance. Matt dropped to a crouch behind a clump of sage and Brandon followed his example.

"Harvey, this is Sheriff Langtry," Matt shouted. "We've come for Jenny. Is she with you?"

Harvey edged back into the shelter of the mine.

Moonlight glinted on the pistol in his hand. "Maybe. Maybe not. That depends on what you got for me!"

"We've got your brother up on the ridge. Bring the girl out here where we can see she's safe and we'll talk about a trade. Otherwise, Marlin goes back to jail and we'll be coming after you!"

Brandon knew that Matt expected him to keep quiet. But if Jenny could hear him, he wanted her to know he had come for her and that he would do anything to get her back.

"Harvey!" he shouted. "This is Brandon Calhoun. All I want is to get my daughter back safely. I've got five thousand dollars for you if you'll bring Jenny out now!"

The long silence that followed was broken only by the distant cry of a coyote. Brandon's nerves had begun to snap by the time Harvey answered.

"Hell, Banker, if you had that much money, why didn't you just help us with the mortgage? That woulda saved you and me this whole stinkin' mess! And you, Sheriff, how do I know this ain't just a trick. You could have a whole damned posse up in them rocks, waitin' to shoot me down as soon as I give up that little gal."

So he had Jenny after all. Brandon felt himself go light-headed with relief. "Jenny's all we've come for, Harvey. Just bring her out here and turn her loose. Then you and your brother can take the money and head for Mexico."

"'Tain't gonna be that easy, Banker," Harvey shouted back. "Your daughter's in a bad way. I got her in the mine, layin' on some blankets, moanin' and groanin' like the devil hisself had hold of her. I ain't no doc, but from the looks of things, I'd say she's fixin' to have that young'un right here!"

From their place behind the ridge, Harriet and Will had heard everything. Harvey's last words left both of them thunderstruck.

"I'm going down there!" Harriet seized the bundled medical kit from behind her saddle where she'd tied it. Will, still mounted, watched her with desperately frightened eyes. Her brother was such a man most of the time, it was easy to forget that he was only eighteen years old. Her heart went out to him.

"It'll be all right, Will," she tried to reassure him. "Dr. Tate showed me how to help Jenny. I have everything I need right here, and I know what to do."

"If it's that simple why were we planning to take her to Denver?" He flung the words back at her. "I'm not a little boy you can pat on the head, sis. Jenny's my wife, she's in danger, and my place is with her!"

"I know." Harriet gazed up at him, heartsick. "But somebody needs to watch things here, and right now there's no one available but you. The best thing you can do for Jenny is to stay calm and help keep things under control."

"But what if she dies? What if I never get to see her or talk to her or hold her again?"

Harriet steeled herself against the distress in his young eyes. "You mustn't even think that way, Will. I'll do everything I can." Impulsively she reached up and squeezed his hand. "We're wasting time. I have to go."

Harriet would never understand what happened next. Marlin had been quiet and docile, slumped in the saddle listening to the exchange between Brandon, the sheriff and Harvey. Maybe he'd been worried about the way the conversation was going. Or maybe he just lacked the common sense to stay put until he could be exchanged for Jenny. Whatever the reason, he suddenly took matters into his own hands.

While Will and Harriet were distracted by their argument, Marlin seized the saddle horn with his manacled hands and drove his hobnailed boots hard into the horse's flanks.

The startled animal screamed and reared, almost striking Harriet and slamming Will's mount to one side as it leaped over the ridge, skidded down the rocks and plunged on a slanting path down the steep, gravelly slope toward the mine.

Marlin clung desperately to the saddle. "Here I am, Harvey!" he bawled. "I'm comin' to get you outta here!"

"Stop, you crazy fool!" Will fumbled with the pistol until he'd regained his grip on the weapon. *"Stop!"* He leaned over the rocks and fired three warning shots, aimed well above Marlin's head. The bullets whined as they ricocheted down the brushy hollow, their echoes sounding like a whole volley of gunfire in the darkness.

"Damn liars!" Harvey screamed. As the nightmare scene unfolded, Harvey began firing back up the slope at the imagined enemy. Matt and Brandon were flattened against the ground when Marlin's horse charged past them. They saw Marlin reel and pitch sideways, over the horse's shoulder. The handcuffs caught on the saddle horn, and Marlin was dragged fifty yards down the canyon before the horse staggered to a halt.

"Hold your fire, blast it!" Matt shouted. Dodging and ducking like an infantryman, he raced down the wash to where the horse stood, its sides heaving. Matt's oaths and curses purpled the air around him.

"Congratulations, Harvey!" he shouted in a fury. "You've just killed your damn-fool brother!"

The primal cry that tore from the mouth of the mine did not even sound human.

Will had gone white with shock. Harriet tore her eyes away from his stricken face. With Marlin as insurance, she had felt relatively safe going down to the mine. Now she would be walking into the lair of a wounded animal.

But that made no difference. No power on earth could keep her from Jenny's side.

Clutching the medical kit, she clambered down through the rocks and emerged on the open hillside.

Half a league, half a league,
Half a league onward...
Into the jaws of Death,
Into the mouth of Hell...

"Harvey!" she shouted. "Don't shoot! It's Harriet Smith! I'm unarmed, and I'm coming down to help Jenny!"

Brandon watched her, his throat tightening as she moved down the slope toward him. She walked proudly, her head high, her shoulders squared, showing none of the terror she must be feeling inside. Her hair had come loose from its pins to flutter around her face like a dark halo. His angel. His brave, beautiful, fierce lioness. He would give up his life for her. But he could not help her now—or even stop her. Her capable hands carried his hopes and his heart.

"Hold it right there, Schoolmarm!" Harvey called as she came abreast of the sage clump where Brandon had taken shelter. "If you want to come down here and play midwife, that's fine by me. But it'll cost you."

Harriet halted in momentary surprise.

"The banker said he had five thousand dollars cash on him," Harvey said. "If his money's as good as his mouth, I want it now. Bring it down to me and I'll let you go back to the little gal. Otherwise, she can damn well have that baby by herself—if she doesn't die tryin'."

Brandon rose to his feet, knowing the hate-crazed man could shoot him anytime he chose. He would never have judged Harvey to be a murderer, but now that he'd killed his own brother, Harvey had nothing to lose. In his grief-crazed condition, he was capable of anything.

"You can have the money, Harvey," Brandon said, "but only if you take it and ride out of here now. The sheriff's given his word that you'll have time to get away. Haven't you, Sheriff?"

"On a stack of Bibles!" Matt's voice rang out from the shadows of the wash. "All we want is Jenny, safe and sound. You, Harvey, can go to Mexico, or to hell for all we care."

"No good," Harvey snapped. "There's nothin' says you won't be after me the minute I clear out."

"Then take me with you!" Brandon heard Harriet gasp as he spoke. "With me as a hostage, nobody would come near you."

"Good idea." There was a manic edge to Harvey's voice. "But you're a big man, Banker. Even without a gun, you could be too much for me to handle. I'd rather take me a woman. She'd be easier to manage and a helluva lot more amusin', 'specially at night."

"Stop this!" Harriet was growing frantic. "Settle things any way you like, but let me get to Jenny before it's too late! After the baby comes and I know she's all right, I'll go anywhere!" She swung toward

Brandon, thrusting out her hand. "Give me the money! We're running out of time!"

Brandon reached into his jacket and retrieved the hefty wad of bills wrapped in a muslin bag. As her hand closed around it, he caught her wrist and spun her hard against him. His mouth captured hers in a forceful, desperate kiss.

"*Mmff*—what—" Startled, Harriet struggled against him, twisting and pushing. Then she felt the cold weight of his pistol sliding into her pocket and she understood what he was doing. Still clutching her medical kit, she flung her free arm around his neck and returned the kiss so passionately that Brandon staggered backward to catch his balance. What had begun as a ruse suddenly became a poignant farewell that contained all the love and yearning there was no time to put into words.

She tore herself away from him then, her eyes welling with tears, as if she were seeing him for the last time.

"Tell Jenny I love her," he said, not daring to say more.

"Yes. Yes, I will." She turned away and rushed down the hill.

"And I love you," he said softly, gazing after her. "My sweet, brave Harriet, I will love you all my life."

As Harriet reached the mine's entrance, Harvey stepped out of the shadows with the old army pistol in his hand. He was dirty and unshaven, and his eyes, lit by the campfire's red glow, reflected a glint of desperation that edged on madness.

"Come on in, Schoolmarm," he said, leering at her. "If I'd knowed I'd be entertainin' two purty gals, I would have cleaned up a bit. First off, I want the money."

Harriet placed the muslin bag into his open hand. Whatever happened, she resolved, she could not let this man know how terrified she was. Her fear would feed his sense of power, pushing him over the brink of cruelty.

He reached out to fondle her. She pushed his hand away. "That's not part of the bargain," she said in a cold voice. "Where's Jenny?"

Grinning, he glanced back over his shoulder, into the pitch-black depths of the tunnel. Without waiting for more of an answer, Harriet pushed past him.

"Jenny!" Her voice echoed off the walls. "Where are you?"

A huge shape stirred in the darkness and she could hear the sound of heavy breathing. Harriet's heart was in her throat by the time she realized it was only a horse, most likely the one Harvey had ridden here.

Nerves screaming, she edged past the horse and moved deeper into the tunnel. "Jenny!" she called again. "Can you hear me?"

In the darkness she could hear the distant sound of dripping water and the fluttering wings of a bat.

Then a thready whisper arose from the shadows. "Harriet…thank heaven…"

Harriet moved toward the voice but could see nothing at all. "Get me a lantern!" she shouted back at Harvey. "Now!"

She had expected some resistance, but seconds later she heard the sound of rummaging. Flickering yellow light revealed rough, sagging timbers festooned with cobwebs. Boxes of canned food and the trash of years littered the floor.

"Git that baby here fast, Schoolmarm," Harvey growled, hanging the lantern on a nail. "I'll be leavin' soon to git a good start afore first light. And baby or no baby, you'll be goin' with me." He spat a stream of tobacco on the ground and lumbered back toward the mine's entrance.

Jenny was lying on a filthy horse blanket. She looked like a child's doll abandoned in a rainstorm, her dress torn and muddied and wet from her own fluids. Her hair was a mass of tangles and her blue eyes were wild with pain and terror.

Harriet dropped to her knees, set her bundle aside and took the small, cold hands in her own. Jenny began to cry softly, tears running down her mud-smeared cheeks.

"Will and your father are outside, Jenny," Harriet said softly. "They'll be here as soon as they can, but first we need to get that baby here. How long have you been in labor?"

"A…long time." Speaking seemed almost too great an effort for her. "The pains started on the way here—on the horse. He wouldn't stop…oh!" The childlike fingers dug into Harriet's flesh as another pain seized her body. Her head rolled back and forth on the blanket. The cords on her neck bulged with strain as the pain built, crested and passed. "My baby," she whispered, "I can't feel him moving anymore. I'm afraid something's happened."

"I need to examine you," Harriet said. "Dr. Tate told me what to look for and what to do. We're going to get you through this, Jenny. Now, hold still."

Raising Jenny's sodden skirt, she probed gingerly with her fingertips. What she felt confirmed her fears.

"You're ready to give birth, but the baby's in the wrong position," she said. "I've got to turn him. It's going to hurt, Jenny. You'll need to be very brave."

"I know," Jenny whispered. "Just save my baby."

Harriet rolled up her sleeves, trying not to think about what she had to do. If she thought about it, she would never have the courage to begin.

Jenny whimpered as another hard contraction took her. Harriet stroked her face, her hands, waiting for the pain to pass. The doctor had told her to work between contractions. But with the pains coming almost one on top of another, she would have to work swiftly.

"Hurry it up back there!" Harvey's voice echoed down the tunnel. "It's time we was makin' tracks, teacher woman."

Harriet's heart shrank in her chest. What if he tried to take her before the baby came? She felt the weight of Brandon's pistol against her leg and she knew that, if need be, she would use it.

The contraction had ebbed. Harriet reached under Jenny's skirts, praying as she worked by touch, groping for the spine, the tiny buttocks, the head. Jenny ground her teeth, biting back screams of agony as the baby shifted. Then, suddenly, it was done. The baby's head slipped naturally into the birth canal. Harriet sank back onto her heels, her heart slamming, her body soaked in sweat.

Harvey's big boots came tramping down the tunnel. A moment later he stepped into the light, leading the horse. "Ain't waitin' for no fool baby!" he growled. "Horse is packed and I'm ready to go! You're comin' with me now, Schoolmarm!"

He took a step toward her. In one quick move Harriet pulled the pistol out of her pocket and thumbed back the hammer. "Take one more step and I'll blow your head off," she said quietly. "Now, unbuckle your gun belt, drop it on the ground and kick it over here."

Rage glittered in Harvey's eyes, but he did as he was told. She ought to shoot him, Harriet thought. That would end the danger to them all. For the space of a heartbeat her finger tightened on the trigger. But even then, she knew she could not take a human life. Harvey Keetch was not a monster, just a grieving, desperate and foolish man.

"Get out of here, Harvey," she said. "You've got the money. Take it and go before I change my mind about killing you."

He hesitated and Harriet could almost see the wheels turning in his mind. Without a hostage, he would be arrested or shot as soon as he left the sheltering tunnel. Better to take stay and gamble on the chance that this woman lacked the stomach to carry out her threat.

"Harriet—" The feeble cry came from Jenny. She was gasping frantically, grunting with effort as she bore down. "The baby! It's coming now!"

Harriet glanced toward the helpless girl. In that second the standoff was lost. With surprising quickness, Harvey sprang at her, seized her wrist and twisted Brandon's gun from her hand.

"Now, Schoolmarm," he growled, pointing the weapon at her. "I'm goin' now and you're comin' with me. Else I'll blow a hole through that purty head of yours."

She willed herself not to look at him. "I'll be no good to you dead, Harvey," she said. "Now leave me alone. I need to deliver this baby."

"Women can have babies by theirselves. My ma done it."

Harriet ignored him. Her hands groped beneath Jenny's muddy skirts. "Almost there," she murmured. "When the next pain comes, push, Jenny. Push for all you're worth."

The contraction came as she spoke. Jenny arched her exhausted body, screaming with effort as, with the last of her strength, she pushed her infant out into the world.

There was an awful tick of silence, then a tiny gasp and a miraculous, mewling cry as the baby filled and emptied its lungs, breathing, kicking, squirming. Alive. Harriet cradled the tiny creature between her knees while she tied and cut the cord. Her emotions were raw and sharp, like a fresh cut. Tears of relief flowed down her face. "You're a mother, Jenny," she said as she wrapped the child in the flannel blanket. "You have a beautiful, perfect little boy."

"Let me hold him." Pale but radiant, Jenny held out her arms and gathered her son close, kissing his puckered rosebud face and brushing back his wet blond curls. "Oh, Harriet, I could never have given him away!" she whispered.

"I know you couldn't. And I think your father knows it, too." Harriet leaned closer. "What you heard back there at the house, that's never mattered to him. He loves you, Jenny. He wanted me to tell you that."

"Thank you," Jenny said, her eyes welling with tears. "And thank you for my baby, Harriet. Now I need Will. And he needs to see his boy."

"He'll be here," Harriet said. "As soon as—"

Her words ended in a gasp as Harvey jammed the pistol's cold muzzle against her throat. "No more stalling, Schoolmarm," he hissed, twisting her arm behind her back. "The little brat's here. You done your job. We're gettin' out now."

Harriet willed herself not to show fear. After all, she had put him off before. "I'm not finished," she protested. "I need to tend to Jenny or she'll bleed—"

"You're finished." He jerked her to her feet, pulling her backward, toward the horse. "But just to show you my heart's in the right place, teacher lady, I'm givin' you a choice."

"A choice?" She gurgled the words as the pistol pressed into her neck.

"That's right," he rasped. "There's a new card in the deck now, and here's how it plays. Either you come with me and behave yourself nice and proper, or I leave you here and take the baby."

Chapter Seventeen

The three men waiting at the mouth of the mine could not hear the words spoken in the tunnel. But Jenny's scream and the baby's cry were sharp enough to echo off the earthen walls and reach their ears.

Will was first to react. He charged for the entrance and would have plunged headlong into the tunnel if Matt and Brandon hadn't caught his arms and held him back.

"Let me go!" he gasped, struggling forward. "Jenny needs me!"

"She doesn't need you getting shot," Matt growled. "Our friend Harvey will pump you full of lead if you go blundering in there now."

"But how can we just stand out here?" Will's hair had fallen into his eyes. He looked young and frightened. "Jenny could be in trouble! The baby could be in trouble! They could even be dying!"

"Harriet's with her." Brandon did his best to sound reassuring, though his own nerves were like shards of splintered glass. "She'll know what to do."

Will sagged in defeat, breathing hard. "I'm all right," he mumbled. "Let me go."

Releasing him, they sank into the uneasy silence of helpless men. Small, ordinary night sounds—the scurry of a pack rat, the cry of a nighthawk, clawed at their senses. The horses, which Will had brought along when he'd come down from the ridge, stirred and snorted in the shadows.

Brandon thought of Harriet with her capable hands, her keen mind and her courageous heart. At a time like this, there was no one he would rather have at Jenny's side. But with a crazed criminal holding them hostage, anything could happen. Before the night was out, he could lose the people he loved, and the words he longed to say to them would remain unspoken forever.

"Sheriff!" Harvey's voice bellowed from the depths of the mine. "I've got the schoolmarm and I'm comin' out. Give me plenty of room and nobody'll get hurt."

"We hear you, Harvey!" Matt shouted. "Let Miss Smith go and we'll give you all the room you want."

"No deal, Sheriff!" Harvey's voice came from nearer the entrance now. "Teacher here's my insurance policy. Anybody comes after me and she won't look so purty when they find her."

Something large moved in the darkness and they

heard the nicker of a horse. "What about Jenny and the baby?" Matt shouted. "Are they all right?"

Harvey snorted, leaving the question unanswered. "Soon as I'm on my way, they're all yours. Now git back, we're comin' out."

A shower of earth cascaded to the floor as the horse moved forward. The tunnel was too low for a rider to sit upright. Harvey and his hostage would have to duck against the horse's neck to keep from hitting the timbers that supported the ceiling. It would be all too easy to trigger a cave-in that would bury Jenny and the baby.

"Careful," Brandon warned the others as they moved clear. "Don't spook him."

"I don't plan to," Matt muttered, but Brandon noticed that his right hand was resting on the butt of his holstered revolver. Will stood poised to dash into the tunnel as soon as the way was clear.

"*Ha!*" Harvey shouted as the horse exploded out of the opening. He was leaning low in the saddle with Harriet crushed in front of him. His pistol was cocked and aimed at her head. Her eyes met Brandon's through the fading darkness.

"Jenny's fine!" she shouted, risking her life to let him know. "It's a boy! Go to her!"

The horse shot out onto the tailings, then wheeled abruptly and plunged up the slope toward the trees. Will sprinted into the tunnel shouting Jenny's name. Matt vaulted onto his big chestnut gelding.

"No!" Brandon caught the bridle before the sheriff could kick the horse to a gallop. "Stay here and help with Jenny. I'll go after them."

Matt's eyes narrowed. "Have you forgotten which one of us is sheriff here? This is my job. Let me do it."

"Listen to me." Brandon gripped the bridle harder. "You're the law. Harvey won't let you get near him, and he'll use Harriet to keep you away. But I'm the one he really wants. He blames me for everything that's happened, and he'll be out there waiting to even the score. I need to go after him alone. It's our one best chance of getting her back."

Matt hesitated; then, seeing the sense of the argument, he drew his pistol and offered the grip to Brandon. "You'll need this," he said. "And take my horse. It's the fastest one we've got. Be careful, and good luck to you."

Seconds later Brandon, armed and mounted, was guiding the cat-footed gelding up the slope along the path Harvey had taken. He was walking a tightrope, he knew. Move too slowly and he could lose the trail. Move too fast and he could spook Harvey into harming Harriet. For now, he could only follow along and hope to understand the game Harvey was playing.

Harriet's life, he knew, could depend on that understanding.

The sky had begun to pale above the eastern hills, showing a faint gleam like pewter emerging from beneath layers of tarnish. The dawn brought streaks of silvery gray, delicately brushed with hues of opal and carnelian that faded to palest blue as the first rays of sunlight stole above the horizon.

Along the trail, dark patches of shadow materialized into rocks and trees and bushes. From far down the slope, a quail greeted the morning with a cry that sounded like *lay-low, lay-low*.

Harriet blinked, squinting as a ray of sunlight struck her eyes. The trail had been winding steeply upward for what seemed like hours. Now, in the distance, she could see a massive, honeycombed outcrop of rocky ledges running above a deep canyon where a creek gushed along the bottom like a thread of liquid silver. Was this where the trail—and her life—would end?

The horse was spent. Its roan coat was lathered and its sides heaved with the effort of carrying two riders up the steep trail.

"You'll kill this animal if you don't rest him," Harriet said.

"He'll git his chance to rest soon enough." Harvey's unshaven chin brushed her ear. His breath smelled of rotten meat and stale tobacco. "What's the matter, teacher lady? Gettin' anxious to start the fun? Ain't never had me no poke at a schoolmarm afore."

"You're a fool!" Harriet said, masking the horror she felt. "Let me go and you could travel twice as fast. You could be in Mexico in a few weeks, with enough money to set you up for life."

Harvey spat off the edge of the trail. "That's just what I mean to do. But not till after I git what I want."

"Why risk staying here?" Harriet persisted. "If you're caught, you'll go to prison for life. But nobody's going to chase you all the way to Mexico, Harvey. The bank robbery failed, and Jenny's safe. The only real harm you did was to your own brother, and that was nothing but a sorry accident—"

"Shut the hell up, woman!" Harvey stormed, jabbing her shoulder with the pistol he held. "You think I'm so stupid that I don't know all that? I ain't leavin' till I git me that banker's ears and balls to nail on the wall of my Mexican hacienda, right over the fireplace where I can see 'em every day. As for you, teacher lady, I didn't just bring you along for fun. I brought you along for bait!"

Harriet's empty stomach clenched as his plan hit home. Harvey had made no effort to cover his tracks. If Brandon was on their trail, Harvey could wait for a good place to ambush him, then kill her and dump their bodies where they'd never be found.

"That's how much you know!" she said carelessly. "Brandon Calhoun wouldn't cross the street for me, let alone risk his life."

Harvey chortled. "I seen that kiss he gave you afore you came into the mine. Strikes me he'd come a long way for another kiss like that 'un."

"Brandon's daughter just had a baby and he'll want to stay with her. If anybody comes after us, it'll be the sheriff."

"Then tough luck for him. And tough luck for you. When I git to Mexico, it won't matter how many bodies I left hid in this canyon."

His words sent a somber chill through her body. She had cooperated with the bumbling Harvey in the hope that he would let her go. But she should have guessed the truth. He planned to kill her, along with anyone who came after her. He was desperate, with nothing to lose. And now, Harriet reminded herself, so was she.

The trail leveled out as they neared the top of the ledges. From her position in front of Harvey, Harriet could look over the edge and trace the meandering deer trail they'd followed upward from the creek bed. Clumps of aspen and scrubby piñon pine screened much of the path, but briefly, through the trees, she detected a flicker of movement.

Harriet squinted into the morning sunlight, not daring to shade her eyes. Maybe it had been an animal she'd seen—a deer or even an elk. But when she saw it again, passing through another open spot, she realized it was a man on horseback, traveling fast.

As the horse rounded the next curve, she recognized Matt's big chestnut. But even from a distance she could see that the rider wasn't the rangy young sheriff. The solid shoulders, dark brown coat and gray Stetson could only belong to Brandon.

An instinctive cry of alarm died in her throat. To shout a warning to Brandon would betray his presence. Oh, why hadn't he stayed at the mine with Jenny? He was riding into a trap, only half-aware of the danger. She had told herself that she had nothing to lose. But now that Brandon was here, all that had changed. He had loved her enough to come after her. She would not let him pay for that love with his death.

How could she warn him? Even if he chanced to look up, Brandon would be unlikely to see her with Harvey. Like him, they were screened from view by rocks and brush. She would have to find another way.

The idea came to her as she caught sight of a twisted gray stick lying across the trail. Thinking fast, she jabbed the horse's sensitive belly with the pointed toe of her boot. The animal flinched and snorted nervously.

"Rattler! Look out!" She jabbed the horse again, harder this time. The horse reared, throwing her back against Harvey and causing him to lose his grip on the pistol. By the time he'd recovered the weapon, Harriet had tumbled to the ground, clambered to her feet and was headed down the trail at a run.

"Stop, you bitch!" He fired a warning shot above her head. Harriet kept on running. Her legs were rubbery from hours of sitting on the horse and she knew she wouldn't get far before Harvey caught her again. But her idea had succeeded beyond her wildest hopes.

As she rounded the first bend in the trail, she heard the sound of hoofbeats behind her. Seconds later Harvey reined up and leaped out of the saddle, brandishing the stick she'd declared to be a rattlesnake.

"You stupid female!" Catching her by the hair, he brought the stick down hard across her back. "Here's your gol-damned snake! I ought to break every bone in your body with it. But I want to keep you purty for a while. Never could git it up for an ugly woman."

With Harvey still pounding on her back, Harriet swung toward the riderless horse. She would never make it into the saddle with the solid grip Harvey had on her hair. But there was one thing she might be able to do.

With all her remaining strength she brought the flat of her hand down on the horse's rump. The startled roan jumped, squealed and bolted down the trail, carrying the food and water, the blankets and Harvey's rifle, which had been slung from the saddle in a leather scabbard.

Flinging Harriet to the ground, Harvey plunged after the fleeing roan. He ran a few steps. Then, seeing the chase was hopeless, he drew his pistol and swung back toward Harriet. The murderous expression in his eyes told her she had pushed him too far. Not only had she cost him his horse and supplies, but the loss of the rifle would prevent him from getting a long-distance shot at Brandon.

"You damned hellcat," he snarled, "I could shoot you here and now, right between those big brown eyes. But I got plans for you when we git to where we're goin'. Move it, you banker's whore!" He jabbed her ribs with his pistol.

"I'm sore from riding," Harriet complained, dragging her feet as slowly as she dared, giving Brandon more time to catch up with them.

"You'll be sore from somethin' else when I'm through with you," he said with a sneer. "We're gonna put on a show for that boyfriend of yours afore I kill him." He jabbed her again with the pistol. "Oh, I know the bastard's somewhere close by. Elsewise, why'd you be actin' so contrary? But I'll git him. You'll see."

He fished a plug of tobacco out of his pocket and bit off a chaw. "When I'm out in the woods and I want to catch me a coyote, all I have to do is hole up somewhere and make a squeal like a wounded rabbit hurtin' real bad. Purty soon that old coyote pops his head up to look, and that's when I git him. Huntin' a man ain't much different, 'specially when I got me such a nice tender rabbit to make the squeal."

Snaking his free hand around her, he squeezed her breast hard. Harriet bit back a yelp of pain. She would never give Harvey the satisfaction of hearing her scream, she vowed. Not even if he killed her.

* * *

Brandon spurred the big chestnut up the slope, keeping to the cover of aspen and maple thickets and avoiding the open game trails where he might be seen from above. He had heard the gunshot and Harvey's raging shouts. He had even managed to catch the loose roan and tether it in a patch of grassy shade. Harvey's rifle, loaded and ready, lay behind the saddle, within easy reach.

Harriet had done a valiant job of letting him know where she was being taken. And if scaring away the horse with the rifle on it had been her doing, he probably owed her his life. Now they were likely on foot and she would be stalling their progress any way she could. But if she continued her tactics, Harvey might lose patience and turn on her.

Sheltered by a stand of young fir trees, he studied the hillside. At the top of the slope, an escarpment of high ledges jutted against the skyline. In such a rock formation, there were bound to be hollows and crevices where a man with a gun and enough ammunition could fend off a small army. Likely as not, Harvey had already set up a hideout, with food, water and extra bullets. Whatever the risk, Brandon knew he could not let Harvey drag Harriet into such a place.

He had hoped for more time to gain the advantage of surprise, perhaps by circling around and coming out above them. But time, he sensed, had run out. His only chance of freeing Harriet was to force Harvey's hand now.

"Harvey!" he shouted up the slope. "I know you're up there and I know you can hear me! Let the woman go now! You can keep the money and nobody will come after you!"

Harvey's crazed laughter echoed down the canyon. "You're gonna have to do better than that, Banker. This hellcat chased off my horse, so I'll take the one you're ridin'. And I'll take you in the bargain. How's that for a deal?"

"Fine!" Brandon swallowed the taste of fear, knowing there was no other way to save Harriet's life. "I'm all yours, Harvey, and so's the horse! But I want your word that Miss Smith goes free."

Harvey cackled. "You got it, Banker. On my sainted mother's grave. Now come out in the open, where I can see you."

Brandon heard the sounds of a scuffle. "No!" Harriet screamed. "Don't do it, Brandon! It's a trap—" The solid crack of flesh on flesh ended her words. Brandon's heart sickened. He could see them now as he moved upward through the trees. Harvey was holding Harriet in front of him, using her as a shield. She sagged in his arms, stunned by the blow. Brandon kept moving up the slope, knowing he had no choice if he was to save her.

The pistol in Harvey's hand was Brandon's own, wrested from Harriet in the mine. He jammed the barrel against Harriet's temple. "That's it, Banker. Climb out of the saddle and toss that six-shooter up here. Then lead the horse up here, nice and easy like."

"You're not a murderer yet, Harvey." Brandon spoke soothingly as he dismounted and moved up the hill. "Your brother's death was an accident, we all know that. But harming a woman, that's different. You'd burn in hell for a crime like that. Turn her loose now, before something goes wrong."

Harvey spat out a vile oath. "You'll be burnin' right there next to me for what you done to my family, Banker. I'm holdin' all the cards now. I got the schoolmarm and the money, and purty soon I'll have you, too. Now, throw that shooter up here and git down on your hands and knees. I want to watch you crawl up here and kiss my boots!"

They were less than a dozen yards apart now. Harvey had stopped just below the rocky ledges. They rose like a solid wall behind him. Brandon could see Harriet clearly. Harvey had his left arm hooked around her throat. His right hand pointed the gun at her head. Where he had struck her, an ugly red welt ran from her cheekbone to her jaw. But the copper-flecked eyes that returned Brandon's gaze held nothing but love and absolute trust.

Brandon prayed silently that his next desperate act would not betray that trust.

"Quit stallin', Banker." Harvey's voice was an impatient snarl. "You heard me. Toss that six-shooter up here. Then git down on your knees."

Brandon's eyes took careful measure of the distance. His thumb released the hammer on the pistol to keep it from firing accidentally and hitting Harriet. Then, with a lightning motion, he flung the weapon so that it whizzed past Harvey's ear and bounced off the cliff face with a metallic clang.

Harvey's reaction was automatic. He jerked his head toward the sound, loosening his grip on Harriet. At the same time, Brandon seized the rifle off the saddle and jabbed the barrel into the gelding's flank. The big chestnut screamed, reared and plunged straight toward Harvey.

"Run, Harriet! Get away!" Brandon shouted as he charged up the hill. He saw her roll clear of Harvey and scramble to her feet. An instant later she had dived off the trail and taken shelter behind a rock.

The gelding veered off to one side. Harvey had been knocked flat by its charge. He came up spitting dirt and fumbling for his weapon. But by then Brandon had reached the level ground below the ledges. His booted foot came down on Harvey's pistol, anchoring it to the ground. His hands aimed the rifle at Harvey's chest and chambered a shell.

Harvey, on his feet now, looked down at the spot where the rifle's muzzle touched his chest. He raised sheepish eyes to Brandon's, his mouth stretching into a little-boy grin that showed his missing tooth.

"Shucks, Mr. Calhoun, you wouldn't shoot a man in cold blood, would you? Hell, I didn't do you no real harm. You said that yourself. And you promised me that if you got your woman back, I could go free. C'mon, I was only funnin' with you."

He took a step backward, toward the rocks. "You ain't the sort who'd shoot an unarmed man in cold blood, Mr. Calhoun. You know that, and so do I." He took another step. Brandon clenched his jaw in frustration, knowing the pathetic little rascal was right. He had never taken human life, and killing Harvey wasn't worth what it would do to his conscience.

Harvey grinned confidently. "You got everything you want, now, Banker, so I'm just gonna walk away. My ma always said you was a good man. You'd never shoot one of her boys."

"But *I* would!" Harriet stepped out from behind the rock, her eyes blazing fire. In her hands she held the pistol Brandon had thrown toward the cliff. Her grip on the weapon left no doubt that she knew how to use it.

"Go on, Harvey," she said. "Take another step. I'd love to blow a nice big hole through your miserable little body!"

Harvey eyed her sourly, but he did not move. For the space of a breath the three of them stood there, frozen like actors in a living tableau. Then a familiar voice rang out from the rocks above them.

"Well, one of you had better shoot the sneaky little polecat," drawled Sheriff Matthew T. Langtry. "Otherwise I might be tempted to do the job myself."

Leaving the sheriff to bring in his manacled prisoner, Brandon and Harriet started back at once. They rode double on Brandon's tall bay mare, which Matt had brought with him. Harriet straddled the mare's rump, her arms wrapped tightly around Brandon's ribs.

The sun had risen on a glorious spring day. The high country aspens were swollen with buds. Chickadees chased each other among the branches, filling the air with their raucous calls. Snow lay rich as ermine on the distant peaks.

Brandon took the steep, meandering game trail as fast as he dared, pushing the mare hard. Harriet, he knew, shared his sense of urgency. Later there would be time to lie in each other's arms and talk, time to say all the things the two of them had left unsaid. They would have days of living and nights of loving, and every moment heaven allowed them would be a precious gift. But right now, nothing mattered more than getting back to Jenny and the baby.

"They'll be all right," Harriet said, her arms tightening around him. "Otherwise, Matt would never have left them. And they seemed fine to me, too. The baby was tiny, but he cried right away. That's a sign of good, healthy lungs. And Jenny's stronger than she looks. She was so brave, Brandon. You'd have been so proud of her!"

Brandon swallowed the lump in his throat. "I just hope she'll give me the chance to tell her that, if it isn't too late."

"It won't be." Harriet pressed her face against his back. "Jenny loves you. All she wants is for you to be part of her family."

"Even after what she heard at the house, that she isn't my natural daughter? You can't tell me that won't make a difference."

"Wait and see." Harriet held him fiercely, her arms offering a haven of comfort. "Everything will work out for the best. After all this trouble, it just has to."

Brandon yearned to believe her. But guilt and worry gnawed at him. He had always believed that people reaped what they'd sown. It defied reason that a man who'd driven his wife to an early death and banished the daughter of his heart should be worthy of love. Even the glorious woman who rode with him now was a gift he'd done nothing to merit. If all the people he cared about were to turn their backs on him, it would be an act of justice, and no worse than he deserved.

"Down there." Looking past his shoulder, Harriet pointed to a hollow between two hills, less than a mile distant. "That's where we left them."

Brandon nudged the mare to a canter as they came down the long grassy slope. Now they could see the entrance to the mine and the shelter that had been improvised just outside with logs and blankets. Nearby a horse was tethered and a lanky figure stood scanning the horizon. That would be Will, Brandon thought. His son-in-law. A good man.

By the time they pulled up in front of the mine, Brandon's heart was pounding. Harriet slid off the horse first, giving him room to swing his leg over and dismount. But she hung back with her brother, giving Brandon a chance to approach the makeshift shelter alone.

He had to crouch to see beneath the blanket where Jenny lay. She looked pale and tired, but her smile was radiant.

"Hello, angel," Brandon whispered, his throat aching.

"Hello, Papa." Her eyes glimmered as she held out a doll-size bundle wrapped in a flannel blanket. Brandon glimpsed a tiny rosebud face crowned by a nimbus of fair hair, the same shade as Jenny's had been when she was born.

Something inside him seemed to melt as he gathered the baby in his arms. Harriet watched them from a distance, her smile radiating pure love.

"I'd like you to meet your grandson, Papa," Jenny said softly. "His name is Brandon. Brandon William Smith."

Epilogue

❧❧❧

Christmas Day, 1885

"Come back here, you little mischief!" Jenny dashed after her son, who was reaching for a tinsel garland on the Christmas tree.

"I've got him!" Brandon, who'd just come into the parlor, scooped the child up and swung him toward the ceiling, setting loose a torrent of happy giggles.

Jenny collapsed into one of the leather armchairs that faced the fireplace. "He's all yours, Papa. I tell you, he wears me out! Every day is like running a race! I'm just glad I didn't have twins!"

Brandon sank into the matching chair and settled his grandson on his knee. "Bite your tongue, young lady," he said. "Harriet saw Dr. Tate yesterday. When he listened with his stethoscope, he thought he heard two distinct heartbeats. Of course, it's too early to be certain, but maybe…" He gave his daughter a solemn wink.

"Oh!" Jenny sprang out of the chair, wide-eyed. "Oh, my goodness! Twins! Wait till I tell Will!" She raced off to find her husband, who was out in the stable readying the sleigh for their after-dinner ride.

The two youngsters were doing all right, Brandon reflected. Will had proven to be such an adept businessman that Hezekiah Moon, the feed-store owner, had raised his pay and taken him on as a partner. When the old man retired a few months later, Will, with Harriet's approval, had used his school savings to buy the store from him. Business was thriving and Will had managed to buy some land with a cozy little house on it. Brandon had repeatedly offered to help the young people with money, but Will and Jenny were determined to manage on their own. Brandon was proud of them both.

"Is this a private party or am I invited, too?" Harriet glided in from the dining room, where the table was laid for Christmas dinner. She looked beautiful with the Hungarian shawl draped around her shoulders and her golden topaz earrings, his Christmas gift, dancing in the firelight. Her skirt was raised in front to accommodate her rounding belly. Brandon ached with love every time he looked at her.

"Come here, Gypsy queen." He lifted Jenny's son out of the way, leaving his lap empty. She curled against him, settling herself like a warm cat before he replaced the child in her arms.

"This may be our last quiet Christmas," she said, nuzzling his chin. "We'd best enjoy it while we can."

He kissed her gently, stroking the bulge that rose below her waist. "Twins. I can't even imagine it."

"And no, we're not going to name them Harvey and Marlin. Especially if they're girls." She wrinkled her nose at him.

"What a tease you are," he murmured. "What happened to that prim-and-proper schoolmarm I used to know?"

"I think you were a wicked influence on her." She snuggled close, cradling Jenny's son against her shoulder. "Have you ever thought about what a mixed-up family this little fellow will grow up in? I started out as his aunt. Now that I'm married to you, I'm also his grandmother. That makes you both his grandfather and his uncle. And our children will be his aunts and uncles, as well as his cousins. Don't you think he might find that confusing?"

"I'd say so. I'm already confused." Brandon laughed, feeling contentment radiate from his head to his toes. Some people asked for blessings that never came. He had been too proud to ask, but the blessings had come anyway, flooding away the wall of pride and bitterness he had built against the world. Whatever happened in the years ahead, he would be grateful for this perfect day, this perfect moment, surrounded by the people he loved.

He would be grateful forever.

* * * * *

The much-anticipated finale to the Moreland quartet!

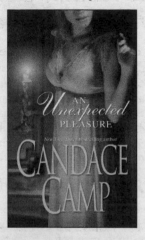

London, 1879

Had Theo Moreland, the Marquess of Raine, killed her brother? American journalist Megan Mulcahey had to know. But to find out, she needed to infiltrate the marquess's household.

The new American governess intrigued Theo. Miss Mulcahey had come to Broughton House to teach his young siblings. Now the strange pull of their immediate desire both troubled and excited him. But why was this delicious vision snooping around his mansion like a common thief?

Available 19th September 2008

Celebrate 100 years of pure reading pleasure with Mills & Boon®

To mark our centenary, each month we're publishing a special 100th Birthday Edition. These celebratory editions are packed with extra features and include a FREE bonus story.

Plus, you have the chance to enter a fabulous monthly prize draw. See 100th Birthday Edition books for details.

Now that's worth celebrating!

September 2008

Crazy about her Spanish Boss by Rebecca Winters
Includes FREE bonus story
Rafael's Convenient Proposal

November 2008

**The Rancher's Christmas Baby
by Cathy Gillen Thacker**
Includes FREE bonus story *Baby's First Christmas*

December 2008

One Magical Christmas by Carol Marinelli
Includes FREE bonus story *Emergency at Bayside*

Look for Mills & Boon® 100th Birthday Editions at your favourite bookseller or visit
www.millsandboon.co.uk

FREE!

2 Books
and a surprise gift!

We would like to take this opportunity to thank you for reading this Mills & Boon® book by offering you the chance to take TWO more specially selected titles from the Historical series absolutely FREE! We're also making this offer to introduce you to the benefits of the Mills & Boon® Book Club—

- ★ **FREE home delivery**
- ★ **FREE gifts and competitions**
- ★ **FREE monthly Newsletter**
- ★ **Exclusive Mills & Boon Book Club offers**
- ★ **Books available before they're in the shops**

Accepting these FREE books and gift places you under no obligation to buy, you may cancel at any time, even after receiving your free shipment. Simply complete your details below and return the entire page to the address below. You don't even need a stamp!

YES! Please send me 2 free Historical books and a surprise gift. I understand that unless you hear from me, I will receive 4 superb new titles every month for just £3.69 each, postage and packing free. I am under no obligation to purchase any books and may cancel my subscription at any time. The free books and gift will be mine to keep in any case.

H8ZEF

Ms/Mrs/Miss/Mr ....Initials ....

Surname ....

Address ....

BLOCK CAPITALS PLEASE

....

....Postcode ....

Send this whole page to:
UK: FREEPOST CN81, Croydon, CR9 3WZ